NIGHT FALL

Books by Nancy Mehl

ROAD TO KINGDOM

Inescapable

Unbreakable

Unforeseeable

FINDING SANCTUARY

Gathering Shadows

Deadly Echoes

Rising Darkness

DEFENDERS OF JUSTICE

Fatal Frost

Dark Deception

Blind Betrayal

KAELY QUINN PROFILER

Mind Games

Fire Storm

Dead End

THE QUANTICO FILES

Night Fall

THE QUANTICO FILES
BOOK 1

NIGHT FALL

NANCY MEHL

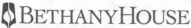
BETHANYHOUSE
a division of Baker Publishing Group
www.BethanyHouse.com

© 2021 by Nancy Mehl

Published by Bethany House Publishers
11400 Hampshire Avenue South
Bloomington, Minnesota 55438
www.bethanyhouse.com

Bethany House Publishers is a division of
Baker Publishing Group, Grand Rapids, Michigan

Printed in the United States of America

Library of Congress Cataloging-in-Publication Data
Names: Mehl, Nancy, author.
Title: Night fall / Nancy Mehl.
Description: Minneapolis, Minnesota : Bethany House, a division of Baker
    Publishing Group, [2021] | Series: The Quantico files ; #1
Identifiers: LCCN 2020046125 | ISBN 9780764237638 (trade paperback) | ISBN
    9780764238185 (casebound) | ISBN 9781493429899 (ebook)
Subjects: GSAFD: Mystery fiction. | Suspense fiction.
Classification: LCC PS3613.E4254 N54 2021 | DDC 813/.6—dc23
LC record available at https://lccn.loc.gov/2020046125

In chapter 15, Revelation 9:17–19 is from the King James Version of the Bible.

In chapter 25, John 3:16 is from the New American Standard Bible® (NASB), copyright © 1960, 1962, 1963, 1968, 1971, 1972, 1973, 1975, 1977, 1995 by The Lockman Foundation. Used by permission. www.Lockman.org

Cover design by Studio Gearbox

Author is represented by The Steve Laube Agency.

21 22 23 24 25 26 27   7 6 5 4 3 2 1

To John Frye,
who knew what it meant to live a life
of service to others.
I'm so grateful to have been given
the gift of your friendship.
I'll miss you, John, until the day comes
when we can dance together again in heaven.

Do you hear the Train Man rumbling in the night?
Can you see his dreadful face grinning with
    delight?
If you hear his horrid wheels clicking round and
    round,
Cover your head and plug your ears to block the
    frightful sound.

For any little boy or girl who hears the Train Man
    speak,
Who feels his rancid breath caress their pretty
    cheek,
Must close their eyes, pretend to sleep, and very
    softly pray,
Or else the evil Train Man may carry them away.

           —"THE TRAIN MAN," A NURSERY RHYME

Prologue

His mother sat in the chair next to his bed, reading from The Book. He was almost twelve now, and she'd been reading it to him ever since he was a little kid.

Adam hated it. It scared him. Did everyone really come from beings in the sky? Were people really born either demons or angels? Mother said they were—and that they had no choice in the matter.

He'd begun to believe he was a demon, but he'd always been too scared to ask her. He suspected she thought he was, though, because of the way her dark eyes bored into his. It made him feel strange inside. But if he was a demon, didn't that make her and Father demons too? Mother said demons could have only demon children, which meant demon children always had demon parents. He didn't want to be a demon. If only he could run away. Go somewhere else. Be someone else. But that would never happen. He was trapped.

He tried to be as good as his mother wanted him to be, but it was hard. Too hard. She considered everything a temptation. Even food. That meant they never had much to eat in their house. Tired of being hungry, he'd stolen a candy bar from the store when no one was looking. He'd stuck it in his pants pockets, and he hadn't been caught.

But would an angel steal? Or just a demon?

The truth was he hated his mother. He was closer to his father, who had a high forehead and large eyes that reminded Adam of a drawing he'd seen of an alien. Maybe The Book was right about where they all came from.

Surely his father was an angel. He gave him treats when Mother wasn't looking. And he made faces at her behind her back, making Adam want to laugh out loud. Of course, they couldn't really laugh at Mother. They were both afraid of her. If Father weren't afraid, he'd just tell her to shut up. He'd ignore her orders to beat Adam with the paddle she kept in the kitchen. But he always did whatever Mother told him to do.

When he wasn't teaching Adam his school lessons or out making what little money they seemed to have, Father spent most of his time in the basement smoking. Mother wouldn't let him smoke anywhere else in the house. When she asked him what he was doing down there, he said he was working on *things*. Adam had no idea what these things were. He wasn't allowed to go down there. He was sure Mother didn't know either. She had a bad leg so she stayed out of the basement. She didn't seem to mind Father spending time downstairs, though. It was clear she didn't like him any more than he liked her. Maybe Father didn't want to be a demon either, but Mother treated him like he was.

Although Adam hated the beatings, he was even more afraid of the times her eyes went dead and she put her hands around his neck. Usually when Father wasn't there. Adam had grown taller in the last year, but she was still stronger than he was. It hurt. He could hardly breathe. Sometimes he wondered if she would stop. Sometimes he wished she wouldn't, but he was afraid of dying. Which planet would he go to when he died? The one for angels or the one for demons?

Most of the time he understood what he'd done wrong when he was punished. He'd stayed outside too long, or he'd forgotten something he was supposed to do. Then once, at one of the special meetings his parents had taken him to every week until a few months ago, he smiled at a man's pretty daughter, who was about Adam's age. That made Mother really angry, and he got a beating that night. She kept telling Father to hit him harder because what he did was so bad. His father acted like he was obeying her, but the paddling got softer and softer.

Adam hadn't been taken to the meetings again. That was all right with him. He liked being home alone. Sometimes he'd sneak food out of the refrigerator, and so far Mother hadn't noticed. He'd also stare at the paddle on the wall, thinking about using it on *her*. The image in his head made him smile.

An angel wouldn't think about hurting his mother, would he? Yet, more and more, thoughts about hurting other people swirled in his mind. The feelings they caused were so strong he had to force himself to think about something else. Otherwise, he might do one of those awful things.

His mother finally closed The Book, then started reciting that scary poem about the Train Man. For as long as he could remember, she'd said it every night so he'd stay in bed and not make any noise.

After Mother turned out the light and left his room, he hooked his hands behind his head and stared up at the ceiling.

It was so dark in here. Not that it mattered. What was there to see? Just a small bed with an old mattress that smelled, a nightstand that wobbled, and the desk and chair his father found next to a trash dumpster.

A few months ago his family visited his aunt's house. Until that day, Adam hadn't even known his mother had a sister. His aunt had kind eyes and a soft touch. And her house was beautiful. Bright and cheerful. He'd looked around the kitchen. No paddle. He couldn't help but wish his aunt could be his mother. When she smiled at him, it made him feel something he'd never felt before. Envy.

Turned out she had a boy Adam's age with a bedroom full of wonders. New furniture. Posters on the wall. Toys. Video games. He couldn't believe it. His envy turned into something even more dark. Anger. He wanted to hurt his cousin and take all his amazing treasures. Why should that boy have everything Adam wanted? It wasn't fair, was it?

They didn't stay long, and after they left, Mother announced they would never go back. She said their house had too many temptations. Maybe that was true, but he didn't know what was true and what wasn't anymore. New feelings had begun to grow inside him. Resentment. Rage. Hatred.

As he tried to force himself to go to sleep, he kept an ear turned toward the train tracks that ran somewhere behind their house. Thankfully, he heard only silence, yet he knew that a train could go by at any moment. Even though Adam was fairly certain the Train Man wasn't real, he was terrified of him. Reluctant to take a chance, he'd stay in bed no matter what.

Someday he'd find a way to leave here. Maybe he could

live with his aunt. But if Adam really was a demon, and she found out, she wouldn't want him there, would she?

His eyelids finally grew heavy, but suddenly the door to his room squeaked open. Light streamed in from the kitchen, and Father stood in the doorway with an odd look on his face. He motioned to him with his fingers. "Come with me," he said.

As Adam followed him, he wondered where Mother was. She'd be mad if she caught them, and he'd get another beating. He wasn't sure how many more of those he could take. His father didn't seem concerned about her, though. And when he stopped at the door to the basement, Adam was confused.

"I have something to show you," Father said.

Adam trailed him down the stairs. When they reached the bottom, his father pointed to something lying on a large wooden table.

Now Adam knew the truth.

He *had* been raised by demons.

1

Twenty years later

Patrick walked next to the railroad tracks as he searched for an open boxcar. November was still especially cold and rainy, and a sudden gust of wind grasped him in its icy fingers.

Clouds above him blocked the moon for several minutes, and surrounded by blackness, Patrick stepped carefully. He stayed on the side of the train where a copse of trees helped hide him from prying eyes. As their limbs shook and bent from the strength of the wind gusts, his tattered coat provided almost no protection. He could feel winter waiting in the wings. He needed to find a Salvation Army soon. They'd let him take a shower and give him clean clothes. Maybe even a new coat to keep him warm.

As he pulled on yet another boxcar latch that stayed tight, his mind drifted to his mother and older brother. Years ago, they'd pleaded with him to come home. He should have, but he was cocky, certain he didn't need them. He'd been raised in church, but he'd wanted a different kind of life—especially after his father died. He craved an existence full of fun and adventure. Well, this sure didn't qualify. His laugh was low and hoarse, and it triggered another spasm of coughing.

Patrick stopped for a moment, then took a partially smoked cigarette out of his coat pocket. He'd found several of them on the sidewalk outside a movie theater in downtown Kansas City, and he'd scooped them all up. He cursed softly when he remembered this was his last one. New packages of cigarettes were impossible to steal now. Almost every store kept them either locked up or in a place inaccessible to the public. Sometimes a smoker would give him a whole cigarette when he asked for one, although that was a luxury. He would smoke only half of it, saving the other half for later.

He coughed again, trying to ignore the pain in his chest. He'd been spitting up blood for a few weeks. He should find a free clinic—maybe here in Independence—but he was pretty sure he knew what they'd say. He didn't want to hear it.

When he reached for the book of matches in his pants pocket, his fingers got caught in a ragged hole. The matches were gone. He could search through the canvas bag he carried with him, but he wouldn't find them. He'd definitely put them in his pocket. His curses echoed loudly through the black of night.

"Are you all right?"

Patrick startled at the voice coming from the darkness. A man walked into the yellow beam provided by a looming light pole behind the train cars. He seemed to have stepped out of nowhere.

Patrick's body tensed. But he saw the person now approaching him was younger than him and held a can of spray paint. A train tagger. Not dangerous.

"You have any matches?" Patrick asked.

The man smiled. "No, but I have a lighter and some cigarettes." With his free hand, he reached into his coat pocket and took out both a plastic lighter and an open, almost-full pack of cigarettes. "I have more smokes in the car. You can have these."

"What about the lighter?"

The man held out his hand. "Keep both."

Patrick grabbed them before the guy could change his mind. "Thanks," he mumbled. "I mean it. Very nice of you."

"Not a problem."

"You're a tagger?"

The man laughed. "I guess the paint can gave me away."

Patrick smiled as he put a fresh cigarette in his mouth. He tried to ignite it, but the wind kept blowing out the lighter's flame.

"Hey, there's an open car down here," the man said. "If you get inside, you can light that a lot easier."

Patrick thanked him again. This was turning out to be a good night. Cigarettes and a place to sleep. He was so tired. His bag held a small pillow and a blanket he got from some do-gooders who'd found him under a railroad bridge a few months ago. They needed to be washed. Or replaced. Another reason to go to the Army when he got to the next city. They might even give him a sleeping bag too. That would help a lot.

He followed the man down several cars to the one that was open. Another light pole illuminated the tag the man had painted. Patrick liked most of the graffiti he'd seen on trains. A lot of it was interesting and colorful. This one was a little different. He stared at it a few seconds, trying to figure out what it meant, then decided he really didn't care.

The man set his paint can inside the open car and pulled

himself up into it before reaching down to help Patrick up. Patrick walked a little way inside the empty car and lit his ciga- rette. He sighed as the smoke entered his lungs. Once again he was seized with coughing, and he fought to control it.

"Sounds like you should give up smoking," the man said.

Patrick's family had said the same thing, but he didn't like anyone telling him what to do. Suddenly, his mother's voice seemed to speak out of the darkness. *Pat, you need Jesus. He can help you. Change you. Save you.*

He could almost see her tear-filled eyes as she spoke those words. Why was he revisiting this now? Something powerful poured through him. Regret? In that moment, he wished he'd listened to his mother. But it was too late. He couldn't go back.

"Thanks for the cigarettes and helping me find a place to sleep," he said. "I'm Patrick." He held out his free hand, and the man grabbed it with a gloved one.

"And I'm Adam." Without letting go, he took a step closer. "Have you heard of the Train Man, Patrick?"

He shook his head. *The Train Man? Who's that?* "I don't think so."

Adam began reciting a strange poem as he smiled in the glow of the burning cigarette. Patrick didn't see the first flash of metal until the last second. Then as life began to drain from his body, he could get out only one word. "Jesus."

Alex Donovan could almost feel the air around her bristle with tense excitement as she took her seat in the Quantico conference room Monday morning, along with two other mem- bers of the FBI's Behavioral Analysis Unit. She still had trouble believing she was part of this elite squad. As coordinator for the National Center for the Analysis of Violent Crime while stationed in Kansas City, she'd been a liaison between local law enforcement agencies and the BAU. Her work with the violent crime squad had earned her respect from the agents she'd worked with in the BAU. Those connections opened a door she'd dreamt of stepping through ever since she was a teenager.

Her goal had always been the same—to get to this place—and she was finally here. It still felt surreal. And now she'd been asked to meet with the BAU unit chief.

She tried to ignore the butterflies in her stomach that seemed to have turned into wasps, stinging her insides with apprehension mixed with anticipation. The door to the room opened, and the chief, Jefferson Cole, walked briskly into the room. Alex noticed the tight line of his jaw. Something was wrong. Something big.

The first time Alex met him, Jeff reminded her more of an accountant than an experienced FBI agent and talented analyst. He was tall and lanky with dark hair and black glasses, and sometimes she almost expected him to ask for a list of her deductible expenses for last year. But the comparison ended when he opened his mouth. Jeff was a man who knew who he was. He always gave his best, and he expected no less from those who served under him.

Even though she could tell the situation was serious, Alex couldn't quell the feeling of exhilaration bubbling up inside her. She clasped her hands under the table and tried to appear like the calm professional agent she knew she was.

Jeff sat down at the table, then gestured toward the phone sitting on it. "I'm expecting a call from Kansas City. They're asking for our help."

Alex nodded, studying the other agents around the table.

She'd noticed Supervisory Special Agent Logan Hart as soon as she joined the unit. It was hard not to. He was good-looking, with kind blue eyes and dark blond hair that always seemed to need a good combing. Alex thought it looked good that way, windswept and romantic. She'd spoken to him a few times and found that his easy smile and manner matched his personality. Some people in the unit called him "Preacher" because of his spiritual beliefs, but they said it with affection. Everyone seemed to like him.

Before she realized she was doing it, she reached up and touched her bangs. Speaking of windswept, November's strong breezes could certainly mess with one's hair. She kept her long dark mane in a ponytail when she was working, though, so the wind wasn't really a huge problem. However, her bangs were another story. She hoped they looked all right. Now that she was thinking of them, she wanted to fluff them out. She fought the urge, but it was difficult to put her hands back in her lap.

She was being ridiculous. She wasn't looking for a boyfriend. Being part of the BAU was everything to her. Her focus was on her career. Any kind of relationship would just get in the way.

Looking across the table, she caught Monty Wong staring at her. She liked him, but he made her a little nervous. He was attentive and serious, and he rarely smiled. He was nice enough but just a little tightly wound. She tightened her lips to hold back a smile when she realized she was describing herself.

"Logan and Monty, you're here because you're seasoned and your work has been exemplary," Jeff said. He turned to Alex. "And you're here, Alex, because you worked with us out of the Kansas City Field Office. The special agent in charge has high praise for you, and your work as our NCAVC coordinator was impressive." He locked his gaze on hers. "Kansas City PD is asking for our help. I want you to coordinate with them and our Kansas City office. Having someone who already knows the KCPD and our agents in that area will be really helpful."

Alex's body tensed. Lead the team? She knew she was respected for her work with NCAVC, but she'd only been here six months. What did Logan and Monty think of this? She quickly glanced at them. Monty's expression hadn't changed. Logan looked a little surprised, but he covered it well. A few extra blinks, but she didn't see any other physical actions that betrayed his true emotions.

"Yes, sir," she said. She had no reason to say anything else. This wasn't a voluntary assignment. When you were told to go, you went. And you did what you were told to do. Period.

Jeff started to say something else, but then the phone rang. He pressed the button for the speakerphone.

"We're here, Stephen," he said.

Stephen Barstow was a well-known figure in the Kansas City law enforcement community. A decorated detective, he'd earned Alex's respect as they worked several cases together during her time in Kansas City.

"Good," Stephen said. "I hear you've assigned Supervisory Special Agent Donovan to help us, is that right?"

"Yes. She's sitting right here."

"Hello, Alex." The smoothness she remembered in his voice came through the phone.

"Hi, Stephen. Glad to be working with you again."

"Same here."

"I also have Supervisory Special Agents Logan Hart and Monty Wong with us."

"Good to have you all on board. So as you know, Jeff, we

have a problem. Four murders. Only a week or two between each one, and they all look random. Nothing about the victims is similar—as if our UNSUB is selecting whoever is in the wrong place at the wrong time. Three men, one woman. Two Caucasian, one Black, and one Hispanic. Three of them younger, one in his seventies. All the bodies were discovered on trains and were stabbed multiple times."

They could hear him take a deep breath before going on. "Unusual tags on the outside of the boxcars. Something like Bible verses, but we've searched several Bible apps to find them, and they're not in any version we could locate. We're not sure what the UNSUB is trying to tell us. He signed his work, but we have no idea what the initials TM mean. His name? Or something else?"

There was a slight pause. "I'm sending you some photos of the tags right now, along with everything else we've got, which isn't much. We don't have any real evidence. This guy is careful . . . and smart. At this point, we're not in charge. He is. Have your team look over this information before they get here, okay? I'll expect them at the command post in the morning. We're setting it up now. Does that work for you?"

"They'll be there, Stephen. Talk to you soon."

The call done, Jeff turned on his laptop and pulled up the information Barstow had just emailed. He sent the file to a large screen on the wall and began slowly clicking through the photos.

In mere seconds, Alex felt like all the blood in her body had frozen, as if time itself had come to a halt. Her mind couldn't seem to process what she was seeing.

How could this be happening?

Logan had listened closely to the detective from Kansas City, but he'd had to fight to stay focused. What was that scent Alex Donovan wore? It was a mixture of lilacs and . . . something else. His mind kept trying to figure it out, which was infuriating. He wasn't interested in Alex. He was a Christian, and he had no plans to get involved with a woman who didn't share his faith.

So why did his eyes drift her way whenever she was in the room? And why did he keep wondering what she would look like if she released her thick, wavy black hair from the band that held it in a ponytail? Alex wasn't classically beautiful. Her bangs were no doubt an attempt to hide a high forehead. Her nose was a little long, and her mouth was too wide. But those slight imperfections faded when you looked into her eyes—gray-blue irises framed by black lashes. The way she outlined them made them seem even larger than they were.

She was also crazy smart, and when she looked at him, he felt as if she knew what he was thinking.

He felt his face flush.

"Grab your gear and get ready to go," Jeff said. "Any questions?"

Logan shook his head and glanced at Alex. Her face had gone white, and her eyes were wide. "Is something wrong?" he asked her.

She was quiet for several seconds before saying, "I . . . I need to speak to you, Jeff." She stared down at the table. "Alone, please."

Her request bothered Logan. "We're a team," he said. "Whatever you have to say, you should say it in front of all of us." His tone was sharper than it should have been.

"Hey," Monty said. "If she wants to speak to the chief alone, that's okay. If it applies to the case, we'll get an update."

"Does what you want to tell me have something to do with this case?" Jeff asked Alex.

She looked up at him. After another few seconds, she nodded.

"Then these agents stay, Alex. If it's something personal, that's different."

"Do you have some idea who our UNSUB is?" Logan asked.

Alex shook her head slowly. She'd hung her suit jacket on the back of her chair, and now, because she wore a short-sleeved blouse, Logan could see the muscles in her arms working as she clenched and unclenched her hands on top of the table.

"No. But I . . . I know what the tags on the boxcars mean."

Jeff's eyebrows shot up. "You understand them?"

"Yes."

"For now, don't tell me how you know. Just tell me what they mean."

"Go back to the first photo," she said, her voice barely above a whisper.

Jeff clicked on the images until he found the images he wanted. "This is from the first murder," he said. "Just outside Kansas City." Then he read, "'Angels walked on the earth. M 4:7.'"

"Stephen's right," Monty said. "That almost sounds like something from the Bible."

Alex stared at it, then her eyes narrowed and her face flushed. Logan could almost hear the wheels in her mind turning.

"No. It's not from the Bible," she said. "Show me the next one, please."

Jeff brought it up. Alex stared at this one for only a few seconds, then read, "'And the angels made war. N 1:21.'"

Jeff shook his head. "So what are those notations? Like you said, these references aren't biblical, but they seem like it, with chapters and verses."

The red in Alex's cheeks deepened. "They're exactly that. Chapters and verses from a book. For example, M 4:7 is Marduk, chapter four, verse seven. It actually says something like 'Angels walked on the earth, but the world regarded them not.' N 1:21 is the book of Nergal, chapter one, verse twenty-one. 'And the angels made war with the evil ones.'"

Jeff brought up the third photo and read, "'He arises. T 7:12.'"

Alex squinted at the image. She was again silent for a few moments before saying, "I can't remember which book T is. Sorry."

Her eyes darted toward Logan and Monty, then back to Jeff. After hesitating a moment, she said, "From the time I was twelve, I was raised by an aunt who believed the teachings in a book that theorized the world is populated by beings from another world. Some good. Some malevolent. Everyone on earth is classified as either a demon or an angel. This is how the people who believe in this book explain the concept of evil. Supposedly, if a person is born with demon blood, all their descendants will be demons. If they're born with angel blood, they're angels forever. The same applies to their descendants. Demons are destined to cause pain and destruction. Angels are called to fight the darkness."

Monty raised an eyebrow. "What if an angel and demon get together?"

Alex shook her head. "Can't happen. According to the teachings, angels are repelled by demons and vice versa."

"Well, that could explain a few relationships I've had," Monty said under his breath.

Despite the seriousness of the conversation, Logan grinned at him.

"You say this woman raised you?" Jeff asked.

"Yes. I lost both my parents when I was young. As far as I know, this aunt is my only living relative."

"What did she say you were?" Logan asked. "An angel or a demon?"

Alex's slight smile quivered before she said, "We never talked about that. I'm not sure what my aunt thought. Nor do I care."

Logan flushed with anger. How could a child grow up like that and be . . . normal? "Well, you fight the darkness every day. That makes you an angel in my book."

As soon as the words left his mouth, he was instantly embarrassed. Alex smiled at him, making him feel a little better.

"Thank you, but our UNSUB isn't following *your* book," she said. "He obviously has a copy of the book my aunt quoted to me."

Jeff nodded. "So our UNSUB is sending us messages from some book. But what is he trying to tell us?"

"We need to use your knowledge to get ahead of him, Alex," Monty said. "Looks like we have a secret weapon. You can help us find him."

"I doubt he's going to make it easy," Alex said. "Show me the message from this last murder."

Once again, Jeff brought up an image. "This is from where they just found the fourth body in Independence."

This time Alex frowned. "'A 13:12. I am the Destroyer.'"

"What does it mean?" Jeff asked.

"This book claims that, at some point, the demons and angels will engage in all-out war and that the Destroyer, one of the chief demons, will wipe out one third of the world's population. It's a prophecy."

"Something similar is in the Bible's book of Revelation," Logan said. "Something about four angels being unleashed and a third of mankind perishing."

"That does sound similar. This verse is found in the book of Abaddon," Alex said.

"The destroyer," Logan repeated softly.

"You know that Abaddon means *destroyer*?"

"Yeah. Again, Revelation. It mentions an angel named Abaddon." He sighed. "I'm not that knowledgeable about end-time prophecies. Sorry, I only remember a few things from reading about it in the past."

"Do you see any other similarities between your aunt's book and the Bible?" Jeff asked.

"I don't know much about the Bible, but I doubt it. This book says the end is already decided. People are either angels or demons. They have no choice, and they will never be anything else." She leaned back in her chair and crossed her arms. "After being brought up by someone who kept trying to ram this stuff down my throat, I don't have much interest in any kind of religion. But from what I've heard about Christians, they believe people can change. They can decide their own fate, isn't that right?"

Logan nodded. "If you mean we can choose the forgiveness Christ offers and become new, then yes. It's referred to as 'being saved.'"

"Then the difference between The Book and the Bible is like night and day."

"You just call it *the* book," Jeff said. "But what's its title?"

"That's it. It's considered so sacred that no one can be trusted with its true name, so they just call it The Book—both words said as if they're capitalized. Followers—the angels—call themselves the Circle, and they're the only people allowed to read it."

"Okay, so what is our UNSUB trying to tell us?" Jeff asked, his voice tight with concern.

"I think he believes he's a demon—the Destroyer called to carry out the destruction I mentioned. Obviously, he's delusional. No one has that kind of power."

Jeff's face went blank, and he was silent for several seconds before he picked up his phone. "Get Agent Suter in here. Now."

Monty started to say something, but Jeff held up his hand, signaling him to be quiet. The silence in the room was thick with apprehension. What was going on? Jeff was never at a loss for words.

A few minutes later, they heard a knock on the door.

"Come in," Jeff called out.

The door was pushed open, and Moreen Suter, a BAU

agent, walked in. Logan admired her. Smart, insightful, and bold, she had helped to bring quite a few initially unknown subjects, referred to as UNSUBs, to justice.

"Yes, Boss?" she said.

"Repeat what you reported to me earlier."

Moreen stared at him for a moment, then said, "We heard from a research lab in Kansas City. They think they may have a problem with a shipment of viruses from Ethiopia. They're not sure yet, though. It's just an alert for now."

"What kind of problem?" Logan asked.

"Before anyone gets too concerned, remember there may not be anything amiss. Sometimes things get misplaced—"

"Deadly pathogens get misplaced?" Alex said. "What kind of Mickey Mouse lab is this?"

"Unfortunately, not all overseas labs have the safety protocols they should," Jeff said. "This has been an ongoing problem for a while now. The CDC is trying to correct the situation."

"What might be missing?" Logan asked.

"Six inactive samples were sent from Addis Ababa to Kansas City for testing. Scientists are trying to develop effective treatments for patients already infected with certain viruses."

"You're talking about a vaccine?" Monty asked.

"Yes, we have preventive vaccines for this particular strain but nothing to combat the virus in patients who are already sick. This is an attempt at a cure."

"Wait a minute," Alex said. "You said these samples were inactive. So they're not contagious?"

Moreen nodded. "Researchers can work successfully with inactive samples. Obviously, it's safer." She took a deep breath. "But after the six samples were received and logged into the lab in Kansas City, the next day they could find only five. Not

long after that discovery, they received a call from the lab in
Addis Ababa. They're missing an *active* sample of the virus.
Right now both labs are checking carefully, trying to figure
out what happened. It could be a simple mistake. Or . . ."

"A dangerous, active virus was shipped to the Kansas City
lab and is now missing," Jeff finished.

"Yes. And this morning the research assistant who received
the samples from Ethiopia didn't show up for work. The lab
called the KCPD, who found he'd moved out of his apartment." Moreen sighed. "According to the head of the lab
in Addis Ababa, the chemist who prepared the samples is
missing as well, and they have reason to worry about some of
his recent actions. Coworkers said he talked a lot about the
ability to mutate certain viruses. Turn them into superbugs."

"Would something like that be more dangerous than
COVID-19?" Monty asked.

"Yes."

The room fell completely silent. Logan was certain everyone was thinking the same thing he was.

"What virus are we talking about?" he finally asked.

Moreen swallowed hard. "It's the Zaire Ebola virus. Already extremely lethal. Incredibly deadly. If it were altered in
some way, it could be the most devastating virus we've ever
seen. We could be talking about an easily spread pathogen
with a ninety percent mortality rate."

"That's it," Alex said, her voice so soft Logan could barely
hear her. "Our train killer has the virus, and he's going to
unleash it. That's how he intends to carry out the prophecy."

3

L et's not jump to conclusions," Jeff said sharply. "We need more information before we can confidently link our UNSUB to the missing sample. If it's even really gone."

He pointed his finger at Moreen. "I want you on this right now. Find out for certain if that sample has really disappeared—and who the missing researcher is. Once you have a name, contact the KCPD and tell them to put out an APB. And run this guy through NCIC and ViCAP. I doubt he has a criminal record since they would have run a background check before hiring him. But maybe we can check the VIN number for any vehicles he's owned, see if he was ever stopped by law enforcement. We need to figure out where he might be."

Alex agreed with Jeff. This guy wouldn't be found in the National Crime Information Center or the Violent Criminal Apprehension Program. He'd probably prepared very carefully. He was hidden away somewhere. Someplace where he felt safe. Checking any past tickets or warnings was a long shot at best, but they had to do everything they could to find him, starting with the all-points bulletin Jeff wanted put into effect.

"Got it, Boss," Moreen said. She left, closing the door firmly behind her.

Alex jumped at the sound. It was as if one of her nightmares had slipped out of the darkness and was crawling into her life. A life she'd worked so hard to create.

"How big is this . . . Circle, Alex?" Jeff asked.

"I don't know, but my aunt told me they have members all over the world. That might have been wishful thinking, though. She used to have meetings at her house, but I don't think she ever had more than half a dozen people there at one time. I wasn't allowed to participate, so I'm just guessing. Her place was pretty small. It wouldn't hold too many people at once."

"How do we get a copy of this book?" Jeff asked. "We need it . . . now."

"Is it on Amazon?" Monty asked.

Alex bit her lip. *Amazon?* "No. According to my aunt, very few copies exist. I don't know if that's true, but she had one of them."

Jeff sighed. "So we need someone in this Circle to give us a copy?"

Alex wanted to give him hope, but there just wasn't any. They had no way to track down members of the Circle—at least not without months or years of investigation. Her aunt had made that clear. Everyone used pseudonyms. Her aunt had called herself Lady X. Alex could still hear her laughing about the moniker. "I've always wanted to be a Lady

X," she'd said. "A woman of mystery. It fits me, Alexandra. Doesn't it?"

Twelve-year-old Alex had nodded, although she didn't think her aunt was the least bit mysterious. She thought she was stone cold crazy. Now, with her training, Alex understood her aunt's mental problems. But living with someone like Willow had been almost unbearable for a child who'd lost the mother she'd adored.

"Your aunt is the only person we know who has a copy of The Book." Jeff leaned back in his chair. "Where is this aunt?"

"In . . . in Wichita, Kansas."

"I'll contact our resident agency in Wichita and ask them to get a warrant to pick up her copy."

"Assuming she still has it, she won't give it to them," Alex said. "She won't even open the door."

"*If* our UNSUB has the virus and you're right about him, he could start spreading it to the general population. We don't have time to mess around here. What she wants doesn't matter. We'll have a warrant. She'll have no choice in this matter."

"I realize that." Although everything inside her fought the next words to come out of her mouth, Alex's sense of duty won out over her long-held vow never to see her aunt again. "I really believe I'm the only one she'll talk to. If I can convince her to give me The Book, we'll save time and possible delays. Even with a warrant, they'll still have to find her hiding place. She worked hard to keep it out of sight. Even I have no idea where she kept it."

"Okay," Jeff said. "We need that book. I'll contact the SAC in Kansas City. Let him know we've been asked by the KCPD to help with their serial-murder investigation. Advise them about this turn of events and ask his permission to send you and Logan to Wichita. I'm certain they'll want to set up a task force, seeing it's possible we're dealing with a weapon of mass destruction. All of CIRG needs to be on board for this."

Jeff was right. The FBI's Critical Incident Response Group was comprised of the most highly trained agents in the world. If anyone could find this virus in time, it was them.

Alex shivered, but she wasn't cold. She'd never planned to set foot in Wichita again. She'd turned her back on her painful past and started over. Facing it filled her with dread.

The door opened suddenly, and Moreen's expression was grim. "Sorry to interrupt, but I think this may be important."

"What is it?" Jeff asked.

"The research assistant who disappeared in Kansas City left something behind. They found it in his desk at the lab. It appears he wanted someone to find it. They just sent me a copy of . . . well, it's a poem."

"A poem?" Jeff's tone held a touch of anger. "Why do we care about a poem?"

"Let me read it, Boss. Then you tell me if it matters."

Jeff sighed deeply and nodded.

Moreen cleared her throat.

> "'Do you hear the Train Man rumbling in the night?
> Can you see his dreadful face grinning with delight?
> If you hear his horrid wheels clicking round and
>   round,
> Cover your head and plug your ears to block the
>   frightful sound.
> For any little boy or girl who hears the Train Man
>   speak,
> Who feels his rancid breath caress their pretty cheek,

Must close their eyes, pretend to sleep, and very softly
        pray,
    Or else the evil Train Man may carry them away.'"

She looked up. "The title is 'The Train Man.'"

The color drained from Jeff's face.

"TM," Alex said, her voice cracking. "Train Man. This guy is definitely our UNSUB."

"Alex, Logan, get to Wichita," Jeff said, his expression tight. "Monty, I want you to coordinate with Kansas City. They'll want the task force there, and you can help them set up a command post. I'll let Stephen know what's going on. Alex, are you certain your aunt will give you this book?"

She shook her head. "I honestly don't know. It's her reason for living. A sacred text that can't be replaced. All I can do is try."

"A serial killer may have an extremely deadly pathogen. We don't have time to worry about her feelings. You bring me that book, Alex," he said forcefully, "or we'll do it the hard way. I don't want to tear apart an old lady's home, but we'll do whatever we have to." He stopped and fastened his gaze back on Moreen.

"What's this guy's name?" he asked her.

"Adam Walker. We're doing a deep search on him now. Trying to figure out where he is. How to find him."

"Has the CDC been notified? Homeland?"

"The lab has contacted the CDC. I'll check about Homeland."

Alex could barely understand the conversation going on around her. Logan was going with her? He would meet Aunt Willow. See where Alex spent her teenage years. It was too much. She had to find a way to stop it.

A thought popped into her head. "I need to confront her alone," she said, trying to keep her voice steady. "If Logan is with me, she won't cooperate. She'll see him as an enemy. Someone she has to protect herself from. I'm the only one who can talk her into giving up The Book."

"If she hands it over to you, fine," Jeff said, looking at her over the rim of his glasses. "Hart will go as backup. He can stay in the car unless he's needed."

He stared at her through narrowed eyes, then leaned forward in his chair. "Look, there's still a slim chance this Walker guy might not have the virus. Perhaps the lab will find their sample. I hope so, but at this point I'd bet money they won't. Everything's starting to line up. The poem and the initials on the trains . . . too much coincidence for me. The bodies have been found in Missouri, and the missing sample was taken from a lab in Kansas City. We need to proceed as if Adam Walker has the virus and intends to use it. Time is of the essence."

He stopped and frowned at her. "Why not just get the virus if that's what he really wanted? Why the murders on trains? Obviously, there's something about trains and this . . . Train Man poem that's important to him. But how do these killings relate to the virus?"

Alex took a deep breath, again trying to keep her voice steady. "We might actually have a little more time than we think. I'm pretty sure six sacrifices are required before the Destroyer brings death on the earth. I think that's what these murders are about. I should have realized it sooner."

"Six sacrifices?" Jeff said.

Alex nodded. "Yes, sir. If I remember right, the sixth sacrifice has to be a virgin. I think he plans to keep going until the last sacrifice has been offered. Then he'll release the virus." She cleared her throat. "Having access to The Book will really help. I tried to forget all this. We can't rely on my memory alone."

Jeff straightened up in his chair. "I'll call Alice and tell her to get a flight arranged to Wichita. I want you and Hart at the airport within two hours."

Alice Burrows was Jeff's capable and reliable administrative assistant. Alex had no doubt the plane would be ready when Jeff said it would.

Alex and Logan answered "yes, sir" at the same time. Although Jeff usually called them by their first names, when it came to a situation like this, the atmosphere in his office changed. He changed. First names went out the door, and Jeff became "sir."

"Do you have any idea how we can find this guy, Donovan?" Jeff asked.

"As you know, we won't actually do a profile now since we know who our UNSUB is, but we can review all the victimology for common elements. We should also develop a questionnaire for use with his neighbors, coworkers, friends. Then we can review the info gleaned and develop some investigative strategies for the task force, including key witness interview strategies. And, of course, we should review The Book. It will give us insight into how Walker thinks."

Alex stopped and thought for a few seconds. Was she forgetting anything? She looked at Logan, but he was quiet. She turned back to Jeff. "I believe we can determine what steps Walker will take next. Maybe if we get ahead of him, we can catch him." She looked up at Moreen. "He's a white male, late twenties, early thirties, right?"

"Yes, white. Thirty-two."

"Most likely he's been raised with parents or guardians who believed in The Book," she said. "I'd look for them. Maybe he went to the place he felt the safest. Home."

"You don't think he's married, do you?" Monty asked.

"No. We all know these kinds of killers are usually loners, unable to create or maintain close relationships. Of course, exceptions to the rule exist. Dennis Rader comes to mind. But this guy is traveling around to different towns in the area, killing. And if he has a deadly virus, would he take it home to his family? Maybe, but I tend to doubt it."

"But he'd take it home to his parents?" Logan asked.

"Again, his place of safety. They understand him." She sighed in frustration and looked at Jeff. "It's just too early. Let's wait and see what we find out about this Adam Walker. That will help us figure out what he might do next."

"Some kids rebel against the values and beliefs of their parents or guardians because they want something different," Monty said. "You did. How do you know this guy, Walker, didn't get involved with the Circle after he left home?"

"It's not impossible," Alex said. "But remember, according to my aunt, few copies of The Book exist. Most of them are probably in the hands of older people who've been part of the Circle for years. That's why I believe Walker was raised on it." She hesitated for a moment. "You are right about one thing, though. He is rebelling—and maybe his parents had a hand in it."

"What do you mean?" Logan asked.

"Only angels are allowed to read The Book. Demons aren't allowed anywhere near it, let alone have a copy and read it to their children. The Circle believes The Book is a road map for the future. Demons aren't supposed to have that kind of knowledge. If the Circle already knows what Walker is doing, that he and his parents have turned out to be demons, they might retaliate if they can find him. They sure won't protect him."

She paused, letting what she'd just said sink in. "The Circle won't accept any demon's role in the prophecy. It's supposed to happen without demons even knowing about it. It's a prophecy, not a plan. Also, Walker wrote those messages on the train cars. No one is allowed to share the sacred scriptures with the world. It's . . . well, it's like the unpardonable sin. Isn't there something like that in Christianity?"

"Yes," Logan said when she turned to him.

She nodded. "This is looked upon in the same light. This guy can never go back to the Circle. Even if he weren't a demon, he's committed several big . . . sins, for lack of a better word. Like I said, his parents may protect him, but the Circle won't."

"Those passages about a war with the angels and the demons? Who wins?" Logan asked. "I mean, if a third of the world is eliminated, that leaves two thirds remaining. Are they angels or demons?"

Alex searched her memory. "I do remember Willow telling me that after the war, some demons and some angels will survive and learn how to reign together. She believed they'd decide that they needed one another, that good can't exist without evil."

"Well, I don't know about that," Jeff said, "but without evil we wouldn't have jobs."

"That proves her point, I guess," Alex said. "The FBI wouldn't exist if there wasn't evil for us to fight."

"One thing I don't understand," Jeff said. "You say those in the Circle aren't supposed to share The Book with anyone else, unless they're an angel. Yet your aunt told you all this?"

Alex shrugged. "I guess if she believed *she* was an angel, then she also believed her sister—my mother—was one, making me an angel too. Angels are allowed to read The Book to their children until they reach ten years of age. After that, the children have to decide if they want to join the Circle. If they don't, their parents must never mention The Book to them again. They're treated as outcasts with the hope that they'll repent and someday decide to become members."

"But you said you were twelve when you went to live with your aunt," Jeff said. "You were already too old."

Alex didn't want to say much more about her mother, but she had to answer Jeff's question.

"My aunt said she thought my mother died so I would end up with her. That she was called to 'bring me into the fold.' Even though I was too old, she believed it was okay to share The Book with me since I'd never had a chance to listen to the 'truth' before. I hated her for saying that about my mother, and when I was fourteen I told her I didn't want to hear anything more about The Book. That if she didn't shut up about it, I'd tell someone in the Circle she was breaking the rules. After that, she left me alone. But she did make me promise to never tell anyone what she'd shared with me. I agreed since I had no plans to ever talk about this again."

"Did she treat you like an outcast after that?" Monty asked.

"Actually, no. Things stayed pretty much the same." Alex sighed. "In her own twisted way, she tried to take care of me. Unfortunately, her mental illness made that difficult for her. And for me."

"Thanks for sharing this with us, Alex," Jeff said. "I'm sure it's not easy."

She met his gaze. "My job is to do everything I can to protect the public. This certainly fits." Jeff's words hit her hard. His concern touched some raw emotions trying to force their way to the surface, but she was determined to hold on to her professional persona, no matter what it cost her. Willow had taken enough from her. She wasn't going to ruin this too.

"Well, I'll be more confident we're on the right track if the lab confirms that virus sample is really missing and it's active," Monty said with a sigh. "I feel like we're still in the dark. Looking for a serial killer is one thing. Trying to find someone who plans to start a pandemic is quite another. It hasn't been that long since COVID-19 ground this country to a halt. We just can't go through that again."

Alex stood. "I truly believe Walker's got it. He's not playing. He's killed four people. We'll see two more murders before he releases the virus. I expect the next one will happen quickly. We need to move."

"Who are these sacrifices made to?" Logan asked, also standing.

"They have a god. He's called the Master. Aunt Willow didn't speak about him much. He's kind of off-limits, I guess. I don't know anything else about him."

"Do they pray to this . . . god?" Jeff asked.

"I don't know that either. I never heard my aunt pray to him. It's possible they feel he's too holy to talk to. Like I said, I've tried to forget everything Willow told me about The Book. I'm surprised I retained this much. It wasn't intentional. I worked hard to bury all this years ago. Guess I wasn't very successful. It's still there."

"Let's leave any other questions about this book for later," Jeff said. "You all get going. We've got to do what we can to narrow the search for this guy so he can be stopped."

"What's the railroad doing?" Logan asked.

"Stephen told me they're guarding their trains the best they can. I'm certain the Kansas City police are doing all they can too, but with all the trains out there, this guy could show up almost anywhere. "

Jeff picked up the folder he'd brought with him and handed it to Alex. "I'm trusting you to do a good job. A lot of lives may depend on it."

"I will."

"I know you will. I'm not worried. Just remember that Kansas City needs whatever you can give them as soon as possible. We can glean a lot from what we already know about this guy and what we can discover from investigators doing a thorough search for information. We need to provide as much help as we can. The lives of at least two more people are at stake. Hopefully, he hasn't already killed them." He stood. "Why the poem? How does it tie in?"

"At first I assumed he chose victims near trains because it's easy to tag boxcars and hide bodies inside," Alex said. "But after hearing the poem, I think he had a fractured childhood. Confusing, especially if his parents never told him whether he was a demon or an angel. I remember wondering the same thing when my aunt first started telling me this stuff, but I got past it soon enough because I didn't believe any of it. I wonder if 'The Train Man' was read to our guy when he was a child."

She paused for a moment, letting everything they knew so far click into place in her mind. "Obviously, Adam Walker decided he was a demon. And not only that but the demon who's supposed to bring about destruction on the earth."

"It seems to me that believing he belonged to the world of demons didn't give him his own, personal identity," Logan said.

"Exactly. And at some point in his life, he identified with the Train Man. Maybe he was originally presented to Walker as someone terrifying, but then our killer decided to face his nightmares by becoming the thing he feared most." She met Jeff's gaze. "I'm probably jumping the gun a bit. This is just my initial reaction."

"Sounds right to me," Jeff said. He looked at Logan and Monty. "You have anything else to add?"

When they both shook their heads, Jeff said, "Okay. Start with that. Give us more when you can."

"Yes, sir."

Jeff turned and left the room. They followed quietly behind him, no one saying a word. Alex was sure they were all thinking about the Train Man. Hopefully, something in the file would help them find him. An inner voice told her they needed to work fast, because this guy was already several steps ahead of them.

Another voice, one that troubled her even more than she cared to admit, told her no one could understand the Train Man more than she could. They were connected by the past, and that connection terrified her.

4

Adam opened the refrigerator and scanned the contents. "Why can't we have something to snack on in this house?" he said loudly. "Some cheese. Crackers. Anything."

"You told me not to buy stuff that isn't on your diet."

Adam jumped at Sally's voice. He hadn't realized she was standing in the doorway. He closed the door to the fridge. "You're right," he said with a smile. "Sorry."

"If you want me to buy you snacks, I will," she said.

Adam gazed at his wife. Her shoulder-length blond hair was tucked behind her ears, and as she looked back at him, he could see the love in her eyes. Before his father died, he had encouraged Adam to find someone he could be happy with. Then not long after he passed away, Adam met Sally. He'd felt so alone with Father gone. Sally came along at exactly the right time. Adam truly believed she was "the one." The perfect woman for him. They'd been married almost nine years now, and he loved her more today than the day they tied the knot.

"No, you're right. I don't need them."

He walked over and took her in his arms. "I'm so glad I have someone who takes such good care of me."

"You shouldn't be on a diet anyway," she said softly, melting into his embrace. "You're too thin as it is, you know."

He squeezed her lightly and laughed. "You're great for my ego."

Sally kissed his cheek. "Pot roast with potatoes and carrots for supper? Your favorite."

"You're too good to me. Next you'll be telling me we're having apple pie for dessert."

It was Sally's turn to laugh. "I'll make sure we do. Not a problem."

"You're the best thing that ever happened to me, you know that?" he said. "I wish you could have met my father."

Sally nodded. "I'm sure I would have loved him."

"Yeah, and he would have felt the same way about you. He was a wonderful man. Taught me everything I know."

Adam got a glass out of the cabinet and turned on the kitchen faucet. He quickly downed the water, then put the glass on the counter. As usual, he remained thirsty. "I still think there's something weird about our water," he said. "It's . . . well, it's not refreshing."

Sally laughed. "You have quite an imagination."

"I guess so."

Just then Gabby and Trey came into the kitchen. Their beautiful twins. They were out of school today. Teachers' meetings.

"When's lunch, Mama?" Gabby asked, her blues eyes sparkling. She had blond hair like her mother, but it was naturally curly while Sally's was straight. Neither Adam nor Sally had curly-headed relatives. Adam used to tease his wife whenever

he saw a curly-headed man. Maybe he was Gabby's real father? Although Sally always laughed, he could tell the jokes
bothered her, so he'd stopped them. Gabby was clearly their
child. She had Sally's blue eyes and his nose. Just like Trey.

"You two go wash your hands," Sally said. "Then come
back for your lunch." The twins scurried away, giggling as
they ran down the hall to the bathroom.

Sally turned toward Adam. "What do you want for lunch?"

He shook his head. "I have to work today. I'll probably be
home late. Can you hold supper off until eight?"

"Sure. I'll feed the kids earlier, then put them to bed and eat
with you when you get home." She smiled. "I'm so glad you
got rid of that apartment. I know you needed a place closer
to work, but now you can be home more. We all missed you."

"I missed you too. I need you and the kids more than I
can say."

As she began preparing lunch for the children, Adam
watched her. She was perfect. The children were perfect.
Even this house was perfect. His father had put the old family
home in Adam's name, and after he died, Adam completely
remodeled it. Today, no one would even know it was the
same place. Except for the basement. He hadn't changed
anything down there. He was also the only one allowed to
go downstairs.

Adam's arms itched. He scratched them, but it didn't help
much. Maybe it was this wool sweater Sally bought him. He
didn't want to hurt her feelings, but he might have to stop
wearing it.

"You're still itching?" she asked. "This has been going on
for quite a while."

He nodded. "Not sure why. Just dry winter skin, I guess."

He paused a moment before going downstairs to get what he needed. "You'll read to the kids before they go to bed?"

She stopped making peanut butter and jelly sandwiches and looked at him. "Of course. We're getting close to being halfway through The Book. I'm so glad we have your father's copy. He taught you well. And I think it's time to tell the children *their* daddy is called to bring destruction to a third of the earth, don't you?"

Adam smiled slowly. "Yes. I think you're right."

Sally took a slow, deep breath, and her eyes grew shiny. "They'll be so proud. I know I am."

"Thank you, dear," he said as he unlocked the door to the basement and prepared to step into his destiny.

With the threat of a possible deadly pathogen being released on the public, FBI's Critical Incident Response Group sent a small plane to get Alex and Logan to Wichita as soon as possible. Monty took the plane Alice Burrows ordered to Kansas City.

The Kansas Bureau of Investigation had been alerted to the situation and requested permission to approach Alex's aunt themselves given concerns about time. Their request had been denied. Alex made it clear she had the better chance of getting Willow's copy of The Book quickly. They were sending an agent from the resident agency in Wichita to pick them up at the airport. Hopefully, Alex and Logan wouldn't have to deal with bruised egos with any agency, the FBI or otherwise.

To be honest, Alex wasn't convinced she'd be able to get The Book either. She hadn't talked to Willow for years. She'd forced herself to call from time to time, but Willow rarely answered her phone, and her landline wasn't set up for voice mail.

As their plane approached Wichita, Alex's stomach tightened, and she began to feel nauseated. She was disgusted with herself. She was a trained behavioral analyst with the FBI. She'd faced the worst the world had to offer. Murderers, rapists, child molesters. Terrorists intent on killing large groups of innocent people. Human traffickers. She'd looked into the eyes of evil many times and had learned to control her reactions. But since seeing words from The Book painted on the sides of train cars, the fear she'd overcome in her twenties was trying to make a reappearance. It was silly. She was afraid of a woman in her sixties who had never hurt anyone that Alex was aware of. Was she being unfair? Was she taking her pain out on Willow?

An incident she'd almost forgotten flashed in her mind, making her wonder if Willow really was harmless. Suddenly Alex wasn't so certain. Maybe that was why she was so apprehensive about seeing her again. She pushed away the memory and instead thought about the day she first met Willow—her mother's only sibling. She knew her mother had an older sister with whom she'd once been close. But her mother told her they'd simply grown apart. That Willow was sweet but had "emotional problems." They'd never visited her aunt, and Alex never thought much about her.

Then her mother died.

The caseworker assigned to Alex must have realized that her aunt was nuts as soon as they arrived at the house. Living in dirty, messy surroundings and dressed like some kind of hippie from the sixties, Willow LeGrand was clearly living on some other planet. One Alex had no desire to visit, let alone stay there until she was eighteen. But the caseworker had just dropped her off and walked away, even though Alex had pleaded with her not to leave her there. It was obvious the woman couldn't have cared less. Just another case checked off her list.

It took Alex weeks to get the house clean and figure out how to feed both of them. Willow had been existing on candy bars, chips, and pop, but she gladly gave Alex money from her disability check so she could go to a neighborhood grocery store and buy food. Within three months, Alex had become the adult in the house. Cleaning, cooking, and paying bills that had been neglected for quite some time. Eventually, things began to run more smoothly . . . until Willow started talking about some crazy book with aliens, demons, and angels.

Then came the meetings. Alex was instructed to lock herself in her room, forbidden to come out until Willow's Circle guests left.

Alex realized she was digging her nails into the armrests. Her fingers hurt as she straightened them. She reminded herself that there was no other way to find a copy of The Book and attempt to get ahead of a man who may have the power to kill thousands if not millions of people. She had no choice but to approach her aunt.

The plane landed at the airport. When she'd left Wichita, it was called Mid-Continent Airport, but in 2014 it was renamed the Dwight D. Eisenhower National Airport. As she peered out the small window next to her, she noticed the main building had been given a needed facelift. She wondered what else had changed, but she didn't plan to stay around long enough to find out. She had to get that book and get out. It needed to go to the lab at Quantico so they could look for fingerprints—although there wasn't much chance they'd find any but her aunt's.

Alex and her team were convinced they weren't looking for an *unknown subject* now. They were confident Adam Walker was behind both the train killings and the virus threat. And Monty had been right—trying to stop a potential mass murderer was different from looking for a serial killer.

Alex was grateful her colleagues weren't treating her strangely. After sharing her past, she'd been afraid they would see her as weird—and different from them. She'd fought hard to free herself of the odd little girl she used to be. The fears that had controlled her. The nightmares that struck terror into her heart. She could feel the beginnings of a panic attack, so she concentrated on her breathing. *In, out. In, out.* It had been years since she'd had to deal with one of these attacks. She couldn't allow them to come back now.

"Kansas City won't give us long to get that book," Logan said as they waited for their pilot to tell them they could disembark.

"I know."

The cabin door opened, and Special Agent Keith Corbin came out. Keith was not only a pilot but a member of the FBI's Emergency Response Team, working out of the Washington field office. Well respected throughout the FBI, he was called upon when agents needed to get somewhere fast or if evidence needed to be delivered to Quantico. Keith was a handsome man with prematurely gray hair and an easy smile.

"You can disembark now," he said as he lowered the outside stairs. "I've been told to wait here for you. Must be an important assignment."

Alex and Logan rose from their seats and grabbed their go bags.

When they reached the door, Logan shook Keith's hand. "They're all important, I guess, aren't they?"

Keith grinned. "The perfect response. Well, whatever's going on, I'm praying for your success."

"Thanks, brother," Logan said.

Alex nodded at Keith and mumbled her thanks before they headed down the stairs to the tarmac. Was Keith a Christian too? It felt as if Logan and Keith were part of a club she wasn't a member of.

She and Logan had just entered the terminal when they heard someone call out their names. They both turned to see a man approaching them. They stopped as he came near them with his hand extended.

"Special Agents Donovan and Hart?"

"Special Agent Monroe, I assume," Logan said. "Nice to meet you." They shook hands, and then Agent Monroe approached Alex, who shook his hand as well.

"You look so familiar," she said. "Do I know you?"

Monroe laughed. "You certainly do. In fact, you're the reason I joined the FBI."

Alex frowned at him. She never forgot a face. Why was she having trouble with this one? In just seconds, as if a rotten wooden door sealed for years broke open, she remembered. She felt dizzy and fought hard to steady herself.

"You used to call me Googly," he said with a big smile. "It's me, Mike. We lived down the street from each other for years. Rode the bus to school together."

Alex tried to speak, but no words would come out. The past was scratching and clawing its way into her carefully constructed life. No matter what she had to do, she was determined to catch the creep who'd opened the door and let it in.

5

lex now seemed more relaxed in the front seat of the car, but Logan could tell something was wrong on the plane, and he'd also seen the way she'd reacted to Mike.

He wasn't sure what it was, but something was still off. He could feel it. What kind of life had Alex endured here? Sure, her aunt sounded a little weird. Okay, very weird. But so what? The idea that a trained FBI behavioral analyst would fall apart when reminded of an uncomfortable childhood didn't make sense. He'd been around Alex awhile now. She was sharp. Hard. Professional. Why was she so affected by this place?

She turned to face Mike. "Why did you say I was responsible for your decision to join the FBI?"

Mike chuckled. "You used to tell me all the time that someday you were going to join the FBI and catch all the bad guys."

"*All* the bad guys?" Logan said from the back seat. "You don't plan on leaving any for the rest of us, Alex?"

She actually laughed. He hadn't been sure it was possible.

"Since then I've decided to leave a few for people like you, Preacher."

"Gee, thanks."

Mike looked at him in the rearview mirror. "Your nickname is Preacher? You got off better than me. After I graduated from high school, I discovered contact lenses. Thankfully, my days as Googly are behind me."

"Yeah, I don't think I'll lose my nickname as easily, but don't worry. I have other things on my mind today. I won't be trying to convert you."

"Thanks, I appreciate that," Mike said, grinning.

"So tell me more about your aunt, Alex," Logan said.

Alex was so quiet Logan wondered if she'd heard him.

"Like I said back at the office, my aunt took me in when I was twelve," she finally said. "After my mother died. She didn't hesitate. I believe she really wanted me."

"She was always kind to me," Mike said. "She was just . . . different."

"What does that mean?" Logan asked. He knew the larger details surrounding Alex's aunt, but he wanted to hear more. Who was she really? Why didn't Alex want to see her? Why hadn't she visited her in all these years?

Another silence. "Look," Mike said. "This is kinda tough for me." He looked over at Alex. "I don't want to . . ."

"Stop," Alex said. "This is just like any other case. Be honest. It won't bother me. We have to find that toxin before it's too late. Hurt feelings are the least of our worries."

Mike took a deep breath. "Okay. Well, she was a nice lady who wore flowery dresses and ballet shoes. Her hair was usually messy, and she would lose concentration in the middle of a sentence. I met her before Alex moved in. I was selling candy for my school once and went to her house. She asked me to come in so she could find some money. When she opened the door, the odor overwhelmed me." He glanced at Alex again. "She didn't seem to know how to clean a house. Something like a dozen cats were running around. And a big pot of cabbage sat on the stove that could have been there for days."

He shook his head. "At least I think it was cabbage. How she ever got custody of you, Alex, is beyond me. I didn't know anything about The Book or the Circle she was involved in until I was given all the current facts of this case. When I got wind you were coming and why, I asked to be assigned to help you here in Wichita—and to bring you the warrant you might need."

"I appreciate that," Alex said. "My aunt got custody because she was my only living relative. The social worker didn't care what Willow or her house were like. Apparently, neither did the court or child services. They just sent me there so they could close their case in an overloaded child welfare system."

"Wow," Logan said. "I can't imagine living in a place like that." He couldn't keep the compassion out of his voice even though he knew Alex wanted to keep the conversation professional.

"It didn't stay that way for long," Mike said. "Alex cleaned up that mess and kept it clean. She did all the housework and cooking. It was like she was the grown-up and Willow was the kid."

"Do you have any idea what we're going to find when we knock on her door, Alex?" Logan asked.

"I assume everything will be as it was before I lived there. Willow didn't have any desire to be an adult."

"How do you think she'll receive you?" Mike asked.

"I really have no idea. She used to tell me she loved me, and in her own way, I think she did. But she never really took care of me. I mean, she gave me a room to sleep in and provided for my basic needs. Of course, she had only a disability check, so all my clothes were secondhand. And if I wanted anything besides food or clothing, I had to buy it myself."

"My mom hired Alex to help around our house," Mike said. "And she passed my sister's clothes along to her."

Alex smiled. "Yes, your mother was good to me," she said. "She was more of a mother than Willow ever was. How is your mom?" She leaned toward him. "Does she still live in the same house?"

"She's fine, and, no, she's moved. Dad was killed not long after you left. Car accident."

"Oh, I'm so sorry to hear that."

"Thanks. Anyway, once my sister and I were out on our own, Mom stayed in the house alone for a while. But a few years ago, she relocated to a senior-living apartment complex. She's really happy there. I'd like to tell her you're in town, but I was told to keep this assignment under the radar. I wish you could visit her. She'd love that."

"I would enjoy that too. But that will have to be a different trip. No time for anything besides getting The Book to the FBI lab."

"Of course you're right," Mike said. "Maybe I could contact you when this is all over and see if you can come back for a visit."

Alex didn't say anything as she turned her head toward the passenger side window. Logan wondered if she really would come back to Wichita to see Mike's mother. Alex was a loner. Yeah, she good-naturedly worked with other agents, but she rarely accepted an invitation to nonwork events. Many times she'd say she had to get home to her dog.

"Mike mentioned your aunt had cats. You have a dog, right?" Logan asked. "What do you do with him when you go out of town?"

"My neighbors take care of him."

"I can't remember his name."

"Krypto. I named him after Superman's dog."

Logan couldn't help but wonder why she'd chosen that name. Did she identify with Superman—someone who couldn't be hurt?

"It's great you have neighbors who will watch him," Mike said.

She nodded. "Yeah, it is. They have kids who like playing with him. Sometimes I wonder if he would be happier with them." She paused for a moment before saying, "But I need him in my life. And the truth is he's really attached to me. Thinks he's my protector, I guess. It's a miracle he gets along with the other people as well as he does."

Was there a hint of jealousy there? Or was it fear?

"This is it," Mike said, slowing the car to a crawl.

Logan looked around. Not the best neighborhood. Lots of older homes, but for the most part the properties were well-kept.

Mike pointed to his left, at a large two-story house painted white with yellow accents. "That's where we used to live."

Logan turned to see Alex staring at a different house on that side of the street. He was shocked to see that her face had gone completely white.

Alex felt her throat close, as if fingers of fear had grabbed her and were trying to choke the life out of her.

Stop it! Remember who you are. You don't have to be afraid of that crazy woman. She's just the means to an end. You're here to get that book, then you'll never have to see her again.

Mike pulled the car over to the curb. "If you can't get her to give you The Book, we'll have to call in help to search her house." He leaned over and took some papers from the glove box. "Here's the warrant and the release document."

Alex took them and slipped them into the inside pockets of her jacket.

"Are you sure you want me to wait out here?" Logan asked.

"Yes. She'll shut down if you're with me."

Even as Alex said the words, she wasn't sure they were true. Maybe the fear wrapping itself around her was caused by her concern Logan would see her as vulnerable if he came inside. If he saw the conditions she grew up in, would he feel sorry for her? She hated pity from anyone. She hated self-pity even more. Alex steeled herself to get out of the car and knock on her aunt's door.

"Give me a little time," she said. "I can't just walk in and ask for The Book. I have to put her at ease first." She placed her hand on Mike's shoulder. "Please don't park any closer. I don't want her to see you two out here."

"Okay. But no kidding, Alex. If you need help, you call us right away."

"You know my aunt. She might be crazy, but she's not dangerous." As soon as she'd finished speaking, the memory she'd recovered popped into her mind again. It made her feel cold inside. How could she have forgotten that for so many years?

"Except someone associated with her might be planning to kill a lot of people. This is different."

"Mike is right," Logan said. "Fifteen minutes, Alex, or the house will have to be searched. We don't have a lot of time for her to get comfortable."

Although she didn't like what Logan said, the agent in her knew he was right. They didn't have time to play games.

"Okay." Without another word, she got out of the car, then walked slowly across the street. Even though she didn't want Mike or Logan to go with her, at that moment she felt completely alone. Almost as lonely as she had when she'd lived in this house.

The November wind suddenly whipped past her, causing her to pull her jacket tighter. It might have helped her body to feel warmer, but it didn't do anything to abate the icy fear in her soul.

Adam sat in the diner, watching the people around him. Three women were laughing and talking two booths away from him, probably making fun of someone. Like other students had made fun of him when he was in college. At a table across from him, tired-looking parents with a small child and a baby ate silently, hushing the toddler several times. When the baby began to cry, the mother reached for a diaper bag. She took out a bottle and stuck it in the baby's mouth. He could tell by her pleading expression that she was embarrassed by her children, yet she hoped they wouldn't have to leave. The father just looked disgusted, as if the baby's cries were somehow his wife's fault.

His gaze shifted to an irritated man who spoke loudly to a waitress as he pointed at his plate. From what Adam could hear, he was livid because his hamburger was pink in the middle. "I asked for well done," he was saying. "Does your cook even know what well done means?"

Without saying a word, the weary waitress picked up his plate and walked off. Adam smiled to himself. He was pretty certain either the waitress or the cook would add something special to the man's burger. Something he didn't want.

Adam sighed. No one here was worth saving. In fact, no one in the whole world was worth saving except his family. These beings didn't know if they were angels or demons, and they didn't care. That made them useless for the Master's plan—the plan straight from the book he'd embraced with his whole heart. Why had he hated it when he was a kid? Probably because his mother was the one who first read it to him. Not his father.

He grimaced to himself. Getting rid of so many of these

cockroaches would actually be a blessing. The Book prophesied that those who remained would rule the earth together as one. Although all he wanted was to do the Master's will, he felt a twinge of jealousy. He liked being part of a small, special group that had wisdom kept from the rest of the world. If everyone were as blessed as he was . . . Well, he didn't like that idea.

But then he reminded himself that he would always be the one who fulfilled the prophecy. That knowledge made him feel better. He would be revered among everyone who survived the Master's judgment.

He smiled to himself again, then went back to his notebook, where he continued to write down his plans. It wouldn't be much longer.

Alex stood in front of Willow's door, shivering. Just standing there made her feel sick to her stomach. She remembered sitting on these porch steps, crying. Wanting nothing more than to go home. She'd even prayed for help from a God who didn't answer. She'd asked Him to get her out of this house. But nothing changed, and she'd had to find a way to exist with a deranged woman. If there even was a God, He obviously didn't care about terrified little girls pleading for help.

She'd also asked Him to make it possible for her to someday become an FBI agent. Her dream of working for the Bureau had come to pass, yes. But she'd made it on her own. Without anyone's help.

With effort that took everything she had, she pushed the ghosts of the past into the dark chasm where she valiantly tried to keep them imprisoned. Her arm felt like lead when she lifted it and knocked on the door. She could hear noises from inside, and she expected to see her aunt swing the door open. But instead, another woman did. She looked to be in her sixties and had curly salt-and-pepper hair, dark eyes, dark skin, and a wide smile on her face.

"Can I help you?" she asked.

Alex was momentarily thrown. The FBI had confirmed that her aunt still lived here. Who was this?

"I'm here to see Willow LeGrand. I'm . . . I'm her niece."

The woman's eyes widened. "Alexandra? Oh my goodness. She'll be so happy to see you." She pushed the door open wide. "Come on in, honey. Willow's told me so much about you."

Alex stepped inside and was shocked to find the living room neat and clean. She'd expected Willow to have let the place go back to the mess it was before she'd moved in. She'd also been afraid entering this house would trigger a reaction she wouldn't be able to explain. But even the furniture was different. This wasn't the house she'd lived in.

"Let me have your coat, honey," the woman said. "I just started a fire in the fireplace. It's nice and warm in here."

"That's okay. I'll keep it," she said. "I'm sorry. I didn't expect to find anyone else here. May I ask who you are?"

The woman had extended her arm for Alex's coat, and she let it drop. "Oh dear. I'm sorry. You're right. I should have introduced myself. I'm Nettie Travers. I live here with your aunt."

"What do you mean you live here?" The words tumbled out before Alex realized she sounded rude.

Rather than look offended, Nettie smiled. "Why don't you sit down? I'll explain everything. Willow is napping, but after we talk, I'll wake her up so you two can visit."

"I don't have a lot of time," Alex said. "I'm here on a matter of urgency."

"Then I don't suppose you'd like a cup of tea?" Nettie asked.

"No. No tea. Thank you."

Nettie gestured toward the couch, and Alex sat down. Nettie took a seat in the matching chair next to the couch. Alex was surprised by how nice the furniture was. Not like the secondhand junk her aunt had once owned.

"I'd been living next door to your aunt for a while before she had a stroke. It was three years ago now," Nettie said. "Some of the neighbors tried to help her, but she needed more care than a few casseroles could provide." She shrugged. "Although I thought the best thing for her was a nursing home, she wouldn't leave. No amount of reasoning would change her mind. My Charlie had passed away two years before, so I asked her if she'd like me to move in and care for her."

She leaned back into her chair. "You see, Charlie was also a stroke victim, and I took care of him for four years before he passed. I felt I had the expertise to help Willow, and she agreed to my suggestion. So I sold my house and moved in. She was living in squalor, Alex. For their sake, I was almost glad all her cats had died by then. I cleaned up, got rid of the furniture, and moved in my own. Hers wasn't in very good shape."

"I don't doubt that." Alex frowned at her. "But what are you getting out of this?"

Nettie smiled slowly. "Sorry. I thought I'd made that clear. I was lonely. Sitting alone in my house was withering my soul. Now I get to help Willow, and I feel needed. Wanted."

"I know my aunt's disability check isn't much," Alex said. "I sent her checks over the years as I could, but none of them were ever cashed. Are you paying her bills?"

Nettie stood and went to a small antique-looking desk against one wall. She pulled open a drawer and reached inside, then brought over an envelope and checkbook. She placed them on the coffee table in front of Alex.

"All your checks are in that envelope," Nettie said softly. "I never wanted you to think I was trying to take advantage of your aunt." Then she pushed the checkbook toward Alex. "All her SSI checks are still deposited directly into the checking account you set up for her, and every penny spent is accounted for. I pay for half of everything." She sighed. "Your address was on your checks. I wanted to write to you—to tell you about your aunt's stroke—but Willow wouldn't allow it. She wanted you to come back on your own."

Alex went through the envelope and then scanned the checkbook. Nettie was telling the truth. She looked up and met her gaze. "I'm sorry. This is just so unusual."

Nettie's eyes misted. "You haven't known much kindness, have you, honey?"

The woman's look of compassion angered her. "Look, I really don't have time for this. Whatever you and my aunt want to do is fine with me. I don't care. I'm here because I need something from Willow."

"What is it?"

"A book. A very special book."

Nettie's kind expression turned guarded. "What's the title of the book?" she asked.

"It has no title. My aunt and people she knows just call it The Book."

From behind her, an unearthly screech rose in intensity, causing Alex to jump. She turned to see her aunt standing in the doorway, a look of terror on her face.

7

Nettie hurried over to Willow. As she helped her to the couch, Alex watched her aunt. Alex hadn't seen her in eighteen years. Although Willow was definitely older and Alex could see the effects of the stroke, she was happy to note how clean her aunt looked. Her wild, curly hair had been cut short, and her clothes were much more stylish. Appropriate for a woman her age. Probably Nettie's doing. Just like the house.

"Willow, look who's here," Nettie was saying. "It's Alex. Alexandra."

Willow stared at her as if she didn't know her. Then the corners of her lips ticked upward into a smile, although one side of her mouth was higher than the other. After her reaction to hearing that Alex wanted The Book, Alex was surprised to see her smile.

"Hi, Willow," Alex said. "It's nice to see you."

Willow mumbled something that sounded as if she were trying to say she was happy to see her too.

Alex glanced at her watch. She'd been here close to fifteen minutes. If she didn't move this along, Logan and Mike would be knocking on the door.

She scooted closer to her aunt. "Listen, Willow. I need your help. A very bad man plans to hurt a lot of people. If we don't find him in time, many will die. Do you understand?"

Willow nodded, her eyes trained on Alex's.

"I know you're not supposed to talk about The Book, but this evil man is using it to carry out a terrible plan. We need it so we can figure out what he might do next." Alex reached into her jacket pocket and removed the search warrant. "This gives me the authority to take The Book by force if I have to, but I'd rather you help me of your own free will."

Willow's body stiffened, and her face contorted with fear. She began to breathe quickly and say, "No . . . no . . . no . . . no . . ."

Alex's gaze shifted to Nettie. What was she thinking? Did she know about The Book? Nettie frowned at her. "I'm sorry, Alex, but Willow needs to lie down again. I'm afraid this kind of stress could bring on another stroke."

Before Alex could protest, Nettie helped Willow to her feet and guided her out of the living room, but not before Willow looked back and shook her head at Alex. Her fear was palpable.

Alex looked at her watch again. Time was up. The house would have to be searched. She wondered how upset that would make her aunt—and her aunt's roommate. When Nettie came back into the room, Alex stood.

"I work for the FBI, Nettie. We have to have that book. I

wasn't exaggerating when I said lives are at stake." She put the warrant on the coffee table. "Unless you're able to give it to me, this house will have to be searched."

"Oh, honey, I wasn't getting your aunt out of the room because I don't want you to take that thing. I just didn't want her to see this." She walked over to a large bookshelf, reached behind it, and pulled out something wrapped in plastic. She handed it to Alex. The Book. Alex removed an evidence bag from her other pocket and put The Book in it.

"Thank you," Alex said, meaning it with every fiber of her being. "If it wasn't for you—"

"No, honey. If it wasn't for the Lord. I knew He'd sent me here. At first I thought it was just to care for your aunt, and that was enough for me. But now I know there's more. I'm here so I can get this horrible thing out of this house."

"You're not—"

"Part of the Circle? Heavens no. I'm a Christian. The first time Willow showed this to me, I knew it was evil. I would have thrown it away, but she made me promise not to do that until she was ready. I've talked to your aunt about the Lord, and she's very close to accepting Him instead of these lies."

"I'm surprised she let you see it. No one but members of the Circle are supposed to read it."

"Willow was beginning to question her beliefs, but I think she showed me out of fear. Fear that someone would come to take it forcibly."

"So you promised her you wouldn't throw it away?"

A smile lit up Nettie's face. "But I'm not throwing it away, am I? I'm giving it to you so you can save people's lives." Tears filled her eyes, and her voice choked.

Alex heard a car door slam. "Hold on a minute, Nettie,"

she said. She opened the door just as Logan reached the top of the porch steps.

"Time's up," he said.

"I've got it." She handed the evidence bag to him, and he took it with a smile.

"Good work," he said. "I'll note the time. We need to get going."

"I'll be there in a minute."

"Did you tell your aunt the FBI will need to get her fingerprints?"

"No. I'll tell her caregiver. Willow has had a stroke. It will be difficult to get her to the local RA for fingerprinting. Tell Mike they'll need to come here to do it."

"I will."

"I still need to get a signed receipt. It will only take me a few minutes. Wait in the car for me."

Logan nodded and headed down the steps. Alex shut the door and turned back to Nettie. "What about the others in the Circle?" she asked. "I'm surprised they haven't been around, trying to find this copy if they suspect Willow is backing away from them. Or at least because she's had a stroke."

"Oh, they've called, more than once, but I told them Willow couldn't remember what she'd done with it." She shook her finger at Alex. "I wanted to tell them I burned the nasty thing, but I couldn't lie. What I said was completely true. About a year ago she hid it and then forgot where it was. I just happened to stumble across it. I haven't told her I found it. She's convinced it's lost. She's searched the house more than once, but I had it put away in a spot she didn't think of looking."

"But she heard me ask you for it."

"She won't remember, honey. Her memory has grown worse and worse." Nettie reached over and patted Alex's arm. "Don't worry about us. We'll be fine."

Alex wanted to do as Nettie asked, but she wasn't certain how vengeful the members of the Circle could be—angels or no. She was worried they'd retaliate in some way if they found out Nettie had given her The Book.

"Do you have a cell phone, Nettie? If so, I need it too. We may be able to find members of the Circle with it."

Nettie shook her head slowly and clicked her tongue. "Oh dear. I had an old flip phone. You know, the kind where you have to buy minutes for it?"

Alex nodded. She had a bad feeling about where this was going.

"I threw that away when I got my new iPhone, and none of those people have called since then. I also recently changed your aunt's landline number, just to be safe." She paused a moment, then her eyes widened. "I'm so sorry. You wanted to see who called me. Track them. Though, I don't think it would help you. I think they use burner phones. You know, the kind you can't trace?" She smiled. "I watch a lot of *Criminal Minds*. I know about burner phones."

Alex smiled back at her. "I'm sure you do. Can you give me the number for your flip phone and Willow's new landline? We may be able to get some records that would help us. And if you hear from anyone from the Circle again, will you let me know?"

"Of course, honey." Nettie walked over to the same small desk and this time took a pen and pad of paper from the drawer. After writing something down, she tore off the top sheet and handed it to Alex. "Here are the numbers. I hope they help you." She put the paper and pen on the coffee table, then sat down on the couch.

"Call me immediately if you need help," Alex said as she handed her a card from her pocket. "If you feel threatened in any way." Then she took the receipt form out of another pocket. "I need you to sign this, please. It just says you turned The Book over to me."

Nettie nodded and retrieved the pen she'd just used. She quickly signed the form and gave it back to Alex.

"Please don't worry about us. I think those people finally gave up." Her eyebrows knit together, and she stared at Alex with an odd expression. "I have to tell you something, honey," she said. "Something God wants you to know."

"Look, I'm grateful you've freed my aunt from the Circle, but your God is just another version of the Master she worshiped." Alex expected Nettie to be offended, but she just smiled.

"No, honey. There's only one true God. He wants me to tell you that He saw your tears, and He's been watching over you all this time. Before this present journey is over, you will meet Him."

A chill washed through Alex. "Are you saying I'm going to die?"

"I don't think so. I hope not. But you be careful, honey. And watch for Him."

Nettie stood and gave Alex a hug.

Alex thanked her for her help before hurrying out the door, closing it behind her. Her emotions were all jumbled up. She wasn't angry with Nettie for believing in a God that didn't exist; she was just upset that she'd pretended to have a message from Him. Yet the words the woman spoke echoed through her mind over and over. *"He wants me to tell you that He saw your tears, and He's been watching over you all this time."*

Alex started down the steps but halted momentarily. Nettie hadn't lived on this street when a young Alex had sat here, crying and asking a silent God for help. And Alex knew Willow had never noticed.

How could Nettie know?

I t was clear Logan wanted to talk about the case on their short flight to Kansas City, but Alex was overwhelmed by thoughts and feelings that seemed to fill every empty space inside her. Voices from the past flooded her mind, each one competing for her attention.

They'd gone to the RA with Mike, where agents had carefully made a copy of The Book. Alex and Logan would deliver it to the command post in Kansas City, and the original would be flown to the lab at Quantico. Keith would take it there after dropping them off.

Logan finally fell silent, as if he understood she needed some time to process the fallout from stepping inside that awful house again. Nettie had obviously worked miracles inside its walls, but enough of the past was left to remind Alex of a childhood filled with strange people and weird beliefs. Secret meetings and lowered voices that only exacerbated the fears that held her in a firm grip. She was warned not to leave her room while the meetings were going on, which wasn't a problem. Alex had no interest in her aunt's creepy friends or the teachings from The Book.

Regardless, Willow would quote passages from its pages for hours on end whenever Alex was in hearing distance. Until she turned fourteen, that is. Willow let Alex know more than once how disappointed she was that she wasn't interested in joining the Circle. Alex didn't care. All she wanted was to get out of that house.

Alex's life had been filled with mind-numbing repetition. She would go to school, come home, feed the cats, and clean the house. Then she'd make supper. After that she'd go to her room and study for several hours before falling into bed until she had to get up, make breakfast, and race to the bus. Some nights she'd get off the bus early and go to the store. At least Willow gave her money for groceries. It wasn't much, but Alex learned how to make the dollars stretch. Lots of rice and oatmeal. Bread, peanut butter, bologna, and cheese were the staples. Sometimes she had enough to buy hamburger or a chicken. Willow told everyone she didn't eat meat, but she never turned down Alex's roasted chicken or juicy cheese-burgers. It might not have been the healthiest diet, but it kept them alive.

Alex also found a cheap brand of food the cats seemed to like. She cared about them even though she had to spend grocery money on them. They were sweet, and sometimes they came into her room at night and curled up on the bed with her. Their purring soothed her.

Although Alex never told Willow about events at school, several times she'd shown up without warning. Her wild hair, long skirts, and ballet slippers created quite a stir. Willow had no idea she was a spectacle. She would walk into Alex's classroom and ask her where something was, ranting and raving that someone had stolen it. Alex would get up from her desk and take Willow's arm, guiding her out of the classroom with giggles and snickering following her out into the hallway. Alex would have to calm her down, tell her where the item she wanted was, whether it was her keys, her purse, or whatever. Although the visits were embarrassing, they made Alex's teachers finally stop inviting her aunt to parent-teacher conferences. That made Alex's life a little easier.

Willow never physically abused her but neither did she try to protect her or encourage her. Her instability made Alex feel insecure, as if she always had to be on her guard. She worried that at any moment, the floor could collapse under her again, the way it had when her mother died.

Alex remembered exactly when she'd decided she wanted to become a profiler with the FBI. It was Career Day at school. Before then, she'd just dreamt about joining the Bureau. But one of the students—she couldn't remember his name now—brought an uncle who'd retired from the FBI's Behavioral Analysis Unit a year earlier. His stories captivated Alex. She was so entranced she could barely breathe. Could someone really do that—study hearts of darkness in a way that made them understandable? Could that kind of knowledge save lives and bring justice? Could understanding evil make her less afraid?

It was all she wanted. To live in the light. So Alex promised herself she'd be an FBI behavioral analyst someday. She got books from the library about serial killers and famous profilers. And as she read about the lives of some of the FBI's most successful profilers, she envisioned herself as one of them.

Alex spent those years working hard in school so she could win a scholarship for college. When she walked out the door for the last time, it was the happiest she'd felt since before her mother died. Her only regret was leaving the cats behind.

She worked her way through college to pay for all the other things she needed. Then she joined the police department in Kansas City and from there, the FBI. And now everything she'd dreamt of had finally come to pass.

"That was hard on you, wasn't it?" Logan said.

Alex was startled at the sound of his voice. She'd been so lost in her thoughts that she'd forgotten he was there. "Yeah. I really had no intention of ever going back there."

"You don't have any feelings toward your aunt?"

Alex sighed. She really didn't want to talk about this. Why was he asking these questions? "I took care of her for six years," she said. "My debt was paid. I wish her well, but she's not my responsibility any longer."

"You said she's the only family you have?"

Alex fought back a sudden surge of anger. What was he trying to say? That she should feel some kind of duty toward her aunt? "Yeah, I think so. I mean, my dad disappeared when I was four. I have no idea if he's alive or dead." She looked out the window, hoping it would put an end to the conversation. They were almost there. Alex could never get over how much the ground looked like a patchwork quilt from the air. They were beginning to descend, so she fastened her seat belt.

"I'm sorry, Alex. I'm not trying to meddle. I'm really interested, that's all."

"Well, thanks," she said, trying not to sound as irritated as she felt, "but it might be best if we keep our personal lives . . . personal."

"Sure. If that's what you want."

Logan turned his head and finished whatever he was doing on his laptop. Then he closed the cover before sliding it into his bag and fastening his seat belt. They stayed silent as they prepared to land.

Alex felt some regret for her response to Logan, but she really wasn't interested in sharing her life with him . . . or with anyone. All she wanted to do was find Adam Walker before something too horrible for words happened. Nothing else mattered.

W e're here," Logan said, as if she wasn't aware the plane had landed.

Alex picked up her bag with the copy of The Book inside and followed Logan to the door. They said good-bye to Keith, then walked down the stairs, where they found a car waiting for them. The man who got out and opened the trunk for their bags introduced himself as Detective Ambrose with the Kansas City Police Department.

It didn't take long for them to reach the CP, a boarded-up warehouse converted for the various agencies so they could work together to find Adam Walker.

Ambrose drove them around to the back, and when they got out, he unlocked a metal door and ushered them inside a busy hive of activity. Monty hurried up to them.

"You made good time," he said. "I take it you have a copy of this book we've been waiting for?"

"Right here," Alex said, holding up her bag.

"Great. Hopefully it will help us come up with an assessment and some strategies to find this guy before he uses the virus."

Monty led them to the back of the large area. He opened the door to a separate room where Alex saw a long table set up with chairs around it. She put her bag on the table and removed the copied pages she'd carried with her from Wichita.

"It's been confirmed," Monty said. "The lab in Ethiopia is missing an active vial of Ebola. They believe it was sent to Kansas City, but the lab here can't find it."

"So everyone is convinced the research assistant who's missing—Adam Walker—took it?" Logan asked.

"Yes. Unless we uncover other information, we're proceeding as if he has the virus." Monty gestured toward the table. "We have a meeting in a few minutes. The assistant special agent in charge is Derek Harrison. He's tough, but he listens." Monty looked around him and then lowered his voice. "CDC and Homeland are here."

Having Homeland and the CDC as part of the task force made the seriousness of the situation clear. Alex could feel the tension in the CP. The FBI and local police were working furiously. Desks had been set up all over the room, and analysts, detectives, and agents were busy looking for something that might lead them to their subject.

A large man with red hair approached them, then pointed at the package in Alex's hands. "Is that the book everyone's talking about?" he asked.

"This is ASAC Derek Harrison," Monty said. "Sir, SSA Alex Donovan and SSA Logan Hart."

"Good to meet you, sir," Alex said, extending her hand. Harrison had a firm handshake, and his expression was serious and determined. Good. They needed someone who would do whatever it took to find the virus.

"Yes, this is a copy of the book we believe our killer is following," Alex said. "We hope it helps." She handed it to Harrison.

"I heard it's just called The Book. Has the original been dusted for fingerprints?" he asked.

"The Resident Agency in Wichita is handling that. Once they have my aunt's prints and her caregiver's, they'll be sent to the lab. The Book is on its way there now."

"We need that information as soon as possible."

Alex cleared her throat. "Sir, I'm as sure as I can be that only my aunt and her caregiver's prints will be on this book. My aunt revered it, and she would never let anyone else near it. Even me. She doesn't know her caregiver found it and hid it from her."

Harrison raised an eyebrow. "I don't understand. So you've never read it? But you recognized the graffiti on the train cars. How could you do that if you'd never read this book?"

"My aunt quoted from it a lot. From the time I was twelve until I was fourteen. It was her attempt to add me to the Circle. Her efforts failed."

"What about members of the Circle? You're certain their prints won't be on it?"

"Yes, sir. I am. My aunt could open it in a meeting and read from it, but that's as close as anyone else could get."

"Okay," he said slowly, drawing out the word. "So if she knew we were going to read this thing—"

"She'd be extremely distraught. Probably never speak to me again. But to be honest, she's always had mental problems, and it seems she's deteriorated quite a bit further after a stroke. That's why she has a caregiver."

"You acquired it with a warrant?" Harrison asked.

"Yes. The RA in Wichita got it for us."

"Good. Let's sit down. We're waiting to hear from KCPD. They're going through Adam Walker's apartment again."

His phone rang, and Harrison picked it up from the table where he'd placed it when he sat down. "Speak of the devil," he said. He answered, then listened for several minutes. Finally, he said, "Okay, thanks. If you learn anything that will help us . . . Yeah, I know."

He disconnected the call and shook his head. "Nothing. Everything is gone except for what came with the apartment. Nothing left that might help us. All we have is that poem he left in his desk at the lab. Walker knew how to cover his tracks." He turned toward Alex. "We're counting on you and your team to help us figure out where he might be. How we can find him. We'll give you anything you need. Just ask."

"We'll get to work on it right away," she said. Logan and Monty nodded.

Just then the back door opened and two men carried in boxes of pizza. "Grab something to eat first," Harrison said. "We'll make more copies of this book and give one to you. I want others going through it too."

"Hopefully, we can give you something solid soon," Alex said. "Did you find anything through ViCAP or NCIC?"

"No, nothing. We're gathering all the usual sort of records, of course. Birth certificate, driver's license . . ." He took a deep breath. "You three will be on our Domestic Terrorism Task Force. You'll concentrate on finding Walker—and that virus. You'll also be working with the CDC and Homeland. Detectives with the KCPD are investigating the murders."

"I believe the murders and the virus are closely connected,"

Alex said. "Please ask the Kansas City PD to keep us updated on their progress."

"I will. Your unit chief has good things to say about all of you. I have confidence you'll be able to give us some insight so we can find this virus before more people lose their lives." He paused for a moment. "The CDC says thousands could die if it's released. Even millions."

Alex just nodded. The gravity of the situation could smother her if she allowed it to. She had to use her training to find Walker, and she was determined to do it.

She looked at Logan and Monty. "Let's get some of that pizza. It's going to be a long night."

10

It took a while for Willow to fall asleep for the night, but then Nettie sat next to her bed and prayed for her. As she called upon the God she loved, she couldn't help but think about Alex.

She'd seen the same deep-seated pain in Alex she'd observed in Willow, which in Willow's case had apparently led to a form of mental illness. But losing both parents and living with a mentally ill aunt would be traumatic for anyone. Alex carried that emotional injury like a suit of armor. No one could get in. Nettie wished Alex realized how much alike she and Willow were.

Willow had trusted Nettie enough to share her history. Willow and Alex's mother had been raised by parents who were absent most of the time, focused on their careers. The sisters were often left to fend for themselves, and Willow had become her younger sibling's caregiver, doing the best she could in a role she was unsuited for. Then Alex's mother went off on her own, leaving Willow alone in her emotionally unstable state. She eventually cut off all contact.

Nettie was certain Willow became involved in the Circle when her sister all but abandoned her. She was looking for something to belong to. She'd wanted her life to be important. Willow had no self-esteem before The Book came into her life. It made her feel special.

Willow mumbled something in her sleep, and Nettie reached over to brush her friend's hair from her face. Even though she hadn't reacted well to Alex's visit, when they talked later, Willow had cried, telling Nettie she'd failed her niece. Nettie told her about the forgiveness of Christ and was able to pray with her to receive a different life full of love, hope, and grace. Finally, Willow was free of the destructive cult that had imprisoned her mind for so many years.

Nettie believed God had sent her to Willow for just that purpose. She smiled. She was content. She'd obeyed Him, and now Willow LeGrand had changed books. Her name was written in the Lamb's Book of Life.

Tomorrow she'd call Alex and tell her it was Willow's love for her that finally changed her life. She hoped Alex would be pleased.

She rose from the chair and tiptoed out of the room, making her way to her own bedroom. She got ready for bed and turned on the TV so she could catch her favorite show before going to sleep, but she was so tired that she began to nod off.

She heard the sound of a footstep in her room only at the last moment. By then it was too late.

———

Logan, Monty, and Alex had been going through the information gathered so far on Adam Walker, but they were still waiting on another copy of The Book. It was late, and they were all tired. Thankfully, a nearby table had a coffee maker. Logan wasn't sure how many cups he'd had since they'd arrived at the CP.

Monty was out in the larger room, consulting with some of the local agents. Alex was quiet and focused. She hadn't said much yet. Logan wanted to talk about what he'd seen so far, but he'd decided to be patient. He didn't want to disrupt her process.

When her phone rang, they both jumped. Who would be calling her at two in the morning?

She picked it up and stared at the display. "It's Mike," she said. "Hey, Mike, what's up?" She listened for a long time. Logan watched as her expression changed. "I understand," she said, her voice low. She disconnected the call and stared at her phone as if she'd never seen it before.

"Alex, what is it?" Logan asked.

He watched as she took a deep breath and looked up to meet his gaze. Her expression had hardened. Her armor was firmly in place.

"The police got a call from Willow's neighbor, who said she heard screams. Willow is dead. Nettie's in serious condition. She's in the hospital."

The news hit Logan like a punch in the gut. Had they made a fatal mistake? Should they have put Willow's house under surveillance? It hadn't occurred to him that the two women would be in any real danger. The Circle sounded like a bunch of nuts, not people who would do something like this. Besides, how could anyone possibly know the FBI had The Book? Maybe this a crime that had nothing to do with the Circle.

"Willow seemed so afraid when I mentioned The Book," Alex said. "I thought it was because she was . . . well, you know . . . not all there. Especially after the stroke. I never took the Circle seriously until the Train Man. I should have done something. I should have gotten them protection."

"Listen, it never occurred to me they were vulnerable." Logan frowned. "Besides, how would anyone know we had that book? It doesn't make sense."

Alex shrugged. "Maybe they told someone. A friend who wasn't a friend. Or maybe someone saw us take it out of the house."

"No one could know what was in that evidence bag. That can't be it. And besides, what good would it do to kill Nettie and your aunt? Even if someone knew they'd given us that book, killing them makes no sense. They weren't any threat." He paused for a moment. "Could someone have been afraid Willow would reveal the names of people in the Circle?"

Alex shook her head slowly. "I don't know. As I've said, no one uses their real name in the Circle. It's not impossible, but in Willow's current state, it's unlikely she could have led us to anyone else. And I didn't get the impression that Nettie had anything to do with the Circle. She hated it." She sighed. "Giving someone else The Book is the worst sin a member of the Circle can commit, though. Willow told me that. It's my fault. Maybe this was an act of revenge. Punishment. Why didn't I listen? This was preventable."

"That's ridiculous. Of course it's not your fault. You know better than that. The fault lies with whoever did this. *If* the Circle committed this crime—and we don't know that for certain—they need to be disbanded forever. This isn't some kind of religion. It's a very dangerous cult."

"I agree," Alex said. Another long sigh escaped her lips.

At that moment, Harrison came into the room. Logan told him about Willow and Nettie.

"I want to go back there," Alex said before Harrison could respond. "We might be able to find something to help us locate Walker."

"Our agents at the RA can do that. The local police will be involved too," Harrison said, frowning. "I think you can do more good here."

Alex stood. "You don't understand, sir. They don't know anything about the Circle or The Book. I do. This attack has to be connected to Walker. I know we're focusing on the virus and you have other people investigating the murders here, but they're all connected. I'm certain of it. Besides, we can share techniques to help investigators ask the right questions of neighbors and others who might have seen something around my aunt's house during the time of the assault."

Harrison still looked skeptical. Logan wasn't sure who was right, but he had to admit Alex had made a good point.

"All right," Harrison finally said. "But I need you to keep working on this assessment. Do what you need to do in Wichita and come right back." He looked at Logan. "Go with her. I'll contact Keith and let you know when to meet him."

Alex and Logan arrived at the airport just as Keith got there, barely back from Quantico. Logan could tell he was tired. Hopefully he could sleep on the plane while they were in Wichita.

Alex was quiet, and Logan didn't try to start a conversation. He sensed that she was dealing with emotions he probably wouldn't understand. All he could do was make himself available if she needed him.

When they landed in Wichita, Mike was waiting for them.

"I'm so sorry, Alex," Mike said when she slid into the front seat next to him. "I was certain you'd want to know right away. One of our agents picked up the report and called me. He knew we were friends. I hated making that call. You don't have to go to the house, you know. We can go somewhere else. Get some coffee. Talk."

"No, I want to go. I need to see."

"Do you think this is the guy you're looking for?" Mike asked as he started driving away from the plane. "Would he do this?"

"No," Alex said without any hesitation. "Walker has an agenda. A calling. He has to kill two more people, but he has to do it big. Leave a message behind. Killing a couple of helpless old women doesn't fit his signature. He wouldn't do anything to contaminate his last sacrifices. They're the only thing keeping him from releasing a deadly virus that will finish out his destiny."

"How dangerous is this virus?" Mike asked. "Kansas City's keeping a lot of this on the down-low."

"We don't know. It's possible . . . Well, it could be catastrophic."

Mike turned his head to stare at her. "We need to warn people, Alex."

She reached over and put her hand on his shoulder. "Listen, we don't have all the facts yet. We're not sure what we're dealing with. Going public now would be a big mistake. We could lose him and the virus. If it comes to it, I'm sure the right decision will be made. But for now, we can't make assumptions."

Mike was quiet, then said, "All right. Just do everything you can to help us find this guy, Alex."

"We will. I promise."

Logan couldn't help but worry. Would they be able to

offer anything that would help investigators find Walker? He
hoped so. But would it be in time? Was Mike right? Should
the public be warned? Frankly, he was grateful that decision
would come from someone with a higher pay grade than his.

He didn't have friends or family in this area of the country.
He was thankful for that. But Adam Walker's actions could
devastate other families. Logan was trying not to think about
the actual results from releasing such a deadly virus. It was
overwhelming, and he needed to stay focused.

He could see Alex's face reflected in the windshield. She
looked tired. It would be hours before they would get some
sleep. They'd been booked into an extended stay hotel in
Kansas City with no idea when they'd actually get there.

They finally arrived at Willow's house. Cars lined the
street—both marked police cars and unmarked cars that
probably belonged to detectives assigned to the case. The
coroner's car was there too. A couple of vans from local news
stations were parked across the street from the house, but it
was clear the police had told them to stay out of the way.
If they hadn't been corralled, they'd be in the front yard,
hounding law enforcement with questions. It had to be below
freezing, but several reporters stood outside, talking to the
cameramen they'd brought with them.

Mike double parked so they could leave when they needed
to. Without saying a word, Alex opened her door, got out,
and headed toward the house.

Logan hurried after her. He'd seen some terrible things
over the years, but this was the first time an agent he knew
had lost someone involved in a case he was working. He
wondered how this would affect Alex. Her armor fit snugly,
but was it strong enough to protect her from this?

11

lex willed her legs to take her toward the house she'd lived in for six years. Twice she'd told herself she'd never have to step foot inside again. Now here she was. But this time it was different. Willow wasn't here. For some reason, that made it worse, not better.

"Are you sure you want to do this?" Logan asked. "You don't have to—"

Alex stopped him by holding up her hand. Her eyes locked on his. "Willow and I weren't . . . close. I'm fine. Really. We need to see the crime scene. It could help us figure out who did this. Remember, Walker was probably once part of the Circle. I'm convinced this was their work."

Logan didn't argue with her. Alex was certain that was because he knew she was right.

Logan held up the crime scene tape placed around the front yard. Lights set up by the police seemed to put the old house in a yellow spotlight. A gust of icy wind tried to whip the tape out of Logan's hand, but he held on to it while Alex slipped underneath.

"Hey, folks, you need to get behind the tape," an officer shouted as he hustled toward them. Logan and Alex removed their credentials and held them up.

The officer nodded. "Sorry. We heard you were coming." He glanced toward the house. "The body has been removed, and the injured woman was taken to the hospital. We're processing the scene now. Our Violent Crimes Unit is here, along with our CSI techs."

"Come up with anything interesting yet?" Logan asked.

"Early in the investigation," the officer replied, "but there's certainly something unusual about this crime scene. I won't tell you about it. You should see it for yourself."

A warning bell went off somewhere inside Alex. She thanked the officer, then walked toward the front porch steps. As she passed the spot where she used to sit and grieve, dreaming of a better life, out of the corner of her eye she thought she saw a figure sitting there. She refused to look because she knew it was impossible.

Suddenly, someone pulled on the sleeve of her jacket. She jerked away.

"Hey, sorry," Logan said. "Didn't mean to spook you."

"I'm not spooked," she snapped. "But next time warn me when you're about to grab me."

She knew her response was overblown, but she was upset that she'd had to come back here again. It was as if someone had decided to make her relive the worst time of her life. She forced herself to remember what she'd just told Logan. It was important for them to see the crime scene. It would help them make a valid assessment.

They reached the porch and were met by an officer who handed them gloves and booties. After they put them on, he opened the door to let them in.

Alex had to bite her lip not to gasp. Blood was on the floor, the walls, the furniture. "This guy was angry," she said under her breath.

"Very," Logan added.

Alex stood on the plastic runner laid down on the floor so those working the scene wouldn't contaminate the evidence.

She frowned as she looked around. "I expected something . . . different. If the Circle did this, I would expect it to be . . . orderly. Planned." She waved her hand around. "This is frenzied."

"But why?" Logan asked. "Do you think somehow Circle members found out we have Willow's copy of The Book?" Logan shook his head slowly. "Although, I still have a hard time believing they could."

"We certainly didn't advertise it." As Alex gazed around the room, she had to admit she was confused too.

A man walked up next to them. His jacket identified him as one of the crime scene techs. "You the FBI?" he asked.

"Yeah," Logan answered. "You've got a mess here. Any footprints in the blood?"

"You're not kidding, and no, the killer managed to avoid stepping into any blood." He pointed out two large stains on the carpet where the blood had soaked through to the wood floor underneath. "Both these women were dragged from their beds and killed here. I'm convinced our guy thought they were both dead when he left, but when the police got here they found one of the victims barely hanging on. A Nettie something. Can't remember her last name right now. She's in the hospital. Via Christi. It's about four miles from here."

"Have you recovered the murder weapon?" Alex asked.

The man nodded. "A crowbar. Looks like he took it from the garage. The tools are neatly organized, and there's one empty spot on the wall where the crowbar fits."

"But that doesn't make sense," Alex said.

The man frowned. "I don't understand."

"If the attacker planned to kill them, he would have brought his own weapon. This scene looks like he decided to kill them after he got here. It wasn't premeditated." She shook her head. "Was anything stolen?"

"Hard to tell. The women had some jewelry. Nothing very valuable, but it looks undisturbed."

Alex stared at Logan for a moment before saying, "So it's probably not an attempted robbery that went wrong. This is clearly personal. But Willow hasn't been involved in the Circle since her stroke three years ago. Why now? And why the rage? I really think this happened because they somehow know we have Willow's book, and they're more vicious than we considered when it comes to their rules. What else could fuel something like this?"

She looked down at the blood on the floor, trying to sort through what they were seeing and what they knew so far.

"I don't know," the tech said, "but there's something else you should see. Follow me."

Alex and Logan trailed behind him, their footsteps making crackling sounds as they walked on the plastic sheeting. Alex assumed they were going to Willow's room, but instead the man turned toward another door. Alex froze, unable to move.

"I can't . . ." she said, her voice breaking. She looked to Logan for help. She could see the confusion on his face. His blue eyes searched hers.

"What's wrong, Alex?"

"This was my room." As soon as the words left her mouth, she realized how unprofessional she appeared at that moment. She straightened her shoulders. "I'm sorry. A lot of memories here, but I'm okay." She hated the way her voice trembled. She fought to control her emotions.

Logan took a step closer to her. "If you want to wait outside, I can—"

"No. I *said* I'm okay." She nodded at the crime scene tech. "Go ahead."

But as they walked into the room, what she saw made her feel faint. She swayed, and Logan reached out to take her arm.

The room was as she'd left it. The awful pink, flowered wallpaper. The pink bedspread with ruffles. She'd hated it. Willow had decorated in a style she thought a girl would like, but Alex was a tomboy. And she hated pink. Although she didn't want to look, her head seemed to swivel on its own. A one-page yearly calendar was still thumb-tacked to the wall. Each day was crossed off up until the end of June. The day she escaped this place.

"You were counting the days until you could leave," Logan said.

Her throat was so tight she couldn't respond. She just nodded.

"This is what I wanted to show you," the tech said, pointing behind them.

When Alex and Logan both turned around, she gasped. On the wall above her bed, a circle had been drawn in blood—with her name smeared inside it.

12

ecause they'd had no sleep, Alex and Logan decided to stay overnight in Wichita. Mike recommended a hotel next to the highway. It had outdoor corridors—not a great feature in November—but the rooms were suites, and it wasn't far from Willow's house.

They would have liked to question Nettie before checking in, but she was still unconscious, and the case belonged to the Wichita PD. If they could prove Willow's murder and Nettie's attack were carried out by the Circle or Adam Walker, then the FBI could step in since it was related to their domestic-terrorism case. But for now, no one could be sure the two crimes were connected. Not even with the image drawn on the wall.

Alex and Logan had briefly met with Police Chief Rogers, who accepted their help graciously. They provided questions designed to help his officers with their canvass of the area, talking to neighbors and anyone else around during the time the killer or killers were inside the house. The questions had been formulated based on FBI experience, but after seeing the crime scene, they'd quickly amended them with information that specifically related to this case. Alex was convinced the chief would pass their suggestions on to his detectives. The Wichita PD had a great working relationship with the FBI.

Logan had called both Jeff back at Quantico and Harrison in Kansas City to tell them what they'd found at Willow's. Harrison promised to get back with them after they got a few hours of sleep. If Nettie regained consciousness, he wanted Alex and Logan to talk to her. See what she could tell them. He said he would talk to the WPD and make sure it was okay with them.

Alex tried to sleep. The hotel bed was comfortable, but she just couldn't drift off. What did the drawing on that wall mean? If Willow was killed by the Circle, why the fury? Whoever killed her was filled with rage. Maybe they did know The Book had fallen into the government's hands and met this unforgivable action with judgment. Was death the price for this sin? Carried out by a mediator who was enraged and full of violence? But why write Alex's name in blood? Did the Circle blame her for Willow's supposed transgression?

Although it made some sense, that possibility was still hard for her to grasp. From what Alex could hear when the Circle met at Willow's house, their get-togethers were docile, not angry. She never heard raised voices. Of course, it's hard to get much information when you're stuck in your bedroom, not allowed to see the group assembled in the living room.

Without warning, a memory flashed in Alex's mind. Something else she must have tried to forget. During one of their meetings, Alex had to go to the bathroom. She'd held it as long as she could, but finally she decided to break the rules and sneak out of her room. She'd opened her door so quietly that no one could have possibly heard her. Then, after making sure she couldn't be seen, she'd slipped down the hall to the bathroom.

After she'd done her business, she'd stood, staring at the toilet. If she flushed it, they might hear it and know she'd disobeyed her aunt. Finally, frustration overcame her fear of getting caught, and she pulled the handle. She waited until the toilet was quiet again, then leaned against the door with her hand on the doorknob. She waited, listening for any sounds that might betray her, but she didn't hear anything. Relieved, she decided they hadn't heard the flush. She slowly opened the door—

Alex jumped at the memory and swung her legs over the side of the bed. How could she have forgotten? This was the second time an old memory had resurfaced since this whole thing started. Why was this happening? She felt . . . out of control. Her mind was deceiving her, and it made her feel weak and afraid. She'd seen one of the members of the Circle and had just now remembered it.

After pulling on a hoodie and slippers, Alex got up and went into the living room, which included a desk and a chair. She turned on a lamp. Sure enough, she found paper and a pen in a drawer, and after sitting down, she started sketching the man she'd seen. She had no idea who he was, but a drawing of a Circle member could help the investigators working the case.

When she was finished, she studied her work carefully. It matched her memory, but this had been years ago. The man could look different now. She thought about aging the image but decided she'd better let an FBI expert handle that. As she tried to envision what the man looked like now, someone knocked at her door. She got up and looked through the peephole. Logan. Alex glanced at the clock on the wall. 5:00 a.m. What was he doing here?

She tugged her hoodie around her body, then unlocked the door and swung it open.

"Sorry," Logan said, huddled in his jacket. "I saw a light on, so I figured you were up." He ran his hand through his hair. He was dressed, but obviously he hadn't combed his hair or shaved. Somehow he looked even better unkempt. Surprised by the unbidden thought, Alex felt her cheeks grow hot. She hoped he couldn't see it in the glow of the dim lighting outside.

"Come on in," she said. "I'm glad you came. I remembered something. Maybe it will help."

A blast of cold wind followed behind Logan as she tried to shut the door. Before it latched, she noticed a few snowflakes.

"We should probably check the weather," Logan said as he turned to look at her. "We don't want to get stuck here."

Alex grunted. "Yeah, I've had enough of this town. Never planned on coming back here even once. If you'd told me a week ago I'd be here two times in one day, I would have said you were crazy."

Logan headed to the couch, slipping off his jacket and tossing it over the back of a nearby chair. He stopped before he sat down. "Hey, they have one of those compressed paper logs for the fireplace here. Do you mind if I light it? I'm frozen all the way through."

Alex frowned at him. "Your room's only two doors down from mine. Why are you so cold?"

Logan didn't answer her as he opened the package and removed the log. He put it in the grate and used the matches provided by the hotel to ignite it. Then he opened the flue before turning back to her. "Honestly? I stood out there for a while. I wasn't sure if I should knock. I don't want to compromise us in any way."

"I appreciate your concern, but someone is out there with a virus that could kill thousands of people. I'm more interested in stopping him than worrying about our reputations."

Logan reached into his pocket and took out a couple of packets. "Stopped by the office and got some extra coffee. Just in case."

Alex took them and smiled. "I take it you'd like a cup?"

"That would be wonderful. It would help me warm up too."

"You drink it black, right?"

He nodded. "I'm not opposed to a latte once in a while, but most of the time I like it strong and black, the way coffee was intended to be enjoyed."

"I enjoy a caramel latte sometimes, but it seems like we're always on the go. I've learned to drink it black. Just made sense." She shook her head. "The things you give up for the Bureau."

Logan laughed and sat down on the couch. He ran his hand over the cushion. "This couch seems a little . . . damp." He turned around to look at her. "And what is that smell?"

"Sorry," she said. "It's disinfectant. I always clean hotel rooms. Germs."

"You sprayed the couch?"

"Sure. But let's move on from my germ phobia and talk about the case, okay?"

He was silent for a moment but then said, "All right. I'm

extremely concerned about what we saw on the wall at your aunt's house. It seems like a clear warning. I think you need to be careful."

"Before we analyze that, let me get the coffee ready. My brain needs caffeine. Especially for complicated conversations. We're supposed to be at the airport around eight thirty. We're not gonna sleep at all, are we?"

Logan sighed. "I think that's a safe bet."

Alex found two cups in the small kitchen and quickly brewed the first cup of coffee. She carried it into the living room and handed it to Logan while the second cup was brewing. When that was done, she joined him again. The idea of sitting next to him on the couch felt odd, though, so she moved his coat to the coat rack by the door and sat down in the chair.

"So what do you think about what we saw in my old bedroom?" Alex asked him. She hated referring to it as *hers*. She'd been so unhappy in that room, and she didn't want to claim it in any way.

"I think the Circle is angry with you. But I don't know if they're telling you your aunt and Nettie were attacked because of that anger or if another revelation is coming."

Alex nodded. "Yeah, I've been wondering the same thing. Truthfully, I think whoever did that wants me to feel the attacks are my fault. My punishment for trying to interfere. But if they plan to get to me, they'll have a tough time. I'm armed, I'm with you, and we'll be leaving in a few hours. I don't think their reach is long enough to get to me in Kansas City."

"I don't know, Alex. Didn't you say the Circle is spread out all over the world—probably including Kansas City?"

"Yeah, that's what Willow said. But really, how large could this cult be? I mean, only a handful of people met at Willow's house when I was a kid. It seems more likely this is nothing more than a small fringe group. Not many people involved. And no indication that they're dangerous." She caught herself. "Until tonight, I guess. If they had anything to do with Willow and Nettie's attacks."

"You aren't certain?"

She considered his question carefully. "Something seems off, Logan. Remember, they see themselves as descendants of angels. I never sensed any indication of violence or hate in Willow or in the people who came to our house. I realize I could only hear them through my walls, but their meetings were subdued. Courteous. *If* the Circle felt they were being threatened by demons and they had to protect themselves or The Book, I would expect them to find another way to deal with it. Not what we saw tonight."

Alex sighed. "I can't believe I'm even having this conversation. Angels and demons. Imaginary beings that belong to an imaginary being that lives in the sky." She shook her head. "How can rational human beings be so delusional? I just can't understand—" She stopped short. "I . . . I'm sorry. I didn't mean to . . ."

Logan smiled and took a sip of his coffee. "Let me ask you a question. If you were attacked by a rabid dog, would you assume all dogs are dangerous?"

"Of course not."

"Then explain something to me. Your aunt believed in this kind of stuff, but does that mean God can't possibly exist? Why do you think they're connected?"

"Look, let's not get into a God conversation, okay? But I see your point. I guess I'm the kind of person who believes in what I can see and understand. Quantifiable data. An invisible being that blesses me if I'm good and punishes me if I mess up? I'm afraid He'd be pretty busy handing out reprimands in my case."

"Wow. Where did you get this idea about Him?"

"Before my mother died, I went to church with a Christian school friend once. The pastor was one of those fire and brimstone types. It scared me. I never went back."

Logan sighed. "Another rabid dog, huh? Sometime, if you want, let me tell you about the God I know, okay? No pressure. I'm not trying to convert you, but there is another side to this. One it seems you've never heard."

Nettie's words drifted into Alex's mind. *"There's only one true God. He wants me to tell you that He saw your tears, and He's been watching over you all this time. Before this present journey is over, you will meet Him."* A warm feeling she couldn't explain ran though her. Could God be real? And could such a being care about her? Given those unanswered prayers on Willow's front porch, she wanted to dismiss the idea as insane. But for some reason she couldn't. It was as if a quiet voice inside her was saying it might be time for something different.

"Maybe. Sometime," she said. "But for now let's get back to what happened here."

"I don't suppose you remember anything about the people who met at Willow's? Something that might make it easier to find them?"

"That's what I want to tell you. I have something that might send us in the right direction." She stood and retrieved the sketch. "I was trying to remember anything that might help. I guess I'd blocked out some stuff, but I recalled one of the members of the Circle who came to our house. He's the only one I ever saw." She handed him the paper.

Logan's eyebrows arched. "This is pretty detailed for someone you saw so long ago. Very well drawn. You have talent."

"Just enough to get by. Not enough to do anything with it."

"I think you're selling yourself short. How long ago was this?"

"Forget the number of years," Alex said with a smile. "I'll start feeling old. Actually, I've got a pretty good memory, so I can't explain why I didn't remember this earlier. Even though, like I've said, I did my best to forget all that stuff about The Book. It's . . . weird." She had no plans to tell him about the other memory that had surfaced.

"Maybe you pushed it so far away it took this situation for it to resurface."

Alex nodded. "You're probably right. We need to run this through facial recognition software. If we get a name, we can run it through ViCAP and NCIC too. I realize this doesn't sound like a pattern yet, but what if it is? What if other people have betrayed the Circle and paid a price, and this guy is involved in that somehow?"

"Right. If we can come up with anything else to assist investigators here, it might help us find Walker faster."

Alex was surprised when her phone rang. Who could that be? "Busy morning." She grabbed her phone from the kitchen counter. When she answered she heard Mike's voice on the other end.

"Sorry if I woke you, but I'm here at the hospital. Nettie's conscious and asking for you. Won't talk to anyone else. She says it's important."

13

After assuring Mike they were on their way, Alex told Logan that Nettie was asking for her. "We've got to go down there."

"Sure. I have everything I need with me, but you might want to change first and—"

"You're right. Give me a minute."

Alex hurried into the bedroom and shut the door. She pulled off her hoodie, sweatpants, and T-shirt, then kicked off her slippers and grabbed her jeans, a sweater, and boots. After dressing, she went into the bathroom, where she quickly brushed her hair and tied it back into a ponytail before applying a little mascara.

Why did Nettie want to talk to her? Did she know the person who attacked her and killed Willow? When she walked back into the living room, Logan looked surprised. "That was fast. I don't think I could have gotten ready that quickly."

"That's because you're so vain," Alex said.

"Yeah, someone once wrote a song about me," he said with a grin.

Alex folded her sketch into the pocket of her jeans before grabbing her jacket, making sure she had everything she needed in those pockets as well. Then they hurried downstairs to the car the FBI had rented for them. Alex was grateful the SUV had four-wheel drive. Safer on snowy streets. It was coming down pretty good now. The streetlights highlighted the large flakes, making them look like brilliant bursts of luminescent prisms. As Logan drove, Alex had to tear her eyes away from the beauty around her and concentrate on what lay ahead. The dichotomy of nature and the evil in the hearts of humans made her ache inside. It was a reality that people in law enforcement had to balance every day. Sometimes they were successful. Sometimes they weren't.

It didn't take them long to reach the hospital. They parked in the large covered parking garage and strode through a walkway to the main entrance. As they entered, they found Mike waiting for them.

"Hi," he said. "You've beat the KCPD. I had to call them too, of course. She's in ICU on the fifth floor. Come with me."

The three of them got into an elevator and headed upstairs.

"How is Nettie doing?" Alex asked. "Will she be okay?"

"Her sister-in-law, Barbara, drove in from Independence as soon as she heard. She told me the doctor said Nettie's chances of recovery are good. But it's hard to be sure with the kind of head injury she has. There was some internal bleeding too, and they had to remove her spleen. Hopefully that will be it."

"Are you keeping a guard on her?" Logan asked.

"She's safe. No one can get into ICU without the nursing staff questioning them. If and when Nettie's moved to a regular room, someone will be posted outside her door. Meanwhile, I'm gonna hang around."

It felt as if the elevator was barely moving, driving Alex crazy. When an orderly got on at the fourth floor, she wanted to yell at him. Silly. She felt uncomfortable. Worried about something she couldn't put her finger on.

When the doors finally opened on the fifth floor, they got out. Mike led them to the ICU nurses' station.

"These are the folks I told you about," Mike said to an older nurse who didn't seem happy to see them.

"You can take only one person in with you," she said, her tone leaving no doubt she meant it.

Alex glanced down at the woman's badge. "Ruth, we're also with the FBI." Alex took her creds from her jacket pocket and showed the crotchety nurse. "I'd like my partner with me when I question Mrs. Travers."

Ruth nodded at Mike. "Then you have to stay out here."

"Not a problem," Mike said, then turned to Logan. "But Nettie made it pretty clear she would talk only to Alex. I'm not sure she'll want you in there."

"Let's try it," Alex said to Logan. "If she objects to having you in the room, you can come back out here. I'd like you there for backup. I don't want to miss anything." Having two behavioral analysts was better than one in Alex's mind. The truth was she'd been shaken by Willow's death, and she hadn't slept. She felt the need for another set of eyes and ears.

"Is Nettie's sister-in-law still here?" Mike asked.

Ruth shook her head. "Once Mrs. Travers was conscious, she went to a hotel to rest a bit. She'll be back a little later."

"Okay, let's go," Alex said.

Ruth gestured toward a large door. "Come with me."

Alex and Logan waited for her to step in front of them, then they followed her through the door and past several rooms before she finally stopped in front of one. She pushed the door open and waved Alex and Logan inside. Nettie was hooked up to both an IV and a heart monitor. Her face was bruised so badly Alex wouldn't have recognized her. Both her eyes were swollen almost shut.

"Come . . . closer . . ." Nettie croaked as soon as she saw them. "Who are you?"

Alex had stopped a few feet from the bed, trying to acclimate herself. Years of working with the FBI had placed her at quite a few horrific scenes with mangled bodies and the evidence of man's hate. But this was the first time she knew the person lying in the bed. Nettie was such a kind, gentle woman that somehow the realization that someone had this much cruelty in their heart struck her like a slap in the face.

She walked up next to the bed. "Nettie," she said softly, "it's Alex. How are you feeling?"

Nettie blinked several times as if she couldn't see clearly. "Alex?" she whispered through her bruised lips. It sounded more like *Aless*, but Alex nodded.

"Yes, it's me. I was told you need to talk to me."

Nettie sighed deeply and nodded. Then she reached for Alex's hand and mumbled something Alex couldn't understand. She leaned closer, trying to hear.

"Say it again, Nettie. I missed what you said." She looked back at Logan, who'd been staying back so Nettie wouldn't see him. Now he took a step closer.

"He . . . he . . ."

"He?" Alex repeated.

Nettie nodded slowly. "Here."

Alex looked around. *Here where?* Wondering if Nettie meant there was something she wanted her to *hear*, she said, "I'm listening."

Nettie suddenly thrashed in the bed as if in frustration. "He . . ." she said again. "He . . ."

"Not much longer," Ruth interjected. "She needs to rest."

Frustrated by her inability to understand whatever Nettie was trying to say, Alex reached into her jeans pocket and took out her sketch of the man she'd remembered. She held it in front of Nettie's face.

"Do you recognize this man?" she asked Nettie.

Her eyes grew wide, and she nodded.

"Who is he, Nettie?" Alex asked. Even if she didn't know his real name, anything she could tell them might help to determine who was responsible for the attacks.

"No . . . no . . ." She started to breathe quickly as if she couldn't get enough air. "He . . ."

"I think you need to go," Ruth said. Alex noticed her watching the numbers on the monitor next to Nettie's bed. It was obvious she didn't like what she was seeing.

Alex, not knowing what else to do, leaned down once more, putting her ear next to Nettie's mouth. "I can't understand you, Nettie," she said quietly. "Try one more time."

Nettie was trying to talk, but she couldn't seem to catch her breath. "He . . . here. He . . . here . . ." Suddenly, she bolted upright in the bed, her eyes full of some unseen terror. "He's here!" she gasped. "He's here!" Then she collapsed back on the bed, and the machine next to her began to beep loudly.

"Out now!" Ruth commanded them. She pushed a button near the bed, and immediately they heard a voice coming from a loudspeaker in the hall. "Code blue, room 7. Code blue, room 7."

Ruth pushed them into the hall. Several medical personnel ran into the room and pushed a large cart next to the bed. Alex and Logan hurried toward the ICU's exit to the waiting area. Mike had come in from the front desk, and when he saw them, he jogged over.

"What's going on?" he asked. "Is Nettie okay?"

Alex shook her head. "I think she's in trouble, Mike."

They stood off to the side, waiting to see what would happen. A few minutes later a doctor walked out of Nettie's room. Behind him, the same medical personnel who'd rushed in came out and walked past them.

"You're the FBI agents who spoke to Nettie Travers?" he asked.

"Yes," Alex said. "Is she okay?"

"I'm sorry, no." His eyebrows knit together in a tight frown. "Can you tell me how she acted before we were alerted to a problem?"

Was he blaming them? "She was trying to tell us something," Alex said. "It seemed important. Then she sat up. It was like she was . . . I don't know. Shocked?"

"In pain?"

"Not really," Alex said slowly, "but it's possible. I had the feeling she was reacting to something that happened suddenly."

"Okay, thanks." He grunted. "She shouldn't have died. She was getting better."

"Will there be an autopsy, Doctor?" Logan asked.

"I'm sure there will be. Her sister-in-law is already here from out of town. I'm about to call her. Relatives can say no to an autopsy, but I'm sure they'll want to know what happened too. She only left after Nettie regained consciousness because I said she was improving." He sighed softly. "This isn't a call I want to make. Excuse me."

"We'll want to see that autopsy," Alex said.

"You'll have to go through proper channels."

He pushed the door to the ICU open, leaving them standing there.

"I don't like this," Alex said as they made their way back to the front desk and waiting area.

"What do you mean?" Mike asked. "People don't make it sometimes. It happens."

"But he said she was supposed to recover. Maybe whoever wanted her dead came back to finish the job."

"In the ICU?" Logan said. "That would be difficult."

"Yes, it would," Alex said. "But not impossible."

Ruth returned with a piece of paper in her hand. "I found this drawing on the floor in Mrs. Travers's room. Does it belong to you?"

"Yes, it's mine," Alex said. "I must have dropped it when the monitor went off." She took the sketch from the nurse. "Ruth, how difficult would it be for someone to get into one of these rooms without your knowledge?"

"Not possible," she said without hesitation. "We watch who goes in and out very carefully. If you're thinking about Mrs.

Travers, no one went into that room who wasn't supposed to be there."

Alex thought for a moment. "Do you check every doctor who enters the ICU?"

This time Ruth hesitated a moment, obviously uncomfortable with Alex's question. "No," she said slowly, "but we know our doctors. We'd notice if a strange one went into a patient's room." She pulled her shoulders back and straightened her spine. "Now if you'll excuse me, I have work to do."

As she walked away, Mike said, "I don't like the way she answered that question. It seems clear to me that someone could get past them if they were wearing a doctor's coat."

"I agree," Alex said.

"Do you think Ruth recognized the man in the sketch?"

"I don't think so. She didn't display any signs of dishonesty."

"Excuse me."

Alex turned around and found a young woman in blue scrubs. Her name tag indicated she was a nurse. "Can I help you?" Alex asked.

The woman looked around her. "I . . . I doubt it, but I might be able to help you." She moved a little closer to Alex. "We really thought Mrs. Travers was going to make it."

"Do you have any reason to suspect that someone . . . helped her along?" Alex wanted to be careful. She didn't want to spook the girl.

"A man came to the desk asking about Willow LeGrand. She was friends with Mrs. Travers, right?" Alex nodded. "Well, I couldn't give him personal information about a patient, but I did tell him the survivor from the attack wasn't Ms. LeGrand. He was very, very upset. He hung around out here for a while"—she gestured toward Mike—"but he left around the time you arrived. It's possible he got through the ICU entrance when we had an earlier code blue. Everyone was concentrated on that. He might have slipped into Mrs. Travers's room unobserved."

Alex held up the sketch she still held in her hand. "Could this be the man you saw?"

The nurse stared at the drawing for a few seconds before nodding. "Yes, that's him. I'm certain of it."

14

As Adam sipped coffee in his favorite all-night diner, he reflected on the fifth sacrifice. He'd chosen a different spot, but he'd had no choice. The train yards were being closely watched now.

The older man destined to be offered had fought back like he was twenty. Adam had been surprised, but of course he prevailed.

He wasn't worried about putting himself or his family in danger. The prophecy said the demon who unleashed judgment on the world would be protected, as would those he held close. Besides, he planned to take Sally and the children someplace safe. He'd saved quite a bit of money, and he had his eye on a place in Switzerland. No extradition treaty with the U.S., and the chalet he'd found was far enough away to keep them separated from those infected. He could still watch the results of his achievement on TV. It would be perfect.

He was usually very careful during the ritual, but the man's struggles resulted in blood on Adam's coat. It wasn't a problem, just an inconvenience. Unfortunately, he'd accidently smeared some of the blood from his gloves on the steering wheel of the car.

After the sacrifice, he'd pulled into the alley behind a butcher shop in a strip mall. No one was around. He'd tossed his coat and gloves into a dumpster filled with the remnants of raw meat the place threw out every day. The blood on his belongings would mix with the blood on the meat, so it was the perfect place to get rid of them. He glanced at his watch. The dumpster would be emptied in about an hour, and the evidence of his deed would be gone for good.

Before he left there, he'd removed a clean coat from the trunk of the car. When he got home, he'd clean the steering wheel with bleach. No sense taking chances. He was certain the police knew his name by now, but he didn't need to give them his DNA. Even though he never worried about the police tracking him, he was careful. And if they ever did question him, they wouldn't learn anything. Not only was he much smarter than everyone else but he was also convinced the Master would ensure he was left alone to carry out his divine purpose.

He took a bite of his scrambled eggs as a man entered the diner to drop off several copies of the local newspaper. He smiled to himself. Today's issue should be interesting.

Mike had notified his SAC about the situation at the hospital and then left right after faxing Alex's sketch to the command post from the hospital administrator's office. They'd use facial recognition to try to identify him.

When police detectives arrived to find Nettie dead instead of conscious for questioning, they called in the chief, who ordered his team to close all the entrances and exits to the hospital. They let in only emergency personnel and relatives of those patients in critical condition. They searched every nook and cranny, but they didn't find anyone who didn't belong. And no one on the night shift in the ICU remembered seeing the man in Alex's drawing except the young nurse.

"We've done all we can," Chief Rogers told them. "He's not here now, but we've put out an APB on him. We'd rather have a photo, though. Hopefully, we'll get something soon."

"Good," Logan said. "We need to question him. We don't know if he had anything to do with Nettie Travers's death, but he may still have important information."

"Understood." The chief turned and left. Slowly, all the police cruisers and unmarked vehicles began to pull away from the hospital. People were entering and exiting now. Some people had been upset about being kept in or out of the building, but most seemed to understand—although they had questions. Law enforcement was instructed to say that a wanted criminal might have been spotted inside the building but that it wasn't confirmed. This seemed to mollify almost everyone except the news media that surrounded the chief as soon as he walked outside.

"I guess we'd better call Keith," Logan told Alex after they'd watched the flow for a few minutes. "Hopefully, we can get out of here within the next hour or two."

"I want to know what's going on at the CP. If they've found Walker yet."

"So do I. Let's call in."

Logan had just taken his phone from his pocket when it

rang. He looked at his caller ID. Harrison. He quickly showed Alex the phone's screen and then answered.

"Logan, what's going on there?" Harrison asked. "I'm sorry to hear about Mrs. Travers."

"We think someone from the Circle might have killed her. It's wild that the one man Alex saw at one of her aunt's Circle meetings could be involved in all this, but there it is."

"You're right. Chief Rogers wonders if the Circle is involved too. Listen, we already got a hit on that sketch of Alex's through our facial recognition software. The man we're looking for is Jimmy Gedrose. He used to be with the Wichita PD."

Logan's mouth dropped open. "He was in law enforcement?"

"Yes. Money went missing from a big drug bust on his watch. The other officers involved swore all the money was there when they turned it over to Gedrose. The story was leaked to the media. They never could prove anything, though, so the charges were dropped. But most everyone on the force was convinced he'd done it. That was thirty years ago. Seems he was pretty angry about being kicked off the force."

"This guy was part of the Circle," Logan said. "Maybe that incident decades ago is what threw him their way."

"Could be."

Logan looked at Alex, who was watching him closely. "We're on our way back to the hotel," he said. "We can be at the airport in an hour."

"No. I want you to stay in Wichita," Harrison said. "The weather's pretty bad here. I'm not even sure Keith can take off, but I don't want to chance it either way. I need you two to keep working, see what you can come up with on Adam

Walker. I'm sending you what little we have on him. See what jumps out at you. Get your thoughts back to me as soon as possible. Monty has done what he can here, but Alex has more experience with this cult. We've run Walker through everything, including dark-web sites to see if he's expressed his odd beliefs online. We've also checked to see if he tried to buy equipment or biological weapons somewhere. We've researched phone records and done deep searches on the people he worked with at the lab."

He took a deep breath. "Nothing so far. It's like he was living in the shadows. We really need your help. I want to know what he's planning next. It might be the only way we can stop him."

"All right," Logan said. "Has someone informed Keith?"

"I'll take care of that next. Look, I need you to work closely with the local police too."

"Okay. Did you tell Chief Rogers we're staying?"

"Yes. He's a good man, and he's more than willing to have the help. They're also dealing with an influx of drugs tainted with Fentanyl. Two people have died so far, and several more have been hospitalized."

"We'll do what we can," Logan said. "When we get back to the hotel, we'll get to work."

"I've got to go, but have you seen the local paper there?"

Logan frowned at Alex. "The local paper? No. It's pretty early here."

"Read it when you can," Harrison said. "I'm sure they picked up a story from Kansas City." Then without a good-bye, he hung up.

Logan looked at Alex, who was still staring at him with a worried look.

"What's going on?" she asked.

Logan told her about Jimmy Gedrose and Harrison's instructions.

"But whatever we can come up with should be presented to the team at the CP in person," Alex said.

Logan shrugged. "I know, but we're not in charge."

"We'll just have to do the best we can. What was that about the local paper?"

"My guess is there's already been a fifth killing. After that, the Train Man needs only one more before he unleashes that virus, right? Let's head over to the hotel. They should have papers in the lobby. If not, we'll just check online. We also need to tell the hotel we're staying."

"What about Keith?"

"Harrison's taking care of that. I guess we're stranded here for a while."

"I hope the WPD makes finding this Gedrose guy a priority."

"I'm sure they'll do the best they can, but they're overloaded with some kind of Fentanyl-laced drugs that are killing people."

Alex sighed. "Too many of those cases. The bad guys never take a day off, do they?"

"I guess not. We'd better get going."

They went out to their rental car and drove to the hotel — slowly. The streets were slick, and the snow kept coming. Logan finally pulled up in front of the building that housed the hotel's office. "I'll be right back," he said.

Inside, a young man walked up to the counter, and Logan asked about extending their stay a few more days. Thankfully, they had vacancies, and they wouldn't have to change rooms.

"Can we get some extra coffee?" Logan asked. The clerk grabbed several packets from under the counter and put them in a plastic bag. "I couldn't get by on one cup a day either," he said with a smile. Logan thanked him and then asked about a local newspaper.

"They're over there. Help yourself." The guy pointed toward a long, thin, dark wood table against the far wall. It also held a coffee maker. Thankful for some immediate hot coffee, Logan poured a cup, then grabbed a newspaper.

The front-page headline stopped him cold: *Killer Calling Himself the Train Man Sends Letter to Kansas City Journal.*

15

lex couldn't believe what she was reading. She and Logan had gone to her room to read the newspaper article. "This guy is different," she said, holding the paper as she sat in the chair near the fireplace. She looked over at Logan, who was making coffee. She wasn't sure caffeine was the best thing right now. She was exhausted and needed to sleep, yet she knew her mind wouldn't allow her to. Not yet.

"This reads like a manifesto," she said. "He's definitely been involved in the Circle—even though I can't imagine he is now since he's gone off the rails. Pun not intended."

Logan snorted. "Go ahead," he said. "I'm listening."

"Here's the letter:

"'The Master has judged the world and found it wanting. He has declared that six sacrifices will precede his first judgment. I am the one chosen to carry out this judgment. You can call me the Train Man. I will deliver a contagion so powerful that one third of mankind will die. To the authorities who wonder if I have the ability to do this, rest assured that I am more than capable of carrying out this assignment. I suspect you know this by now.

'The police and the FBI will try to stop me, but they will fail. The words of The Book declare that the Master is God. There is no other. He is the one who holds the keys to all things. He has given them to me to carry out his will. He began all things, and he will end all things. He created the demons and the angels for his pleasure. He looked at the evil he created and found it good.'"

Alex looked up and stared at Logan. "Wow. He's extremely delusional."

Logan joined her, setting two cups on the coffee table and then lowering himself onto the couch. "Even though the Circle doesn't follow the Bible, some of this is certainly similar. In the Bible, the one who rules over the demons is Satan. God created the angels, although some of them fell and decided to follow the devil. But the most important beings are mankind. This book claims we're all either demons or angels and human beings don't exist. Whoever wrote it wasn't trying to mimic the Bible. It would be easier to understand him if that were the case."

"What do you mean?" Alex asked.

"We profile a lot of people who hate the normal interpretation of God. Usually it helps us understand that there may be some kind of resentment toward religion that helps to shape their psyche. But this is something new. Seems to me that whoever wrote The Book was angry with theology. He felt . . . superior over other religious people. He created something

different. Something unique." He paused for a moment and
frowned. "I think his anger is directed at mankind. Possibly
because so many of them follow the God of the Bible. That's
why he wants them wiped out."

Alex nodded. "Makes sense. If mankind doesn't exist, he
won't have to compete with them anymore. Or care about
them. You know, Willow used to say The Book was written
centuries before the Bible. That the author was a superior
being who wasn't from this world." She shook her head. "Boy,
when I say that it sounds nuts. Somehow, though, she made
it sound a little bit sane." She frowned. "So you think the
author of The Book has read the Bible. He's stealing words
and ideas, but he isn't a Bible scholar."

"Yeah. He's been exposed to the Bible at some point. Not
enough to really understand it, but enough to know he hates
it." He stared at Alex for a moment. "I can't even begin to
comprehend what it was like growing up with someone like
Willow as a parental figure," he said after a long pause.

"Everyone has tough stuff in their lives." Maybe once, a
long time ago, she'd wanted someone to feel compassion for
her and reach out to help. But it had never happened, and
she had learned how to take care of herself. She believed
that, in some ways, Willow had made her stronger. Better
prepared for life. When she moved out she was already able
to cook, clean, pay bills, and file her own taxes. She'd also
fought back the dark fears that had tried to destroy her. Then
she worked hard to get into the FBI and now the BAU. She'd
learned that she didn't need anyone else. She could get by
just fine alone.

"Alex, I was thinking about something you said early on.
That Walker must believe he's a demon but he identifies

more as the Train Man. Is he killing as the Train Man? Or as the Destroyer?"

"I think he decided he was a demon, just like you and I believe we're human beings. Then he needed an identity. You're Logan Hart. I'm Alex Donovan. He's the Train Man. His identity as Adam Walker became nothing. Useless. Logan Hart and Alex Donovan became FBI supervisory special agents. He became . . ."

"The Destroyer," Logan finished for her.

"Exactly. And I would say his calling as the Destroyer is driving him to kill. That what's pushing him forward. He wants to fulfill the prophecy. It makes him feel important. Special. The Destroyer is his reason to exist." She took a deep breath and blew it out. "We really need a copy of that book. I think it will help us understand him even more. But we never got our copy."

"You seem to know a lot about it already."

Alex leaned back in her chair and pulled her legs up, wrapping her arms around them. "Not as much as you might think, even though Willow talked about it constantly. She hoped I'd hop on board the Circle train." She laughed lightly. "Pun intended this time. I guess it's like your Bible. People talk about it a lot, but have they read every word?"

"Actually, I have," Logan said. "But some chapters I probably won't read again. Let's just say the book of Numbers isn't for everyone."

Although she wasn't quite sure what that meant, Alex laughed again. "Doesn't sound too exciting."

"You'd be right." Logan grinned at her.

"Aren't blood sacrifices mentioned in the Old Testament?"

Logan nodded. "I was thinking along the same lines. Yet

the Train Man doesn't seem to have any concept of the purpose of the sacrifices in the Bible. That they were setting
up mankind for the final sacrifice that brought eternal forgiveness. He believes his sacrifices precede a terrible act of
judgment."

"The virus," Alex said.

Logan put his head back on the couch and sighed deeply.
"Everyone's going to be calling him the Train Man by tomorrow, you know."

"Yeah, I know. I'm sure he'll enjoy that." She frowned. "You
said this idea of one third of the world dying is mentioned in
the Bible. Can you read that portion to me?"

Logan took his phone out of his pocket and tapped several
times on the screen. "Here it is, Revelation 9:17–19. I'm
reading from the King James Version.

> "'And thus I saw the horses in the vision, and them that sat
> on them, having breastplates of fire, and of jacinth, and brim-
> stone: and the heads of the horses were as the heads of lions;
> and out of their mouths issued fire and smoke and brimstone.
> By these three was the third part of men killed, by the fire,
> and by the smoke, and by the brimstone, which issued out of
> their mouths. For their power is in their mouth, and in their
> tails: for their tails were like unto serpents, and had heads,
> and with them they do hurt.'"

"What is that supposed to mean?" Alex asked.

Logan shrugged. "Sorry. Like I said, I'm not an end-times
expert. Some say it's a guy who lived two thousand years ago
trying to describe some kind of military plane or helicopter.
I think that makes as much sense as anything."

"Wow, that's some benevolent God you have." Alex felt a little irritated. Who could understand this stuff?

"This talks about something that will happen," Logan said. "It doesn't say God caused it." He leaned forward with his arms on his knees. "You know, the Bible's actually pretty easy. God loves, heals, restores. Satan kills, steals, and destroys."

"But doesn't your Old Testament have a lot of killing, stealing, and destroying?"

"Yeah. But people were under judgment then. Now, because of Jesus, we're under grace."

"Yet there's still evil in the world. You and I know that better than most. I think whoever wrote The Book and the people who believe in it are just trying to understand the concept of good and evil. Is that possible?"

Logan nodded. "I think you're right about that." He frowned.

"What are you thinking?"

"It doesn't have anything to do with this. It's just . . ."

"Tell me."

"This . . . book. The Bible tells about a God who gave the most precious thing he had because He loves humans more than anything. Yet The Book erases them from the earth. It's . . . sad."

Alex chewed on her lip as she thought. "Maybe it makes believers easier to control because it takes away their human identity and tells them they're destined to be one thing or another."

"I guess so." Logan sighed. "I feel sorry for anyone who falls for this." His gaze met hers. "Your aunt must have felt she needed some kind of importance in life, just like you think Walker does. An identity. Makes me think she didn't have one before the Circle came into her life."

Alex looked away. "I don't want to talk about her. Let's get back to Walker."

"Okay," Logan said. "I didn't mean to upset you."

Alex didn't say anything. Instead, she took a sip of her coffee. The resentment she felt for her aunt had been stoked by this case. Willow was gone from the world, but she still lived in Alex's mind. It was getting in the way of her job. She just wanted the woman out of her life.

"Walker seems to be completely committed to The Book," Logan continued. "He even believes he's mentioned in it. So why rebel against what he's supposed to believe in? Why share parts of The Book in public? Like you said, the Circle can't be happy with that."

"Yeah, that's bothering me too."

"What if this thing about demons being forbidden to read The Book is only an opinion? Maybe it's not actually mentioned in the text."

Alex stared at Logan for several seconds. "You could be right. Don't people have opinions about the Bible that have nothing to do with reality?"

Logan gave her a lopsided smile. "Yeah, like when they make snarky comments about God's benevolence."

In spite of herself, Alex laughed. "Point taken. You know, I don't remember Willow ever reciting anything from The Book about that. It may have simply been her own idea. If it's not actually in there, Walker might feel he has every right to read The Book and fulfill its prophecies, even as a demon."

"Maybe so. Okay, until we can see what's in The Book, let's drop the idea that Walker is rebelling. I think those concepts have caused us some confusion. Let's say he hasn't rebelled. That this guy knows what's in The Book, and he's following it to the letter. That will make figuring out his next steps much easier."

"I agree. But we really need to see what's in that book for ourselves," Alex said. "And soon."

16

Adam was grateful to be home. It had been a busy night. Even though he'd had coffee with his breakfast, he was dead tired.

"There you are," Sally chirped when he came in. "I was worried about you. Is everything okay?"

He nodded. "Number five has been sacrificed."

"Another coat?" she said, pointing at the outerwear he'd forgotten to take off.

"Yeah, good thing you bought all those secondhand coats. I've needed them." He smiled. "Only one more sacrifice to go. The most important one."

She held out her hand. Adam shrugged off the coat and handed it to her. "I'll be glad when this is over," she said.

"I just want to make sure the Master is satisfied. We need his protection."

"No one has ever served him better than you, honey," Sally said, her sweet smile warming his heart and chasing away the cold. He sat down at the kitchen table. "I need to sleep." He didn't tell her about the letter. He wasn't sure she'd approve. It really wasn't her business anyway. All she needed to know was what he decided to tell her.

"Well, you go lie down for a while. I'll see to the kids and make sure they're quiet, so they won't disturb you."

Adam wanted to climb into bed and fall asleep, but for some reason, every time he lay down he started itching. It was irritating. Sally must be using some kind of laundry detergent he was allergic to. He wanted to ask her about it, but he didn't want to hurt her feelings. She worked so hard. Sometimes, without her knowing about it, he'd rent a motel room so he could wash up and sleep without feeling as if he wanted to scratch his skin off.

"I've got to clean the inside of the car," he said. "Got blood on the steering wheel."

"Do you want me to do it?"

"No, you already work so hard." He put his palms on the sides of her beautiful face and kissed her gently. "I don't know what I'd do without you," he said, circling his arms around her.

"You never have to. I'll always be here for you, and so will the kids."

As if on cue, Gabby and Trey appeared behind her. "Daddy!" Gabby said. "I missed you so much." She ran over and wrapped her arms around his legs. Trey stood back a bit, trying to be a young man, but when Adam gestured to him he grinned and joined their group hug.

"Have you been serving the Master?" Trey asked, his eyes wide with obvious pride in his father.

"I have, and I'm tired, Trey. Gotta get some sleep. You guys be good today, okay? Obey your mother."

"We will, Daddy," Gabby said. "We want to be just like you."

Adam smiled to himself. His life was perfect. His family kept him going. He was so grateful to the Master for rewarding him for his work.

"Let's go," Sally said, disengaging from their hug. "Daddy needs to rest."

Adam watched them leave and then went back to his bedroom. He was so tired he fell asleep before the itching started.

Logan stood. "More coffee?" he asked.

Alex nodded and handed him her cup. "Thanks."

As she waited, she continued thinking about Walker. She'd begun to realize they were a little similar. Both of them had troubled childhoods. Walker had found his identity in a book, and she'd found hers in the FBI. Different choices, different paths.

It took Logan a few minutes to brew the coffee. He brought her cup over and put it down on the coffee table in front of her.

"Have you looked outside?" he asked as he lowered himself onto the couch again.

Alex turned her attention to the window in the front of the room. Maybe Harrison was right. The snow was coming down pretty fast. She'd been so concentrated on their case that she hadn't noticed. *Cases*, she corrected herself. With Willow and Nettie's deaths, now there were two cases, not one. She and Logan weren't assigned to the Wichita murder case, but she knew the two cases were connected. She couldn't ignore the women's murders. Of course, until they had an autopsy report, she couldn't prove Nettie was murdered. Maybe her death had been natural, but it didn't seem right. It felt like something else. Something wrong.

"Hopefully, this snow won't cause us more problems," she said. "We should be in Kansas City. At the command post. Not stuck here."

Logan shrugged. "We can do almost everything from here, you know. Let's talk about what happened to Willow and why. It may be tied in to our guy."

"I think it is. But I wonder if we're *supposed* to assume it's the Circle punishing Willow for not protecting its book, especially given the drawing above my old bed. But again, why? It still seems odd that *angels* would have such vengeance. Unless . . ."

"Unless what?"

Alex cleared her throat. "Unless it's not about The Book, Logan. What if it's about a person? Someone they don't want us to find."

"Who?"

"I don't know. Maybe this Gedrose? Maybe they know I saw his face when I was young, and they want to silence me. Maybe they killed Willow and Nettie to scare me. To force me to keep quiet."

"But if this guy is so important, why send him to the hospital where you might see him? Doesn't make sense. They could have ordered someone else to kill Nettie."

Alex nodded. "You're right. The guy we're looking for probably isn't that far up in the chain of command. Maybe he's just a private in their twisted army."

"Can you remember anything else about him?"

"I've tried, but that one incident was the only time I came face-to-face with any of them."

Logan frowned. "Your room wasn't all that far from the living room. Did you ever overhear anything that might help us?"

Alex shook her head. "I didn't want to hear them. Most of the time I listened to music through headphones. They didn't always meet at Willow's house, by the way. They had other meeting places too. I assume they took turns hosting their little soirees."

"Well, at least we have this guy's name. We know he used to be a cop. It's more than we had before you remembered him."

She nodded. "Even though he didn't say a word to me, something about him frightened me. He—"

Someone knocked on the door. Alex glanced at her watch. Nine o'clock in the morning. "Must be housekeeping," she said as she rose from her chair. "I'll tell them to skip it. What about your room?"

"I'm good."

For a second, Alex wondered if she should make sure it was housekeeping before she opened the door, but then she decided she was being paranoid. How would anyone from the Circle know where she was staying?

She opened the door, expecting to see a maid with a cart. Instead, she looked into the face of the man she'd met as a child. The one in her drawing—only older. She reached for her gun, but she wasn't wearing it.

17

Alex heard a sound beside her. Logan stood there with his weapon aimed at the man's chest. She backed up so she wasn't in his way.

"You better tell us right now why you're here," Logan said. "And how you knew where to find us."

The man held up his hands. "I just know how to track people. I'm not armed." He looked around him, and Alex could see the nervousness in his face. "When I found out the police were searching the hospital for me, I decided to find you. Look, I was with the Circle once, but I'm not anymore. I left years ago. But I've kept an eye on them."

"Why?" Alex asked. "And why were you at the hospital? Did you kill Nettie?"

"No," he said, shaking his head. "I wouldn't be here if I had. When I heard what happened at the house, I went to the hospital to protect Willow, hoping she was the one who'd survived. But . . . she hadn't. Not that I wanted Nettie to die either, but Willow's death . . ." He looked behind him again. "Could you point your gun at me inside? I'm afraid of being seen."

Logan glanced at Alex. "What do you want to do? Call Chief Rogers?"

"No. At least not yet. Let him in."

She backed up and grabbed her own gun. She'd left it on the kitchen counter, and now she pointed it at Gedrose.

"Come in and sit down," she said. "You have fifteen minutes to convince me you didn't kill Nettie, if not Willow. If you don't dispel my doubts completely, I'll call the police and tell them you're here. Right now you're their prime suspect."

Gedrose stepped inside the room, and Logan closed the door behind him. He wiped his feet on the small rug in front of the door, and when Logan gestured toward it, he moved to the chair next to the couch.

"Do you mind if I take off my coat before I sit down?" he asked.

"You have two guns pointed at you," Alex said. "And we're both trained to take you down with one shot. You have no chance of survival if you try something. Just remember that."

Surprisingly, Gedrose smiled. "Warning noted." He slipped off his black coat and put it on the back of the chair. He was dressed in dark slacks and a dark blue pullover sweater. He had to be at least in his sixties, but he carried himself like someone much younger. His beard was neatly trimmed and matched his gray hair. He could pass for Santa Claus, but he wasn't overweight.

He sat down and waited, apparently for them to decide what came next. Alex took a seat on the couch. She wanted to keep a comfortable space between them. She had no intention of allowing him to grab her gun. Logan stood behind her.

"You're Jimmy Gedrose," Alex said. "I saw you a long time ago. At my aunt's."

Gedrose nodded. "So you do remember me." He pointed at their guns. "You don't have anything to worry about. I . . . I loved your aunt, Alexandra. I know you thought she was unbalanced, and, well, she was. But I got to know the woman she could have been. Against the rules, we became friends to the point we told each other our real names. She was Willow to me, not Lady X. She had a generous, kind soul beneath all her problems."

"You didn't really know her," Alex snapped, ignoring the echo of her mother's words in her mind. She'd said Willow had been sweet too. "I had to take care of her as if she were a child. I kept the house clean, shopped, made the meals, fed the cats, paid the bills. She was completely irresponsible."

"But she gave you a place to live, didn't she? I know you may not believe this, but she really cared about you. When you left, it almost destroyed her."

"You're right. I don't believe you." She was certain her aunt cared for her on some level. But was she destroyed to see her niece leave? No. Not unless losing a captive caregiver was that important to her.

Gedrose shook his head. "I saw the police going through her place. Have they found her will yet? She left everything to you, you know."

Alex was so surprised she wasn't certain how to react. "Great, so I get her debts?"

"You get the house, and everything in it. As far as debts, she has none. The house is paid off."

Alex pushed back the anger that bubbled up inside her. "That's not true. She could never have paid it off, even in the eighteen years I've been gone. She owed thousands of dollars on that dump."

"I helped her pay it off, Alexandra. You'll learn it's free and clear now."

"Will you quit calling me Alexandra? I'm Alex."

Gedrose smiled. "Sorry. Your aunt always called you Alexandra. It's a beautiful name."

Alex put out her hand. "Give me your wallet."

He reached around and slowly pulled his wallet from his back pocket. "If you're trying to rob me, you'll be disappointed."

Alex didn't respond. She didn't find the situation funny. She took the wallet from his hand and opened it, then pulled out his driver's license and stared at it, trying to decide if it was real. It looked legitimate and was issued to a James R. Gedrose. She quickly looked through the rest of the wallet. Credit cards, gift cards, vehicle registration—all with his name and a Wichita address. She put it on the coffee table and wrote down his address in a notebook. "If you pull anything, or if we find out you're lying to us, we will call the police. Do you understand?" She handed the wallet back to him.

"Yes, I get it."

"I understand you have quite a history with them."

Gedrose's smile slipped. "I guess you know I was given early retirement from the department. They thought I'd stolen money from a drug bust. I don't suppose you care that I didn't do it."

"Sure," Alex said. "We don't hear that often enough in law enforcement."

Gedrose shrugged. "You've made up your mind, so I won't

waste my time trying to convince you. But there was never any evidence that I took the money. However, if you'll look through the file from back then, you'll see that my partner seemed to suddenly have a lot of luck at the casinos in Kansas City."

"The department would have been looking for that."

"Not if your partner is the chief's son."

"Look," Logan said, "let's concentrate on what happened at the hospital. Do you know how Nettie died? Do you think she was killed?"

"I don't know. I didn't see anyone at the hospital who aroused my suspicions, but you need to know that more members of the Circle are around than you think. The actual number would shock you. I've only met a few of them."

Alex snorted. "Only four or five people used to show up for my aunt's meetings. I think we can handle that."

"But that wasn't the only meeting place in Wichita. And across the country? Thousands of people are in the Circle."

"Wait a minute," Logan said as he sat down on the arm of the couch, his gun still pointed at Gedrose. "You're trying to tell us it's true that thousands of people believe in this stuff? That's absurd."

"Yes, it is. I finally realized that. I got involved with the Circle shortly after I was pushed out of my career and forced to make a living any way I could. I won't bore you with my job history, except to say I did okay." He swallowed. "My wife hated the Circle. She was a Christian and tried to tell me that I'd been deceived and The Book was false. She said that Satan can't create anything so he attacks what God has designed. That The Book is one of the devil's ways to keep people from Him."

"You said she *was* a Christian," Alex said. "You're not married anymore?"

Gedrose hung his head. "She died about ten years ago. Embolism. That's what drove me to the truth. My parents made me attend Sunday school when I was a kid, but I didn't pay much attention. But I had to know if my wife was in heaven. If I could really see her again. So I read the Bible all the way through. When I was done . . . I believed. I prayed for God's forgiveness and asked Jesus to give me a new life. A new mind. I asked for His Holy Spirit to live in me. Make me the man He wanted me to be. And He answered my prayer."

He shook his head and smiled. "Being in the Circle only caused me to fear others. But God filled me with love and changed me completely. I'm not the same. That's the miracle, isn't it? Seeing people change. No other god does that."

Alex sighed. "That's great, but it doesn't explain what happened to Nettie."

"The more I think about it, the more I'm convinced the Circle got to her in the ICU. Nettie wasn't worried that they knew Willow had a copy of The Book, but I wasn't so sure. I warned her they might try to take it."

"Wait a minute," Alex said. "Just before she died, Nettie indicated she recognized you from a sketch I made, but she never mentioned you when she gave me The Book."

"She wouldn't," Gedrose said. "She was protective of me. Even though she wasn't worried about herself, she was concerned about me. She kept my connection to the Circle and to her a secret. She and I were working together to free Willow from the Circle's clutches."

"So you think someone from the Circle tried to kill Nettie because she was trying to free Willow? Then they finished the job at the hospital? But why kill Willow?" Logan asked. "She was one of them."

"I don't know. To be honest, I find it strange that Willow and Nettie were attacked *after* Nettie gave you The Book."

"How did you find out about that?" Alex asked.

"Nettie called me. Told me about it."

"That's convenient," Alex said. "Then you told the Circle about it and caused their deaths. Maybe you even killed them yourself."

Gedrose's expression darkened. "First, I don't know anyone in the Circle who would attack two women—and so violently. And second, even if I were a killer, which I'm not, do you really think a former police officer would assault those women the way they were? I went in the back door after the police left Willow's house. I have a key. What I saw was rage. It was messy. I wouldn't have done it that way. No one in law enforcement would."

Alex couldn't argue with that. Gedrose would have simply shot them.

Logan sat down on the couch next to Alex, his gun lowered. "Let's say we believe you," he said. "Why are you here?"

"I want to help if I can. Like I said, I loved Willow, and I might be the best link you'll ever have to the Circle." He frowned at Alex. "Nettie said you removed The Book in a bag. If someone was watching, they might have guessed what it was."

Alex shook her head. "I really don't see how."

"We might be barking up the wrong tree," Gedrose said, "but ultimately, I can't see any other reason for killing these women. You both need to be careful. The people you work with know about The Book. Maybe someone with the police department or the FBI alerted the Circle."

"I can't believe anyone in law enforcement would be involved in some kind of cult," Alex blurted.

Gedrose looked at her strangely. "Well, I was, and I was a good cop. LEOs are just people. Not all of them are perfect, Alex."

"Law enforcement officers are the angels. Criminals are the demons." As soon as the words popped out of her mouth, she gasped.

"What did you say?" Logan asked, his expression one of astonishment.

"I . . . I don't know." Alex was stunned. Where had that come from? "Forget it. Channeling my aunt, I guess. I'm . . . sorry. I don't really believe that."

"Willow was always trying to jam that stuff into your head," Gedrose said gently. "I see some of it got through."

"No." Alex shook her head vigorously. "I rejected all that crazy stuff years ago. I'm just . . . tired. I need some sleep." She glared at Logan. "I'm all right. Just ignore what I said." She knew she sounded a little manic, but those words flying out of her mouth made her feel violated.

"It's fine." Logan nodded toward Gedrose. "Can you nose around? See if you can find out what's going on?"

"So you've decided not to shoot me?"

"For now," Logan said. "But we don't trust you completely, so—"

"I think he's telling the truth," Alex said abruptly, reaching for the training she knew she could believe in. Could trust. She'd been speaking to Logan, but she never took her eyes off the former cop. "He made direct eye contact. Didn't fidget. Didn't look away. Leaned in to talk to us. I believe him. Gedrose, if you really cared about my aunt, then help us find out who killed her." She took a deep breath. "If you had to pick one person most likely to have done this, who would it be? Don't think. Just react. Now!"

Gedrose blinked several times, then blurted, "Marcus Pannell."

"And who is Marcus Pannell?" Logan asked.

"He was in our group. The one that met at Willow's. He's the only member who could possibly do this. He's a big man, and sometimes he acted like he was in charge. I eventually realized not everyone in the Circle considered themselves angels, and—"

"I thought you weren't supposed to give your real names," Alex said. "How do you know his?"

"I didn't until after I left the Circle. I saw him one day in a local hardware store. He was checking out, so I hung back until he left. I'm friends with the owner. I told him I'd met the guy but couldn't remember his name. My friend told me he was Marcus Pannell. I guess he owns an advertising firm in Wichita."

"Sounds like an educated guy," Logan said. "How could he buy in to this stuff?"

Gedrose just stared at him.

"Sorry," Logan said. "I didn't think."

Gedrose shook his head. "It's okay. I guess we're all looking for answers. The Circle came at the right time, and they made sense to me—in the beginning. The devil is a deceiver. I was certainly deceived."

"Why hasn't the Circle come after you in some way?" Alex asked. "Why haven't they seen you as a threat?"

He smiled. "I was diagnosed with prostate cancer not long after I became a Christian. It's under control, but they don't know that. I told them I just wasn't feeling well enough to be involved—at least until I was cured." He shrugged. "They accepted that and never bothered me again. I'd been one of their most dedicated members. I guess they trusted me."

"But now?"

"I need to be careful."

Alex's phone rang. It was Harrison. "We need to get to work," she told Gedrose. "Give Logan your contact information. We'll let you go for now, but the police will want to talk to you, so expect them. We'll be in touch as well."

She got up and grabbed the phone. "We've got more information about the missing pathogen," Harrison said after she answered. "And it's not good. I want to video conference with you and Logan in fifteen minutes. I'll give you the information then. Will that work for you?"

"Sure. We'll be online." She said good-bye and made eye contact with Logan. "Harrison wants to talk."

Logan grabbed the notebook Alex had used. Turning to a clean page, he handed it and a pen to Gedrose. "Write down Pannell's name too, so we'll know how it's spelled."

"Please call me Jimmy," Gedrose said. "I want to do anything I can to assist you. But call only this number. It's an old burner phone that can't be traced."

Logan frowned. "So you really are worried someone might be following you?"

"A little. But like I said, I didn't notice a tail. Still, I'm giving you the address of a safe place where I plan to hang out for a while. I really believe I can help you if you give me a chance." He shook his head. "To be honest, I never thought the members of the Circle were dangerous. Until now. I really don't know what to think anymore."

"We'll pass this information along to the folks in charge," Logan said. "Again, they *will* want to question you."

Jimmy nodded. "I'll be waiting."

Logan walked him to the door. When he closed it behind him, Logan turned around, his expression tight. "I hope we haven't made a mistake," he said. "Not just letting him go, but I'm also concerned about his safety. He's not a young man."

"And I'm worried that the Circle might have sent him to us. They could be trying to get involved in the investigation."

"I thought you said he was telling the truth."

"He appeared to be, but he was in law enforcement. He knows how to make himself look innocent."

"Well, I hope he's exactly who he seems to be. He really could be an asset."

"I guess we'll find out. Hopefully, partnering with Jimmy Gedrose isn't a decision we'll live to regret."

18

Logan and Alex sat down in front of Alex's laptop. Within minutes, Harrison's video call came through. Logan thought he looked worried.

"You've seen the paper?" he asked, forgoing any kind of greeting.

"Yes," Alex said. "Have you secured the letter?"

"It's on its way to the lab."

"I doubt they'll find anything. Walker's too smart for that."

"Can you tell us more about him yet?" Harrison asked.

"No, sorry," Logan said. "We had a visitor, and that took up some of our time. Jimmy Gedrose. The man in the sketch Alex drew and facial recognition identified. He wants to help us."

"Sounds like you don't think he killed these women, but I don't want to bring someone we can't trust into our investigation."

"He seems to be on the level," Logan said. "He was in the Circle. Knew Willow and Nettie. He did give us a name.

Someone in the Circle he thinks could have been involved in what happened at Willow's. A Marcus Pannell."

Harrison wrote down the name as Logan spelled it. "We'll check it out."

"You said you had additional information about this pathogen?" Alex asked.

"Yeah. I figured if you knew more about what we're dealing with it would help you."

"It could," Alex said. "I'd also like to know about the chemist in Ethiopia. If he was working with Walker, it might help us to understand how far he was willing to go to help carry out this so-called prophecy."

"The chemist's name is Martin Kirabo. According to his coworkers, he was brilliant but troubled. Kept to himself a lot, but in the past few months he talked more than usual. Brought up concerns about someone getting their hands on a sample of Ebola and reengineering it into a superbug. Something that couldn't be easily contained if released into the general population."

"Didn't the people he worked with find this odd?" Alex asked.

Harrison sighed deeply. "I guess these science nerds like to bounce around all kinds of theories. No one was really all that concerned. Until now. With the missing sample and the missing chemist, they're more than a little worried. And before you ask, yes, he followed some kind of strange religion. Didn't talk about it much, but I'm pretty sure we all know what it is."

"Did he ever mention knowing someone in the States?" Logan asked.

"No, not really. But some of his coworkers said he would

go off by himself to talk on the phone the last few months he was there."

Harrison rubbed his forehead before going on. "Here's what we're concerned about. The thing Kirabo brought up more than once was how to make this strain of Ebola airborne."

Logan's stomach felt as if it had suddenly flipped over. "Did you say *airborne?*"

"Yeah, you heard me. Let's just say that if he was able to do that, we're looking at a virus that makes COVID-19, H1N1, and MRSA look like mild colds."

No one spoke for several seconds.

Then Alex said, "Walker believes he's carrying out some kind of sacred destiny. He won't be stopped easily."

"Yeah, that's what I was thinking," Harrison said. "These kind of perps are harder to catch because they're usually prepared to die if they have to. They're bold and determined."

Logan grunted. "So now we have a virulent virus in the hands of a dangerous psychopath who has no conscience. No reason to change his mind. He intends to release this virus to the public. There's no way to reason with him."

"What about putting his own family in danger?" Harrison asked.

"I don't think it would make any difference to him," Alex said. "He places his calling above anything else."

Logan didn't disagree with her. She was right.

"If the guy in Ethiopia truly is with the Circle," Alex said, "then this cult really is worldwide. Willow used to tell me it was everywhere. I didn't believe her. I assumed it was one of her many delusions, but Jimmy Gedrose said the same thing."

Harrison cursed and rubbed the back of his neck this time. "It took several days for the lab to realize there was a problem. Handling deadly viruses, inactive or not, should be overseen a lot better than this. It would have helped if we'd had a heads-up sooner. I'm pretty sure this lab will be shut down—at least until they can make certain it's being run the way it should be."

"Do we know any more about Walker?" Logan asked, trying to redirect Harrison to the information they needed.

"Not a lot more. His qualifications are perfect. Graduated at the top of his class, no arrests, no problems. The lab in Kansas City hired him without reservations. Nothing in the information he gave them raised red flags. His boss says his work was top-notch. He was a bit of a loner. Didn't really spend time with his colleagues after work. Used to talk to some of them about his wife and kids. Seemed like a dedicated husband and father. The people he worked with figured he was committed to his family and didn't have a need for other friends."

"He . . . he's married?" Alex said slowly. "I didn't see that coming."

"Me either," Logan said.

"Well, he lived in that small apartment near the lab, but he told coworkers his wife and kids lived somewhere else and that he went home on weekends. He just never mentioned where that was. We haven't been able to trace it. Can't find any cell phone records with calls or purchases he made with his credit card anywhere except in town. No property in his name. He's a master at hiding his tracks. Detectives have been trying to find his family. Nothing so far. I'll send you the details, and we'll go over them when you get here, but that's the gist of it."

He frowned. "One of his coworkers said he hated Christianity. Once a guy mentioned he and his family were going on a church retreat. He wasn't even talking to Walker, but Walker overheard it and went ballistic. Ranted about how he was worshiping a false God and he'd been deceived. Guess his outburst was reported to their boss, who cautioned Walker. It never happened again."

"That's interesting," Alex said.

Harrison paused for a moment. "You know, this guy may have passed the virus on to someone else. We have no proof he's still got it."

Logan glanced at Alex, who raised her eyebrows. They were both convinced Walker had the virus. He wouldn't let anyone else fill the role of the Destroyer.

"He's got it," Alex said. "Remember, he thinks he's fulfilling a prophecy. He won't let someone else take the glory."

"You're probably right, but keep an open mind. We don't want to miss something because we jumped to conclusions. As soon as we end this call, I'll send you everything new we have on him."

"Where is Walker's dad?" Logan asked.

Harrison shrugged. "Dead about ten years."

Harrison put something into the printer next to him and clicked a button. "I'm sending you a photo of Adam Walker now. The lab where he worked finally dug it up. It's similar to his driver's license photo. File to follow."

Alex opened the file that came through. A few seconds later she and Logan were staring at a young man who wasn't bad looking. Dark hair with blue eyes. His face was plain. Nothing in his expression would make anyone think he was capable of murder. She noticed a scar on his chin. That made it easier to identify him, unless he'd taken measures to hide it.

"How can this be our guy?" Logan asked. "We were told he's thirty-two, but he looks a lot younger. Early twenties."

"Walker *is* thirty-two," Harrison said. "But he does look younger. That might actually work in his favor. If someone saw an older man tagging a train, it would seem strange. His youngish looks make him seem like any other tagger." He blew out a quick breath. "The KCPD is doing everything possible to try to stop him from killing again, but they just don't have enough information to get ahead of him. Neither do we."

"We've been running behind finding these bodies," Alex said. "Number five may be waiting somewhere."

"I hope you're wrong about that, but the truth is we need to move faster."

"Alex and I still need a copy of The Book, especially the part about the six sacrifices and the Destroyer."

"I'll send you those pages as quickly as I can, then give you a complete copy later. I need you back here as soon as possible so you can share your assessment with our team. Looks like the snow will have moved out of our area by tomorrow morning."

"Okay," Alex said. "But I have to tell you, this guy's a little different. He confuses me some."

"Well, that concerns me."

"I really didn't think he'd be married. I have to rethink a few things. Most serial killers have compulsions that can be easily understood. They hate their mothers, or they just hate women in general. Some of them are sexual sadists. Each one has his reason for what he does. It's his signature. But this guy . . . I don't know if the prophecy is enough. I'm still wondering about his childhood."

Alex stood and went to the desk, then pulled out the file they'd brought with them from Quantico. "I noticed some confusion in the way the Train Man left the bodies too." She took out some of the photos and placed them on the table in front of Logan. "Look, he lays them out straight with their hands folded. Usually that would mean he has some kind of concern for them. Some remorse. But he stabs them. That's up close and personal. Shows anger."

"This guy is complicated," Logan said. "Like I said, I'm not sure he's going to be easy to understand."

Harrison opened a folder in front of him and flipped through the pages. "The people at the lab said his wife's name is Sally. The kids are Gabby and Trey. Not sure of their ages, but he acted as if they were young. Under ten. Problem is the police can't find them either. Neither is enrolled in school in Kansas City—Missouri or Kansas—or in any surrounding school district. They had to comb through almost one hundred Gabby or Trey possibilities. Good thing their names aren't John or Mary."

Logan wasn't sure many kids were named John or Mary these days, but he understood the point. "So none of these kids led back to Adam Walker?"

"Not even close. The police were careful to check out every single parent. Nothing." Harrison sighed. "Look. Do what you can. I realize this isn't an actual profile since we know who we're looking for, but I still need everything you can give me about this guy. Work it up and send it to me. We need to get it out to law enforcement right away. Like you said, the fifth sacrifice may have already been made. We've been finding these bodies several days after they were killed. The first body wasn't discovered for almost a week."

"But trains are still being watched carefully, right?" Logan asked.

"Yes. By railroad authorities and personnel and the police. But some of the trains are long, and it's almost impossible to keep an eye on every single car."

"If we make it too hard for him to use a regular train car, is it possible he might make a change?" Alex asked.

Harrison looked alarmed. "To what?"

"All kinds of trains are out there. At zoos, entertainment parks, even in malls."

Harrison stared at them through the computer screen. "I don't like the way you're thinking, but you might be right. We can't ask the police to leave the trains unprotected, but I guess we have to tell them to find a way to expand their efforts."

Alex sighed. "If it's not already too late."

"This is one time we can't allow Walker to stay ahead of us. We have no idea when or where he'll release that virus."

"He has a plan," Alex said. "Trust me. He knows exactly what he's doing."

"She's right," Logan said. "How long was this Martin . . ."

"Kirabo," Harrison said.

"Martin Kirabo. How long was he at the lab in Ethiopia?"

"Twelve years."

Logan glanced at Alex, whose expression made it clear she was thinking the same thing he was. "Twelve years is more than enough time to create a new virus. Something different. Ebola plus."

"Okay, give me what you can as soon as possible," Harrison said. "I'll get those sections of The Book to you." He broke the link without another word.

Logan turned to Alex. "I know we're both exhausted, but let's get to work."

19

Adam checked several times to see if the police had found the fifth sacrifice. Nothing. He cursed loudly. These fools were so incompetent and slow. Would he have to lead them to it? He was itching to get on with the sixth sacrifice so he could put his next plan into action. Once it was done, he'd get Sally and the kids away from Kansas City. Far away from the destruction that would quickly spread.

He had the perfect plan to multiply the virus, and those fools would never figure it out in time. He was told it would take a while for the symptoms to show up. By the time they did, the virus would have spread all over the area, and others would be sharing it around the world. The results would be much worse than any outbreak mankind had seen.

He went to his desk and pulled on his gloves. He always wore them when he was working. Then he penned a letter to the police in block letters. When he was finished, he put it in an envelope, then sealed it and placed a stamp on it.

Adam left his office and went into the living room. Sally was reading a book, her lovely legs tucked under her as she sat on the couch.

"Going to the post office. Be back soon," he said.

"Okay, honey." She smiled. He leaned over and kissed her, then left the house. It would all be over shortly, and then he would have fulfilled his destiny. The Master would reward him, and Adam would live the rest of his life with the knowledge that he was one of the most important people who'd ever lived.

Logan reached over and pulled a large spiral notebook lying on the coffee table toward them, next to the remnants of the Chinese food they'd ordered in. "So what do we know now?" he asked.

Alex had just started to answer him when the fax machine they'd hauled from Quantico began spitting out pages. Logan got up and snatched them.

"They're from Harrison," he said. "The information about Walker and Martin Kirabo." He gathered the papers, waiting until the fax machine fell silent. Then he brought everything over to the couch. He was worried. This virus could be incredibly deadly. Still, it would be almost impossible for it to spread the way the Train Man wanted it to. Especially since they'd had a heads-up. The CDC would have already issued a warning to hospitals and doctors in the area.

Yet Logan felt a strange uneasiness about this guy. He was smart enough to get away with these murders, leaving no evidence behind. Was he on his own? Or was someone helping him? Were the murders of Willow and Nettie connected to him? Or did the Circle really mete out punishment so severe? They didn't have answers to these questions, but they did know Walker understood deadly viruses. Why did he think he had something so lethal that unleashing it would kill millions of people? Could this really be a mutated form of Ebola?

"We need to know more about these men," Alex said as Logan sat down next to her. "Something doesn't add up. Adam Walker and Martin Kirabo worked in labs. They had to know their theft would be discovered." She slowly shook her head. "Don't you find that odd?" She'd taken her long hair out of the band that usually held it, and her hair flowed onto her shoulders, just like it had when he'd come to her hotel room the first time. Her gray-blue eyes locked onto his. Logan's throat constricted, and he had to take a deep breath to get the words in his mind to tumble out of his mouth.

"Yeah . . ." He cleared his throat and tried again. "I was just thinking about that. Ebola is dangerous. Walker had to know the lab would notice the discrepancy."

"He clearly wasn't worried about it. He must have been planning this for a long, long time. Already knew when he'd get the sample. Had probably already moved out of his apartment. He may have shifted to where his family is or secured someplace else close to the lab even before the sample arrived. Like I said before, a place where he thought he'd be safe."

Alex nodded. "This was carefully planned. Down to the last detail."

Logan realized he was holding his breath and quickly blew it out. "That means . . ."

"That means Martin Kirabo probably had plenty of time

to prepare this shipment of his superbug." Alex turned her head and frowned at him. "They waited until they had the exact virus they wanted. I think this thing may be exactly what Walker says it is. Something powerful enough to kill a lot of people."

Logan didn't respond. There was nothing to say. He put his hand on his chest and tried to calm himself. His heart felt as if it would pound right out of his rib cage.

"Let's look through this information before we start writing up our assessment," he said. Logan silently handed her the report about Adam Walker, then began to read the information gathered on Martin Kirabo.

He'd barely started when Alex said, "Adam Walker is left-handed."

"We were certain he was since, based on the writing on the boxcars, the Train Killer is too. But that helps to confirm they're the same person."

"Yeah. You know, there's not a lot here. Like Harrison said, his coworkers don't have much to say about him. No one ever saw him outside of work. He has a cousin who lives in Michigan, but he told investigators he met Adam only once. When they were kids. This guy is a ghost."

"Could Kirabo have come here to help Walker with this plan?"

Alex was silent as she considered his question. "I don't think so. But after you read that report, tell me if you think it's possible. I'm sure flights from Africa are being checked carefully. If our colleagues find out he came here, they'll tell us."

They both went back to reading the paperwork in front of them. After Alex finished hers, she pushed her file toward Logan. Then she got up and went to the kitchen to brew more coffee. When she was done she brought the cups in and put them back on the coffee table. By then Logan had finished reading and had picked up the file on Adam Walker. As she'd said, not much was there.

"Martin Kirabo doesn't fit the profile of a serial killer," she said after a few minutes. She pulled his photo from the file and put it down between them. Logan had to agree. He had a nice smile. A friendly face. He was married and had four children. His mother lived with them. How in the world did he get caught up in this? Not just the Circle but this plot?

As soon as Alex finished speaking, the fax machine beeped and more pages began to slide out. Logan grabbed them before they fell on the floor, then returned to the couch and held them out to Alex.

"Pages from The Book," she said, her voice choked and low.

He was alarmed by the expression on her face as she stared at the papers in his hand.

He recognized that look.

Alex Donovan was afraid.

Once again, Alex felt as if a life she'd ignored for years was rushing at her, determined to drag her back to the pain she'd endured as a child. Hiding in her room, overcome by fear. She'd sat on the floor, leaning against her bed, repeating one of several mantras. *I will not be afraid. I will overcome this. I will be okay. One day I'll do something great.*

She'd made other declarations, but she couldn't remember them all. She'd shut her mind from recalling those years, but obviously not everything had been banished.

"Alex, please. Tell me what's going on."

She looked up at Logan and was surprised to see the concern on his face. She realized she was rocking back and forth, just like she had as a teenager. And she'd been mouthing the words *I will not be afraid. I will be okay.* She forced her body to relax, but it wasn't as easy as it should have been.

"Tell me about moving in with your aunt," Logan said gently. "Please. It clearly traumatized you. Help me understand."

Anger flared like a fire igniting inside her. "Let's get back to work. I'm fine. It's just a shock seeing this again."

"I thought you never read it."

Alex took a deep, calming breath. "I didn't, but like I said, Willow was always quoting from it. She thought she was trying to *save* me, but I didn't want her kind of salvation. All I wanted was freedom. You probably can't understand that."

"I think I can." He leaned toward her. "Please let me in. I really want to help."

Alex pulled the papers from his hands and put them on the table. "If you want to help me, let's figure out a way to assist law enforcement in catching this guy."

Logan didn't move. She realized her response hadn't satisfied him. She didn't want to tell him the truth. She wouldn't risk her career by letting people know who she really was. Had been. But before she could stop herself, words suddenly flowed from her mouth unbidden.

"I don't know why my father left us when I was four. He just walked out the door one day and never came back. But his leaving destroyed my mother. She'd been great, you know? The kind of mom who baked cookies and took me to the park. She'd tuck me in bed at night and sing a song or tell me a story. She was . . . wonderful. Until she wasn't."

Alex closed her eyes. "She never smiled after he left. She struggled with depression for years, and we lived off welfare because she couldn't hold down a job anymore. By the time I was ten, she spent most of her time inside the house, completely overcome. She was there in body, but she wasn't the mother I'd known. I had to do all the cleaning. Make sure our clothes were washed. She'd go to the store when she could manage it, but I had to write out the grocery list. That's where I began to learn to take care of myself without anyone to depend on. I know I've made it sound like I learned to cook and all the rest once I arrived at Willow's, but the truth is those last years with my mother . . ."

Alex cleared her throat and tried to choke back the stream of words pouring out. "When . . . when I was twelve . . ." She put her hands up to her mouth. Why was she saying these things? Why couldn't she stop?

Logan reached over and gently pulled down her hands. "Don't be afraid. You can trust me, Alex."

A wave of fury broke inside her, and she stood, facing him, wanting to break him down. Stop him from caring.

"Trust you? Trust you? I don't even know you, and I don't trust anyone." He reached for her, but she pulled away. "When I came home from school that day . . ." Tears streamed down her face, but she couldn't stop them. "I found my mother hanging in the hallway. Our house had two stories, and she'd looped a rope off the staircase railing, fashioned a noose, put it around her neck, and jumped off. It wasn't like I'd seen on TV. It was ugly . . . awful. . . ."

Logan was on his feet, pulling her close to him. She didn't want to be held. She didn't want sympathy. She began to beat on his chest, but her blows grew weak and useless, and she melted into his arms. She had no more strength. She couldn't fight anymore.

After a few minutes, Logan gently sat her down on the couch. "Your coffee's cold. I'll warm it up."

She watched him as he put her cup in the microwave. When he brought it back, she tried to thank him, but she could only gulp. What had she done? Had she just thrown away her career? Would Logan tell Jeff she was unstable?

Logan sat down next to her.

"You never got counseling?"

"Some woman at the child welfare office talked to me before I was hauled off to Wichita, but I didn't listen. I was too numb."

"Well, listen to me now," he said quietly. "When we push too many painful things behind a door in our minds, one day it finally bursts open. It's too crowded in there. It doesn't mean we're unbalanced. It only means our minds are telling us we've got to deal with those feelings. That hurt. We can't do it if we won't acknowledge what's going on."

Alex wiped the tears from her face and picked up the cup he'd brought her. After forcing several sips of the hot liquid down her throat, she put the cup down and looked at him.

"How can you possibly understand?" she asked. "You probably had a perfect life. A perfect family. I doubt if you know how it feels to lose the people who were supposed to keep you safe and then end up with someone like Willow. Once again, I was the adult. She was the child. She needed even more help than my mother. I did everything. She did nothing." She took a deep breath. "I couldn't have friends. Couldn't invite people to the house. Whenever someone came over other than the Circle—a repairman, whatever—Willow would act crazy. Tell them the end of the world was coming."

"But Mike was a friend?"

Alex nodded. "He was nice to me. We weren't that close, but he'd seen Willow at her worst and didn't mind. His parents seemed to understand my situation and welcomed me into their home. Made sure I had enough clothes to wear and school supplies. They were very kind. They were the bright spot in an otherwise miserable life."

"Alex, there's something I don't get. The feelings you have toward Willow . . . She may have been disturbed, but she doesn't sound mean. Certainly not dangerous."

"Not dangerous?" She stared at him, wondering if she should tell him everything. "At first it was just . . . frightening. House full of trash. Empty refrigerator and cupboards. A woman living mostly on junk food. The food she'd tried to cook was left on the stove, no doubt for days. The smell was horrific. Dirty dishes piled up. Clothes all over the floor. I'd just found my mother's dead body. I was alone in the world, shipped off to live in another town with a crazy aunt. I worked hard to overcome it. I cleaned and cleaned . . . Finally, things were better. I didn't complain about cleaning up after her. At least I had a roof over my head. And then one night I woke up, probably because I heard my door open. Willow was standing over my bed . . . with a knife."

Unable to look at Logan for his reaction, Alex picked up the most recent pages Harrison had faxed. She shuffled through them until she found what she wanted and read aloud.

"'When the Virgin who shall be washed in blood, the final sacrifice, is offered to the Master, the demons will be unleashed, and the angels will make war with the evil ones. This sacrifice will be holy, and the one who offers it will be elevated in the Master's kingdom. He is the Destroyer. The one called to fulfill the will of the Master. Long live the Master!'"

"Isn't part of that one of the verses Walker wrote on a train car?"

Alex nodded.

"Your aunt thought you were the virgin to be sacrificed?"

"That night, I think she did."

Logan looked stunned. "What did you do to protect yourself?"

Alex looked down at the floor. "I was seventeen when this happened. A senior. I know I said Mike and I weren't close, but I had no one else to turn to, so I told him. I was too scared to tell his parents, and so was he. We were afraid I could end up in the system. Even though I would be eighteen in two months, the idea of ending up somewhere even worse than Willow's terrified me. Mike knew a guy at school. . . ."

She looked up at him. She'd gone this far. She might as well finish it. "Mike got me a gun—a loaded gun. I slept with it under my pillow until the day I left, when I dropped it in one dumpster and the bullets in another."

"Why didn't you call the police?"

"Like I said, I couldn't take the chance that some social worker would take over my life. Willow had no memory of what happened." Alex sighed. "I realized then how sick she really was. I really didn't want to get her in trouble, and frankly, I was afraid of the Circle. If I called the police, would they retaliate? Would I have more problems than I already had?"

She clasped her hands together. Talking about this was harder than she thought it would be, yet she felt like some of the anger inside her had been released. "I'd forgotten about that night until we were on this case. I guess it just popped out from behind that door you mentioned. That memory is probably why I've seemed so angry with Willow. It was fear masquerading as something else, I guess."

"I'm glad I was here to talk to. It will stay between us."

"Thank you," Alex said. "I imagine I'll have to be nice to you from now on."

Logan laughed. She loved his laugh. It was one of his best features. "Nah, no blackmail. You can still be mean to me if you want."

She smiled at him. "I feel much better."

He grinned at her but then grew serious again. "Hey, I thought there had to be five sacrifices before the virgin is sacrificed. So how could Willow get it in her head you were . . . you know."

"I think it must have been a combination of reading that stupid book and being overmedicated. I'm not sure the doctor she saw from time to time truly cared about her well-being. She seemed shocked when I told her what happened. In my opinion, she was walking in her sleep. Now that I know more about how people with her illness think, I'm almost certain she wouldn't have actually stabbed me. I know she felt bad about it. Neither one of us ever mentioned it again."

She sighed. "As soon as I graduated from high school, I moved out. I got a job at a local restaurant. It was barely enough to get by on, but I found a room to rent and was able to buy food. Willow had given me a small, white Chevy Aveo that had been parked in her garage for years. The car needed to be repaired, but I worked out a deal with a nearby garage. They got the car going and let me make payments." She smiled. "That thing got me to college in Lawrence, Kansas, that fall, where I'd been granted a scholarship. But then it died, and I didn't have the money to revive it. I did a lot of walking, but thankfully friends at school chauffeured me around quite a bit."

"Did you go all through college without a car?" Logan asked.

"No. In my senior year, a girl offered to sell me her Volkswagen Bug for four hundred dollars. She even let me make payments. That's how I ended up with my first Volkswagen. I liked it so much that when it broke down, I bought another one. It made me feel good to take care of myself."

Thankfully, the rush of words finally slowed. Alex had no plan to talk about some of the hurt that had imprisoned her because of the trauma she'd endured. But these were small things. Even waking up to see Willow standing over her with a knife. She could have handled that. She understood it even though she might not be able to truly forgive it. But the big monsters were still behind that door. The things that gave her nightmares. One in particular. One she would never tell anyone. She would keep it locked and shuttered away. If she ever let it out . . .

She pushed the thought away. It would never happen. She'd defeated everything the past had thrown at her. She'd do it again, and she'd do it alone. "Let's get back to work now. And . . . and thanks for listening, Logan."

"No problem. I'm here anytime you need to talk." When she didn't say anything else, he picked up the papers and stacked them on the table.

Alex lifted her pen and opened her notebook. All she wanted to do was figure out this Walker guy and ensure he was caught before he killed anyone else. Nothing could interfere with that goal.

Nothing.

21

Tim Austin was sorting the mail for the different offices and employees at the *Kansas City Journal* when he came across an envelope mailed locally and addressed to the editor in chief. The block letters and the lack of a return address got his attention. Had the Train Man written again? He yelled at a coworker, telling her he had to leave for a few minutes, then he hurried upstairs to the editor's office. When he reached the secretary, he handed her the envelope. She took it, thanked him, and called her boss, Peter Gardner.

Tim left before Gardner came out of his office. As he walked toward the elevator, he looked down at his hands. He'd heard the whispers between the various reporters, wondering how the Train Man planned to kill so many people. Several had mentioned superbugs and viruses that could do the job. The country wasn't ready for another plague. It was too much to ask of anyone. He prayed quietly that the Train Man would be stopped before something horrible happened.

When the elevator door opened, Tim turned away and hurried to the bathroom, where he washed his hands until they were red.

Alex and Logan met Keith at the airport at 8:00 a.m. with time to turn in their rental car. Logan was exhausted. He and Alex had worked until they were satisfied with their assessment. They'd sent it to Harrison around two in the morning. Logan should have felt relieved, but he'd noticed that something was still wrong with Alex despite her claim that she felt better after unburdening herself. She worked hard, but it seemed like part of her was somewhere else. They were both short on sleep, of course, but what he'd seen was more than fatigue. It was as if she had a war going on in her mind. She seemed tense, not herself. Was she sorry she'd shared her pain with him? Would things be okay between them?

Alex had a stellar reputation. As young as she was, she was almost a legend in the FBI. Her coworkers in Kansas City said she had the ability to see things no one else did. Like the way she determined how tall Walker was by the position of the messages he wrote on the boxcars, and that he was left-handed. Logan was looking more at his MO, his motivation, his signature. All important aspects, but Alex's kind of input was helpful when they needed to narrow possibilities.

Once they were on the plane, though, he was pleased to see her relax and focus on their case, wanting to go over it again to make sure they hadn't missed anything.

"You're kind of quiet this morning," Alex said. "Anything wrong?"

Logan shook his head. "Just tired. Why aren't you drag-ging? We didn't get much sleep."

Alex laughed. "The answer, my friend, is coffee, coffee, coffee."

"I think I'm coffeed out. Is that a word?"

"Coffeed? I doubt it, but I understand what you mean. I guess that makes it okay."

Logan smiled. Today she wore black pants and a match-ing jacket with a soft aqua blouse underneath. Her hair was pulled back and secured with a black band with silver beads. It was simple but strangely feminine. She was the epitome of professionalism, yet nothing could distract from her natural beauty. Yes, she was beautiful.

Logan leaned back into his seat and closed his eyes. It took around twenty minutes to fly from Wichita to Kansas City once they were in the air. Not enough time for a real nap, but at least he could rest his eyes. When Alex put her hand on his arm and said, "We're here," he felt like only seconds had passed. He must have fallen asleep after all.

The cockpit door opened, and Keith came out. "Good luck with whatever you're working on," he said. "I'm praying for you guys."

"I appreciate that, Keith," Logan told him, extending his hand so Keith could shake it. He and Keith had been friends for a while. Logan hadn't known he was a Christian until he saw him at a local prayer breakfast. It was nice to have a brother in the Bureau. Keith and his wife, Donita, had recently started coming to Logan's church. They were a fan-tastic couple and a blessing to know.

He and Alex said good-bye to Keith and hurried off the plane. An agent was waiting for them, and it didn't take long to reach the CP. When they came in the back door, the quiet outside was shattered by the buzz of conversation and clicking of computer keyboards and printers. Harrison stood near a large dry-erase board. Next to it was an even larger corkboard almost filled with photos and papers speared by colored pins. He turned around and saw them.

"Glad you're back. We got your assessment, and I'd like to go over it with you. Let's go in the back room."

Logan and Alex followed him to the meeting room. A few people were gathered around the table, working. They appeared to be searching through papers. Logan had spent many hours doing the same thing on missions. Medical records, dental records, school records, property records . . . whatever it took to understand an UNSUB. It was one of the most thankless jobs an agent could be assigned, yet more than once information had been uncovered that helped field agents find their suspect. Even though this time they knew their subject's identity, they would still need to meticulously pore through everything they could in an attempt to locate him.

Logan and Alex took seats at one end of the table, away from the agents working through the files.

Rather than sitting down with them, Harrison made a call, asking someone to join them in the back room. After he hung up, he sat down. "Alex, we've called in your replacement in Kansas City, Karen Harper. She'll be coordinating the team investigating the murders. I'm keeping her updated on your progress since we believe the Train Man is the person in possession of the virus."

The door opened, and Karen walked in. She was short and stocky. Logan had heard she was a bulldog when it came to her job as the NCAVC Coordinator in Kansas City. Alex had mentioned how relieved she'd been when Karen was assigned. Alex was confident she would do a great job.

Karen sat down next to Alex. "So you're convinced our UNSUB is Adam Walker?" she asked. No time spent greeting her fellow agents. Right to work.

"Yes," Alex said. "Everything we've seen points to him. We're sure he has the virus, and he's identified himself as the Train Man. The only thing we're unsure about is if he's working with someone else."

"As I'm sure you know," Logan said, "most serial killers work alone. That's brought some confusion to this situation. We're not sure how the two cases fit together."

"Wichita tells me a circle was drawn with blood on a wall inside the house," Karen said to Alex. "With your name in the middle. Do we need to provide you protection?"

"No. I believe that was done by someone who is connected to the Circle—and knows I'm with the FBI—just so I would back off. It seems likely they knew I took Willow's copy of The Book. But they thrive on secrecy, and even though they might have killed my aunt and her caregiver, harming someone in law enforcement would certainly increase the chances of bringing them out of the shadows." She smiled. "Besides, I'm capable of taking care of myself."

"Why do you think they knew you had The Book?" Karen asked.

"The more I think about it, the more I believe the Circle was watching Willow's house regularly because they wanted her copy of The Book after she had her stroke and stopped hosting Circle meetings. Nettie wasn't cooperating with them, and then they saw me take away the bag from the house and suspected I had it."

"If the attacker was someone from the Circle, the only thing that makes sense is that he knew The Book wasn't there," Logan added. "Nothing was disturbed. Not a drawer, not a closet." He paused. "Unless the attacker didn't care about The Book."

"Couldn't he have just tried to make it look as if the Circle was involved?"

Alex shrugged. "Maybe. But the Circle is so secretive, there's very little chance someone who's never been a part of it would know enough to draw that symbol above my . . ." Alex stumbled for a moment. Logan realized she'd started to say *my bed*. "Above the bed," she finished. "I realize it sounds as if we're speculating, but I understand the Circle better than anyone who isn't actually a member. The point is, my experience tells me that Adam Walker is the Train Man and that he has the virus. I believe someone else killed my aunt and Nettie Travers. Somehow it's all related. I think we have to keep looking at the Circle when it comes to these murders in Wichita."

"I'm still concerned about your safety," Harrison said. His eyes narrowed. "I want you to stay at the command post as much as possible. Anytime you leave, I want to know."

"I'm with her almost constantly," Logan said. "We'll be careful."

"See that you are." Harrison crossed his arms and leaned back in his chair. Logan could see the weariness in his face. "Before Nettie Travers died she tried to tell you someone she knew was in the hospital. Tell us more about that."

"First," Alex said, "she recognized Jimmy in the sketch I made of a man I saw when my aunt had a Circle meeting at her house. I was probably around thirteen by then, maybe fourteen. And as you know, sir, Jimmy showed up at our hotel in Wichita yesterday. He admitted he was at the hospital, even inside Willow's house after the police had gone. He says he was part of the Circle once, but that he didn't hurt either woman. He was just trying to protect them. Now he wants to help us find whoever killed them. We think he's on the level. And since he said he'd nose around and let us know if he learned anything new, we let him go for the time being. He's willing to be questioned further, though, and we know where to find him."

She paused. "Second, Nettie said *he* was there, but I don't think she meant Gedrose. I believe she recognized someone else at the hospital, but she died before she could reveal a name. The doctor told us she should have recovered, so she may have been killed somehow. We're waiting to see the autopsy report."

"We suggest you bring in Jimmy Gedrose and talk to him as soon as possible," Logan said. "We think he might be able to help us, and if he's on the level, he may need WITSEC."

"We've already talked to him, as has Chief Rogers," Harrison said. "We're bringing him in, and I've alerted the U.S. Marshals. They believe he would definitely qualify for the Witness Security Program."

"Good," Alex said. "He can at least shed more light on what it's like to be inside the Circle."

Harrison reached for a pile of papers and pulled off the top one. "I agree with you about the murders of those women. I doubt it was Walker. And not only because the timeline doesn't fit. Seems he's been busy sending another letter to the *Kansas City Journal*, telling them where we could find sacrifice number five. Thankfully, the paper contacted us and promised not to print the letter . . . for now."

"I wish they hadn't printed the first one," Logan said.

Harrison shrugged. "I guess they thought it would interest the public. At least they're willing to work with us this time. We impressed on them how dangerous printing this letter could be. We don't need this guy glorified, and we also don't want him to know what we know." Harrison sighed. "He's trying to be more creative. He knows we're watching the trains closely. Frankly, if he stuck with the trains, we'd be more likely to catch him. Now we have no idea where he could be. We can't even find the car registered to him. I'm hoping this letter will tell you something I'm not seeing."

"When was it mailed?" Alex asked.

"I know why you're asking. The postmark indicates he was somewhere near Kansas City when your aunt was killed in Wichita."

"That settles it for me, then. I don't think he killed Willow or Nettie. In fact, I'm confident of that. The timeline doesn't work with the first letter from him, and the MO between the murders here and the murders in Wichita doesn't match."

Logan took the copy of the letter Harrison handed him and began to read it out loud.

""The Master has judged the world and found it wanting. The fifth sacrifice has been offered. The worldly, blind police still haven't found him. Here is your clue. This is the only help I'll give you.

'I've sadly benched our number five. Too late to find our friend alive. Instead, I've staged a great grand hunt. Don't rail against my latest stunt.

'The last sacrifice is already being prepared. It is time for the Virgin to be offered. When this happens, the demons will set the earth on fire. The angels will fight for mankind, but they will lose. The world will know the Master is God. It is the will of the Master, and I delight in serving him. Do not make the mistake of thinking you can understand the plague I will visit upon the earth. You cannot. It is stronger and more dangerous than you can comprehend. We have created something so powerful there is no cure for it. And as you die, I will laugh. LONG LIVE THE MASTER!

'You should close your eyes, pretend to sleep, and very softly pray,
        or else the evil Train Man may carry you away.
'The Train Man.'"

"I hate that poem," Logan said. His throat felt tight, and he had to clear it. "So what does this clue mean?"

"It's Union Station," Alex said.

"How do you get that?" Logan asked, surprised.

"The words," she said, looking at Logan as if he were simple. "*Grand* refers to the Grand Hall. *Hunt* is the Jarvis Hunt Room. Of course, *rail*—"

"I get it," Harrison said. "And *stage* is probably the City Stage Theatre."

Alex nodded. "I think our victim is sitting on a bench somewhere near or on the stage."

Harrison stood and hurried across the room to where a group of detectives from the KCPD had gathered in front of a large map of the trains that ran through their target area. Karen stood and followed him. After the two spoke to them, the detectives grabbed their coats and hurried out the back door, obviously headed for Union Station. One of them already had his phone up to his ear.

"Did you notice this letter says the virus has no cure?" Alex asked Logan.

He nodded. "What does that mean?"

Harrison returned to the room. "We should find our victim soon," he said. "Karen is staying here so she can coordinate the search."

"We were just talking about this part of the letter," Logan said. "'We have created something so powerful there is no cure for it.' He said *we*. Do you think he's talking about the chemist in Ethiopia?"

"Seems likely, but here's a new twist to the story. A few hours ago local authorities in Addis Ababa found Martin Kirabo dead. They think he's been murdered."

Alex couldn't believe her ears. "By whom?"

"We don't know, but we're wondering if it was the Circle."

"I have to say I'm surprised," Alex said. "People keep telling me the Circle is bigger than I thought it was. That's hard to believe if it's true that very few copies of The Book exist, but I'm beginning to think they're right." She shook her head. "Everyone has to use a pseudonym. They're not allowed to use their real names. How could such a huge group come from that?"

"I don't know," Harrison said. "But somehow they've managed it. The way they've organized this thing has made it almost impossible for us to track them down. That's why Jimmy Gedrose is important to us. He's the only known member of the Circle left alive we can talk to."

"What about Marcus Pannell?"

"Dead end. Really dead end. The guy died a few months ago. Nothing sinister. Kidney disease."

Alex looked at Logan. "I wonder if Jimmy knew that. Maybe that's why he gave us that name."

"Maybe," Logan said. "At this point, we can't be sure."

"If the Circle is so deadly, why is Jimmy still alive?" Alex asked. "I have a hard time understanding that. He says he told the group he was ill and could no longer attend the meetings, and it seems they've left him alone even though he's actually recovered. But he presents a hole in their secrecy. Even though I tend to believe him, we need to be careful. He could be a plant."

"Noted," Harrison said. "I'll contact the Wichita office and suggest they proceed with caution. Hopefully he's who he seems to be."

"I think that's wise," Alex said. "If he is for real and the Circle finds out he's helping us . . ."

"I've distributed your assessment and recommendations," Harrison said, "but I want you to go over it with our team. You know the drill."

Alex nodded. "We'll do that here?"

"Yes. I'll gather the troops."

A few minutes later the agents assigned to the case and several of the detectives assigned from the Kansas City field office were gathered around the table. Karen was with them. Alex recognized some of them, but others were strangers to her. The group also included crisis-management agents and an attorney should they need warrants or legal advice. Alex was pretty sure she'd spotted the attorney when she came in. Black suit, shiny shoes, manicured nails, and carefully coifed hair all said *lawyer* to her.

Monty slid into the chair next to her. "Glad you guys made it back," he said. He lowered his voice. "Between you and me, we've hit a wall. Hopefully, your friend in Wichita will help us."

"I hope so. They're picking him up today."

"Good idea to keep him safe. People are dropping like flies." He shook his head. "I've never been involved in a case like this. It's crazy. It really is."

"I understand," Alex whispered back. "But we'll get him."

"As long as we're in time."

Monty hadn't needed to mention time. Alex was certain everyone was thinking the same thing. She could almost hear the tick-tick-tick of an internal clock that wouldn't shut up. When someone put a hand on her shoulder, she jumped, then looked up to find Mike smiling down at her.

"Mike," she said. "Good to see you."

"I asked to be assigned to the CP. Since I lived down the street from your aunt for years, I'm hoping I can help identify people coming in and out of her house. I'll be working with a sketch artist."

"That's smart. You had a better chance of seeing them than I did when I lived there. I was busy hiding in my room."

Mike sat down next to Logan and opened his notebook. Everyone around the table had either paper notebooks or electronic tablets.

Stephen Barstow came up to the table and sat down across from Alex. He smiled at her. "Good to see you again, SSA Donovan."

"Good to see you too." The detective's dark hair and deep blue eyes made quite an impression. She noticed a female agent sitting a few chairs away from him reach her hand up to check her hair. Then she wiped the sides of her mouth with her finger, no doubt trying to remove any clumped-up lipstick. Alex was pretty sure the woman would have grabbed her purse and checked herself out a little more if she'd seen Stephen before he sat down.

Harrison moved to the end of the table and stood there flipping through some pages in a large notebook. Finally, he sat down, still looking at the information in front of him. The sound of fingers on keyboards created a steady hum from the other room as analysts searched for anything that would help them with the case.

Harrison cleared his throat. "Some of you know SSA Logan Hart and SSA Alex Donovan. We've given you all copies of their assessment, but I want us to go through it with them in case you have any questions. Also, I need to tell you that we've heard from the Train Man again." He picked up another pile of papers and passed it to his left. "This is a letter the *Kansas City Journal* received early this morning. Read it, please, before we start."

He waited a couple of minutes until everyone at the table looked up at him.

"We'll go through the assessment first. Then we'll talk about this letter." He turned to Alex and Logan. "Let's just hit the high points. Like I said, everyone has read the information you sent us."

He turned back to the group. "We're convinced we're looking for a man named Adam Walker, and we're pretty sure he's part of the Circle. As you know, the local newspaper received a letter where the Train Man boasted about having a contagion that could kill millions of people."

He gestured toward a woman sitting at the other end of the

table. She was short, about sixty, and had blond hair streaked with silver, cut to just above her shoulders. Her expression was solemn.

"This is Dr. Grace Greene from the CDC. Grace, will you tell us what you know about the virus Walker may have?"

Grace nodded. "We're trying to piece the puzzle together the best we can. First, we know a chemist in Ethiopia named Martin Kirabo colluded with a lab research assistant in the United States—the man we've identified as Adam Walker."

Harrison jumped in. "And Kirabo has been found dead—possibly murdered, maybe by the Circle. We don't know for sure. Authorities in Addis Ababa have retrieved his cell phone. He called the same number in the United States over thirty times. We discovered that number belonged to Walker based on information from his workplace. That definitely connects them, but that phone is no longer working. We suspect Walker has disposed of it and secured a new one." He nodded at Grace to continue.

"We have a lot of concerns about the sample Walker may have. As I said, Kirabo was a chemist, and it's possible he altered the sample. He may have attempted to turn it into something far worse than Ebola itself. Something we have no vaccine for."

"Is it airborne?" a woman asked. Alex had no idea who she was.

"We hope not. Ebola is normally spread by contact. An exchange of bodily fluids—and before you think I'm just talking about sex, I'm not. A simple kiss on the cheek can spread the virus. The person kissed touches their face and contact is made. Someone coughing without covering their mouth can do it too. Unfortunately, then, it's very easily spread. And we have no idea how this sample has been engineered. It could be much more lethal than a regular strain."

One of the detectives raised his hand, and Grace nodded at him. "My understanding is that we have the capabilities to contain an Ebola outbreak, but you're saying this guy may have created a superbug? One we can't control?"

"We've come a long way in our handling of viruses. Our experience with COVID-19 has allowed us to be better prepared. We know outbreaks are usually in one area, and if we can track everyone who comes into contact with an infected person before they travel outside of our containment zone, we can usually stop the spread. But if someone releases Ebola in different areas of the country at the same time, or if it's spread through different kinds of transportation — planes, ships, even cross-country buses — we could suddenly have such a high number of infected individuals that it would be difficult or impossible for us to locate everyone and contain the virus."

"How do you think Walker might spread it?" Harrison asked.

"I have no idea. But he has the knowledge to spread it in a way that will affect the most people." She sighed. "Walker is the worst kind of person to get their hands on one of these virulent viruses. His expertise makes him extremely dangerous."

"But it's just a small sample, right?" Stephen asked.

"It doesn't take much to start the cycle."

"Are you surprised Walker was able to get his hands on this virus?" one of the detectives asked.

"Yes, I am. The lab here in Kansas City is a biosafety level 4 facility. BSL-4 is the highest rating for labs that work with infectious agents. It was set up during the COVID-19 pandemic. You have to remember that the lab believed they were receiving inactivated samples, and a technician they trusted received those samples. Not until someone in Addis Ababa noticed that one of their active samples was missing did they become concerned. Of course, when Walker went missing the next day, as did the chemist in Ethiopia, that rang alarm bells." She sighed. "The lab in Addis Ababa has been shut down, and the lab here is under investigation. I can guarantee you that something like this will never happen again."

"If this thing has been reengineered, what are we looking at?" Harrison asked.

Grace took a deep breath, then let it out before saying, "*If Kirabo created something new, we could see an outbreak beyond anything the United States has ever seen. And as I said, if infected people travel to other countries . . . Well, we could completely lose track of it. The good news is we do have ways to prevent infection. A drug called Ervebo can keep people safe as long as the virus hasn't been altered too much."

"But that drug is preventative," Stephen said. "What happens if someone is exposed to Ebola?"

Grace paused a moment, then said, "We don't have a magic drug that kills it. One on the horizon shows great promise, but it hasn't been approved for use in the United States. And before anyone asks, no, the drugs that worked for COVID-19 won't treat Ebola. For now, all we can do is hydrate victims, balance their fluids and electrolytes, maintain their oxygen status and blood pressure, and treat them with antibiotics to address any secondary infections." She shook her head. "But again, if the virus has been altered, we may not be able to do anything to help."

"What's the mortality rate for those infected with Ebola?" Mike asked.

"Around ninety percent. All of you who will be in the field will be vaccinated with Ervebo. I hope it keeps you safe, but as I said, we don't know what we're dealing with. Will this vaccine work for a mutated strain? I can't answer that. All we can do is go by what we know now. If you pray, this is the time to do it."

Although Alex felt a call to prayer wouldn't help, it was clear Grace was extremely concerned. All Alex had wanted since that day at school was to be a behavioral analyst for the FBI. For the first time, she wished she was back in the field. She wanted to go out there and find this guy. But that wasn't her job. She and Logan had to narrow the possibilities so the field agents could capture the Train Man before he unleashed the virus. And she intended to do just that.

A lex stood, and with their notes in front of her, she
began to go through the assessment she and Logan
had put together.

"I know Monty's been working with you, giving you some
preliminary ideas about our subject. But things have changed
because we now have a solid suspect. What we're giving you
today isn't a profile, since that's a procedure we go through
when we don't know who our subject is. But I'm going to
present this assessment as if we didn't believe Adam Walker
is our suspect. With that approach, I think you'll learn some
things that may help you find him."

She reached down and, lifting her cup, took a sip of water.
As she put it back she said, "We were certain from the beginning that our subject was probably a white male between
twenty-five and thirty-five—"

An agent she didn't know raised his hand. "I can remember

only one time when the BAU presented a profile where they believed the UNSUB was over forty. Why is that?"

"I guess it's because almost all serial killers are white males between twenty-five and thirty-five. All we're really doing is following statistics. Of course, there have been some exceptions. Even female serial killers. Aileen Wuornos comes to mind. And Black serial killers—Wayne Williams, Samuel Little. Little claims to have killed ninety-three women."

Alex looked around the table. "I also want to point out that there's a big difference between our subject and the other serial killers I mentioned. Wuornos killed men she believed had raped her or were planning to rape her. Whether or not that was true, she had a particular target for her inner rage. Samuel Little killed only women, most of them marginalized, women addicted to drugs or involved in prostitution. When asked why, his answer was 'Well, God put me here to do this.' I believe his inner anger was directed toward his mother, who was a prostitute. In his mind, he was killing his mother.

"But our current subject is different from Wuornos and Little. His killings are based on the availability of his victims. He's not looking for a specific kind of person to murder. His victims have been two white males, a Black male, and a Hispanic woman. His signature is his complete commitment to The Book. One thing that does connect our subject to Little is that he also believes his actions are directed by some kind of divine being. Usually we would call a killer who chooses victims at random an unorganized killer, but this guy has a specific plan. The victims aren't important, but the MO is. He's presenting a sacrifice. And he always chooses trains to display his bodies. That's why I say he's an organized psychopath."

"He leaves the victims lying on their backs," Stephen said, "with their hands folded. Usually that's a sign of remorse, right?"

"In most cases that's true," Alex said. "But remember, he stabs his victims. It's personal. Usually that's a sign of anger. Most people who commit murder don't enjoy it. They have a goal. A reason they consider valid. They may be angry, but they don't want to get their hands dirty, so they either poison or shoot their victims from a distance. Much more tasteful."

A twitter of laughter erupted around the circle, but she ignored it and looked at Stephen. "You asked about the subject showing remorse. That's not what he's doing. He's showing respect toward the being he calls the Master. This is a divine sacrifice. In his mind, it should be treated as such."

"So we can't predict his next move," Karen said. "His victims are random. This makes it much harder."

"That would be true, except we do know what he plans to do next." Alex took a sheet of paper out of her notebook.

"'When the Virgin who shall be washed in blood, the final sacrifice, is offered to the Master, the demons will be unleashed, and the angels will make war with the evil ones. This sacrifice will be holy, and the one who offers it will be elevated in the Master's kingdom. He is the Destroyer. The one called to fulfill the will of the Master. Long live the Master!'"

"That's from The Book, isn't it?" Stephen asked.

"Yes. Walker believes he's called to be the Destroyer. He won't change his mind. Reasoning with him won't work. Nothing will stop him because he believes his orders are from above." Alex stopped and took another drink of water. When she put down her cup, her gaze traveled around the table again. "Every sacrifice we've found so far has been several days old. From his letter to the newspaper, I think the fifth sacrifice has already occurred, and we'll find it today."

"As you know," Harrison said, "detectives are on their way to Union Station. We have reason to believe that's where the fifth body will be discovered."

"We've notified the Kansas City Southern Railroad," Stephen said. "They've sent our message to all personnel, and they're keeping a strict watch on all their trains. But so far they haven't found anything."

"This sacrifice may be a little different, but it will be train related," Alex said. "Our subject has to stick to his MO."

"But the sixth sacrifice has to be a virgin?" Stephen asked. "What does that mean and why?"

One of the detectives made a joke about Stephen not knowing any virgins. Most of the men around the table laughed, but she noticed Logan didn't.

It was hard for her to get out the next words. "He will want to be certain the sacrifice is a virgin. Our worst fear is . . ."

"You're saying he might kill a child, aren't you?" Karen said.

Alex nodded. No laughter this time.

"A child?" Stephen said. "We can't let that happen. Tell us how to stop him."

"We'll get to that in a moment," Alex said. "Let me finish telling you more about our subject. He was brought up in unusual circumstances. It twisted him. He doesn't think like you or me. I'm convinced that his parents worshiped The

Book and read it to him. He was also acquainted with a very dark nursery rhyme." Alex read the Train Man poem.

"Yeah, we've seen that thing," one of the detectives said. "Who in their right mind would read it to a kid?"

"Exactly my point. Walker's upbringing was unusual, but he believes he's finally found his destiny. His purpose for living. He believes he's a demon, and the only thing in The Book for a demon to do is bring about this war. The Train Man is doling out judgment."

"Is he doing this at the bidding of the Circle?" Karen asked.

"We don't know. Maybe. Members are supposed to be angels, not demons, but it's possible someone wants the prophecy to come to pass sooner than later and is using Walker to do it. Meanwhile, we're trying to untwist the truth according to The Book from the opinions expressed by my aunt. For example, a lot of people think the quote "cleanliness is next to godliness" is in the Bible. It's not. It was first used in this context by Sir Francis Bacon. Some of what we think is truth expressed through The Book might only be Willow Le-Grand's personal beliefs. I know you're going through it carefully, but it's massive, and much of the language is archaic."

"Has this guy ever hurt children that we know of?" a detective asked.

"No. And this is where our normal profile goes against what we know about Adam Walker. We're certain he's obtained the virus. He's admitted he has it, and he's quoted The Book. I believe he's the person we're looking for, but I can't explain some things. For example, according to his coworkers, he's married and has two kids. Seems to adore his family. Left work early or begged off company parties more than once so he could be with them—or because a child was sick. He said his wife's name is Sally and his children are Gabby and Trey. But no one has been able to find a marriage license or locate the children in any school in the area around the killings. I doubt he's traveling far distances to make his sacrifices. Missouri is important to him. I believe he was raised in this part of the country."

"Is it impossible for him to be from someplace else?" Grace asked, looking at Alex but then glancing at Logan.

Logan answered. "No, not impossible, but unlikely. All we can do is draw conjecture based on this guy's actions and what we've learned from other serial killers. Hopefully, we're right, and it will help you narrow the search." He glanced up at Alex. "I agree completely with SSA Donovan. I must admit that the family thing is unusual and gives me pause, but everything else we know lines up."

"Are his parents living?" a detective asked.

"His father, Charles Walker, died quite a few years ago," Alex said. "We haven't been able to locate the mother. Is that information correct, Stephen?"

Stephen nodded. "We found both their birth certificates and their wedding license, Adam's birth certificate, and the father's death certificate, but no death certificate for the mother, Agnes. We talked to neighbors in Independence, where Adam spent his teen years, and they said he and his father lived alone. One of them said Charles told them his wife left when Adam was two, but we know that's not true. Adam was around seven when they moved away from their house in Kansas City, and the neighbors there said his mother was with them when they left."

He took a deep breath. "We don't know where the three moved to when they left Kansas City, but he was probably close to twelve when he and his father landed in Independence without the mother. That makes their whereabouts when he was between the ages of seven and twelve unknown. We're not sure where they were living those five years, and we have no information as to what happened to the mother during that time. We've searched for her but found nothing."

He went on. "The neighbors in Independence confirmed that Adam's upbringing was strange. The father wanted nothing to do with anyone else. Never accepted invitations from the neighbors, and Adam never spent time with the other teens in the neighborhood. Father and son spent all their time together. It seemed the father homeschooled Adam. We talked to the college Adam attended." Stephen sighed. "They had his records, but no one actually remembered him. Well, one professor recalled him, saying he was brilliant because of the work he did, but he couldn't describe Adam. It's like he was a ghost."

"No other relatives?" an agent asked.

"One cousin. Adam's family visited Agnes's sister only once, when the boys were both around eleven. That's another reason we know Charles was lying about Agnes leaving when Adam was two. We're not sure why. Maybe he just didn't want to deal with questions. The cousin, a Randall Burkhart who now lives in Michigan, remembers the visit. He said Adam was so odd it gave him the willies, so he was just as glad they never came back. Randall's mother passed away two years ago, but he says she had no idea where Adam is. They never heard from her sister or him again."

"So did the father stay in Independence after Adam went to college and got the lab job in Kansas City?" Harrison asked.

Stephen shrugged. "Maybe he would have, but he died.

Lung cancer. We're stuck when it comes to other relatives. Charles was an only child, and Agnes had just that one sister. The cousin is no help at all. All the grandparents are deceased."

"This doesn't make sense," a detective from Wichita interjected. "Didn't the father or mother work? Didn't they have jobs?"

"When he and Adam lived in Independence, the father had a job with a local trucking company. But before that we can't find any employment records for either parent. And they didn't seem to pay taxes. That might mean they worked for people who paid cash. No way to track that. There wasn't a checking account or a credit card. All the family's bills in Kansas City and Independence must have been paid with money orders. Same for wherever they were in between."

"How could Adam afford college?" Logan asked.

"He got a full ride. The guy is really smart. Aced all his classes. Went to work for the lab in Kansas City as soon as he graduated."

"What do you think happened to the mother?" Harrison asked.

Stephen shrugged again. "When we couldn't find a trace of her after they left Kansas City, we asked the Independence PD to check out any house where we know Adam and his father lived. They were searched from top to bottom, even checking the yards and pulling up the floors in the basements, just in case. Nothing. The people living there now weren't too happy about it, but we needed to know that they hadn't killed the mother and buried her somewhere on the property."

"Nice thought," Mike said.

"Well, she went somewhere. Frankly, I think maybe she

just got tired of living off the grid and wanted a new life. Changed her name and is living a life of ease somewhere. We just don't know."

Alex waited to be sure Stephen was finished before saying, "Thanks. I think you can see why we believe Adam Walker is our UNSUB. I believe his adolescence was abnormal, so he was looking for an identity. We know he was aware of the Train Man nursery rhyme, and we believe he has the virus. We're also certain that he planned this thing with Martin Kirabo."

"So how do we stop him?" Karen asked.

"By understanding him," Logan said. "Remember, he believes he's fulfilling a calling. He isn't doing this because he's angry or wants attention. He's committed to becoming this Destroyer that The Book talks about. Dump any investigative techniques you've used tracking other criminals. He's different. Try to understand him. Try to understand The Book. It's our best bet to get in front of him." Logan looked at Harrison. "And talk to Jimmy Gedrose. Besides The Book, he's the best tool you've got."

When Logan finished, Harrison stood and gazed around the table. "Okay, we have our suspect. I want you to go over every word of that book. We'll get Gedrose here as soon as possible." He stopped for a moment and looked down. When he raised his head he said, "Anyone else have ideas of how to stop Walker before he releases that virus?"

The silence from those looking back at him spoke volumes. Would they be able to find Walker in time? Alex wasn't so sure.

24

red Voorhees had been working at Union Station for forty years. He was in charge of maintenance and had a large crew to supervise. In all that time, he'd never been involved in anything as weird as what was happening now. The police had shut down the station. They were looking for a body, and they were convinced it was here somewhere. Fred had offered to help them look, but they'd turned him down. Yet so far they hadn't found anything. He doubted they would. If a dead body was anywhere in the station, he and his crew would have found it.

He was about to tell one of them they were wasting their time when he remembered something. He'd heard them say something about a bench, and a while back he'd put a broken bench in the storage room where they kept damaged equipment. He shuffled to the door that led to the room, but before he opened it, he stopped long enough to spit the tobacco he'd been chewing into a trash can and shove a fresh wad into his mouth. It was a bad habit, but his wife wasn't here to lecture him about mouth and throat cancer. He didn't chew around her. And when he retired, he'd stop. But for now, this was one pleasure he wasn't willing to give up.

As he rounded a corner in the storage room, he saw the bench. It had something on it. At first he wasn't sure what it was, but as he got closer, he picked up a strange odor. He'd fought in Vietnam. He knew that smell. He walked slowly toward the bench. As he pulled back the tarp that covered it, he already knew what he was going to find. When he saw it, he backed up, spit out his tobacco, and then threw up. When he was certain he was finished, he pulled out his phone.

As he punched in his boss's number, he wondered if waiting two years to retire was about two years too long.

Most of the team believed they knew the identity of their target and that the fifth victim would be found at Union Station, but they still had to find Walker. As they all returned to their stations, Harrison ordered Logan, Monty, and Alex to stay at the CP in case they could help the team further.

Monty had left the room, and Logan was frustrated with their lack of progress as he and Alex sat at the large table, going over their assessment. They'd been running behind on finding the bodies from the beginning. So many trains, so many cars, and so much time when no one was around to see what was happening to trains waiting for their next run. So far, the Train Man had had plenty of time to prepare his sacrifices without being interrupted.

They needed to concentrate on what he would do next. If there was any way to find him before he killed his sixth victim, their time in Kansas City would be well spent. But there just wasn't anything new as they pored over all the records dug up by the team. Mike had given them descriptions of people he remembered visiting Willow's house, especially those he thought could have been there for Circle meetings. But except for Jimmy Gedrose and Marcus Pannell, they hadn't been able to match his information to anyone specific.

Thankfully, authorities in Wichita had picked Jimmy up, and he would be here tomorrow. Logan was grateful he *was* safe, and that he would probably be put into WITSEC. If the Circle was as large as he'd intimated, that was the only way to keep him away from those who would see his cooperation with law enforcement as betrayal.

"Where was the family when Adam was between seven and twelve?" Alex asked suddenly. "I know we're concentrating more on who he is and where he is now, but this bothers me, Logan. I think it's important."

"Why? Because of the missing mother?"

"That's one reason. Where is she? Why can't anyone find her?"

"You think she's dead?"

Alex rubbed her forehead as if the action would release the answers they were looking for. "If she's dead, where's the death certificate?"

"If she was murdered . . ."

"It's possible. We don't know enough about the father to draw that conclusion. Of course, Adam's world was so small that if his father did kill his mother, think how horrifying that would have been to him."

"Maybe that's what made Adam so twisted."

"Maybe," Alex said slowly. "But I think reading that awful

nursery rhyme to him didn't help. And bringing him up on that warped book." She stopped and took a deep, quivering breath.

Logan was touched to realize she was feeling compassion for the boy Walker had been. He found it ironic that both Adam and Alex had been handed harsh circumstances as children. Alex had become an FBI agent, and Adam made plans to destroy. The angel and the destroyer.

"I don't know if we'll ever find answers to some of these questions," Logan said. He studied Alex for a moment. "Do you think we've described him correctly?"

She sighed. "Yeah, I do. But I keep getting the feeling that we're missing something."

"If he plans to unleash the virus here, don't you think he'll move his family out of the area first? Maybe figuring that out will help us find him."

"But we can't stop every vehicle with a family inside. I wish we had some kind of description for the wife and kids."

"I don't see how we'll get that if we can't find anyone who's met them."

Two of the analysts had left to pick up pizza. They came in the back door carrying several large boxes, which they brought to the table where he and Alex were working. When working at a CP, pizza was a staple. Good thing he liked it. They'd ordered several different kinds, including vegetarian for those who wanted it.

They grabbed some paper plates, utensils, and napkins from a small cart in the corner, and everyone began to form a queue. Small talk broke out, interspersed with laughter as weary workers took a much-needed break.

Logan got up, leaned over, and grabbed two plates. He

opened the boxes closest to him and found pepperoni pizza and supreme pizza. He slid one of each kind onto both plates, then sat back down and handed one plate to Alex. Although he had cut into the line, no one cared or got upset. They were a team, each one looking out for the others.

Logan prayed silently over his food and then lifted a piece of pepperoni pizza, guiding it to his mouth. He'd just taken a bite when Harrison walked up to the table.

"Eat quickly, everyone," he said, his face tight and solemn. "We just found number five."

25

After Harrison and Karen briefed the teams about the discovery of the fifth body, Logan and Alex headed to the hotel the FBI had booked for them. Monty had his own car rental and said he'd be returning to the hotel soon.

Alex was more concerned about the sixth sacrifice than the last one. It was important to Walker. He wouldn't risk choosing a woman he wasn't convinced was a virgin. Would he really kill a child, then? But how could he when he had two of his own? She started bouncing scenarios off Logan, trying to open up the possibilities.

"What about nuns?" she asked.

"Yeah, but some of them decide to be nuns after living rather promiscuous lives, right?"

Alex looked over at him. "How would I know? Are you asking me that because I'm a woman?" He'd looked at her with surprise, and she felt bad that her joke had upset him. "I'm not being serious," she said, "and I have no idea. It's certainly a possibility, though. Surely he'd have the same question."

"I'm still afraid he'll choose a child," Logan said. "Harrison asked the local police to issue a warning to local schools."

"If that gets out . . ."

"The press will cause a panic." He shrugged. "But if it saves a life, I can live with that."

"But it might also cause Walker to leave town and hunt somewhere else. And if that happens we could lose him."

Logan looked over at her. "We can't be absolutely sure he's near Kansas City, can we?"

"That's true, but most serial killers live near or in their comfort zones. You know that."

"Yeah." Logan stopped at a red light. "What about the new letter? Have you come up with anything else that will help us?"

"No, but Harrison has people looking through The Book, trying to find that passage. We should know more tomorrow."

"'The Master selects a young woman, a virgin washed in blood. . . .'" Logan shook his head. "You know, when a person becomes a Christian, we say they're 'washed in the blood.' Of course, we're talking about someone who receives the forgiveness of Christ and has become new inside."

"So if a prostitute became a Christian, she would be seen as a virgin?"

"Actually, yes. Once someone gives their life to Christ, they receive His righteousness and become a new creation." He cleared his throat. "But why would someone like Walker believe that?"

"Right. Based on what his coworker said, we know he hates Christians. In his mind, they're the enemy. They compete with his . . . religion." She gasped slightly. "That new creation thing would put someone like Jimmy right in Walker's cross hairs, wouldn't it?"

"As the virgin?" Logan asked dryly.

"Hardly. But if he finds out Jimmy lied about why he quit going to meetings . . ."

"I see your point," Logan said, any hint of humor gone from his voice. "I'm glad he's safe for now."

"I could be wrong about this, but the idea bothers me. What if he's looking for a single woman who's a Christian? Would that fulfill his desire to find a *virgin*?"

"Maybe, but how would he know someone like that? He doesn't have any friends. Never even connected to the people at work. So where does he find her?"

Alex could tell they got the same answer at the same time.

"At church!" Logan said, his voice strained. "And it's Wednesday night. Church night."

Alex pulled the phone out of her purse and called Harrison.

Adam could barely contain his disgust with these people who were worshiping a god that didn't exist. How could they believe this drivel? It was repulsive. At least he'd been taught the truth. He knew exactly who he was and what he was called to do.

He forced himself to sit through the music as the words to the songs were projected onto screens on the wall. Most of them stood while they sang, but he couldn't bring himself to do that. If he had to, he'd limp out when the service was over so they'd think he couldn't stand comfortably. Many of them also raised their hands while they sang. What did that mean? At first he was afraid he would be volunteering for something if he followed suit, but when no one came around to recruit them, he decided to raise his right hand several times just to fit in.

It felt as if the music would go on forever. Yet Adam had to admit that he might have been touched by some of the songs if he didn't know the Master. But he had truth on his side, so he could stay strong through the attempts to play with his emotions.

Finally, the music stopped, and a man stepped onto the platform. He asked for first-time visitors to raise their hands. Of course, Adam didn't. He wanted no record of his visit. As he looked around at the people, he almost wished he'd brought the virus with him. He would get great satisfaction from infecting these silly sheep. But they didn't fit into his plan. He wanted people who would leave the city and spread the virus before they even knew they were infected. People at hospitals too. He was confident he had time. The police were stupid. They'd never figure out his full plan fast enough. Yet he still felt an urgency inside. A feeling that he needed to move as quickly as possible.

After greeting the people, the man on the platform walked over to a lectern where he opened what Adam assumed was a Bible and began to read.

"'For God so loved the world that He gave His only begotten Son, that whoever believes in Him shall not perish but have everlasting life.'"

Adam wanted to laugh. Everyone knew that Bible verse. It was repeated constantly. It was even on billboards. But it meant nothing to Adam. It didn't make any sense.

"What does this really mean?" the man asked. "Do you realize this one Scripture sums up everything between the covers of this book?"

Adam tried to focus on something else as the man spoke. He assumed he was the church's pastor, but he didn't really care. Yet Adam found himself listening more and more. The man talked about what love was—and what it wasn't. Some of the things he said made Adam uncomfortable. Anger, hate, selfishness weren't love. Putting others before yourself and laying down your life for others was love. Supposedly, Jesus had done just that. It seemed Jesus didn't care how bad you'd been. He loved you anyway. His offer of eternal life applied to everyone. Not just the good people. The angels. It even applied to bad people, the people Adam had been taught were demons, like him. Some of what the pastor said was confusing, but one thing was clear. This pastor believed God loved everyone—all people. But Adam knew better. People were either angels or demons. There weren't just *people*.

With great effort, he tuned out the message and waited. Then about thirty minutes after the pastor had started speaking, the members of the band returned to the stage and began to play and sing softly. Something about surrendering to God.

This was the moment Adam had been waiting for. When his research about Christianity would pay off. He watched the crowd, waiting for those who would "answer the call of God," as the preacher called it. As he waited, something he couldn't identify began to fill the room, and he had a strange feeling. He looked around him. What was it? Then he felt something drop onto his shirt. He looked down and saw a wet spot. He put one hand up to his face and found his cheek wet.

Anger coursed through him. The man on the platform

must be an angel, trying to stop him from his mission. He wouldn't allow it. He hardened himself against what he was feeling. Something he'd never experienced before. Angels were tricky. You had to be careful around them. As he sat there, trying to watch who would respond to the call the pastor had given, a man with long brown hair walked up to him. He knelt down and said, "Adam, God loves you. There's nothing He won't forgive if you'll put yourself in His hands."

Then the man stood and walked away. Adam sat rooted to his seat. He found it hard to breathe. Who was that man, and how did he know Adam's name? It was impossible. Once again, he hardened himself against the thoughts that tried to take over his mind. It wouldn't do the angels any good. He'd never bend. He knew who he was and what he had to do.

As several people stood and walked toward the front of the room, he watched them carefully. A young blond woman slowly approached the pastor. Adam rejected her. She looked too much like Sally. But then a twentysomething woman with dark brown hair that hung to her shoulders made her way up front. She reached out for one of the people the pastor had called "prayer partners." An older man took her hands and leaned close to her, probably to be sure he could hear what she was saying above the music. Adam wished he could listen in on their conversation. For just a moment, he thought about standing next to them, but he didn't want to get too close to anyone.

Every minute or so he glanced around, trying to find the man who'd spoken to him, but he didn't see him anywhere. If his final sacrifice didn't have to be a virgin, he would have seriously considered following the man home and adding him to the Train Man's body count.

Now the young woman with the dark hair was weeping, and then she and her prayer partner prayed. Finally, she looked up. The man said something to her, and she smiled. In fact, she laughed, right along with him. What was so funny? Adam couldn't understand this. He wanted to run out. He felt odd in here. Ill at ease. But he needed his final sacrifice. He hoped the Master would accept her.

At first, Adam couldn't work out how to make certain a woman was really a virgin. He wouldn't choose a child. He was certain the sacred book was talking about an adult. That had to be right. Adam would do anything for the Master, but he wouldn't hurt a child. Every time he thought about it, all he could see in his mind was Gabby. Thankfully, he'd not only found another way, but he believed this was actually what the Master wanted. A virgin washed in blood. He smiled to himself. And here she was. Washed in the blood of "the Lamb." Perfect.

One by one, the new converts made their way back to their seats. People smiled at them. Patted them on the back as they walked by. The atmosphere was joyous, excited. Adam glanced at his watch. How much longer would he be forced to sit here?

Finally, the pastor released the crowd. Adam moved to a pew not far from the young woman he'd chosen, who was now talking with some older woman. He took a card from a pocket on the back of the pew in front of him, then lowered his head and pretended to fill out a questionnaire just so whoever might be encouraged to talk to him would decide to leave him alone. It offered free counseling and encouraged the reader to go through a special class before joining the church. It also asked for a name, address, and phone number, and Adam wrote in nonsensical words.

Finally, the young woman he'd chosen made her way to the doors at the back of the sanctuary. Adam stuck the questionnaire into the wooden pocket and stood. As he followed her, he spotted the man who'd spoken to him. He was standing next to one of the exit doors.

"This is your last chance, Adam," he said as Adam walked by.

Fury exploded inside him. Who was this guy? How did he know him? He didn't look familiar. How dare he try to stop the prophecy from happening?

He ignored the man and strode outside. The woman was walking toward the parking lot. If he were a praying man, he'd pray that she would leave alone. He smiled when she got into a compact car by herself, then he slid inside the car he'd been using since right after the last sacrifice.

Hanging back as far as he could, Adam followed her car until she turned into the driveway of a small house on a dark street. He made a note of the address and drove away still smiling. He hadn't been ready to take her tonight, but he'd come back.

He'd make his last sacrifice soon. As he drove home, he couldn't wait to tell Sally what he'd found.

A lex had told Harrison she and Logan would return to the CP if they were needed, but he'd said they should get a good night's sleep and come back in the morning. Meanwhile, he'd call the Kansas City chief of police and inform him that the Train Man may be targeting women attending Christian churches in the area. If their guess was right, Alex hoped an increased presence around those churches would cause Walker to wait for a more opportune moment. That would give them more time to find him.

The police had sent out a BOLO for Adam Walker. Alex wanted to believe they had a jump on him, but she was certain they didn't. Adam was probably aware that they knew who he was. That the missing Ebola sample had been reported. He hadn't tried to hide his identity. And even though they had no direct evidence tying him to the Train Man, he was smart enough to know it wasn't hard to connect the dots after he'd left a copy of the poem in his desk.

This hotel had indoor corridors. She and Logan stood outside her room still talking, but Alex was so tired she suggested they go inside. She was committed to helping investigators find the Train Man, but she was exhausted. She hoped Logan wouldn't stay long.

Their rooms in this extended stay hotel were smaller, but she still had a kitchenette along one wall, a desk in the small living area, and another fireplace. Overall, it was nicer than the hotel in Wichita. As she put her bag on the king-sized bed, she thought a fire sounded nice.

Before she had a chance to say so, Logan asked, "Do you mind if I start a fire?"

She smiled. "That would be great." Alex opened her bag and took out the can of disinfectant spray she always had with her. She kept a smaller can in her purse. "The room might smell for a few minutes."

Logan, who was tearing open a packaged log, turned and frowned at her. "You really do have a germ phobia, don't you? You know the hotels clean the rooms before their guests check in."

Alex shook her head. "You'd be shocked to learn how many germs are left behind by maintenance staff who rush through a cleaning." She quickly sprayed the room and the bathroom. By the time she was finished, Logan had the fire going.

"So now I sit down on a wet couch?" he asked. "I think I'm getting used to it, though."

"Very funny. It dries quickly."

"Actually, it smells pretty good."

Alex grinned at him. "Lilac Spring. I like it."

"When I smelled this scent at Quantico, I thought it was you."

Alex laughed. "I have cologne with the same scent. I like lilacs." She walked over to the kitchen. "Let me see what we've got to drink." She opened the fridge. Water. Then she checked a basket with lots of packets stuffed inside. The last thing she wanted was coffee. She hoped to get a good night's sleep. She needed it. She spotted something that seemed to fit the bill. "How about a cup of hot chocolate?" she asked.

"Perfect."

As the fire blazed and warmed the room, Alex took two cups from the shelf next to the sink. She examined them carefully. They looked clean, but you never knew. She rinsed them both with hot water. Then she took a bottle of water from the refrigerator and filled each cup before putting them in the microwave. As she waited for the water to heat, she glanced around. The counter looked clean, but when Logan left, she'd sanitize it. You couldn't be too careful.

When the microwave dinged, she took the cups out and stirred in the chocolate mix. When the little clumps of powder had finally dissolved, she carried the cups back to where Logan waited on the couch. He stood when she neared.

"I'm sorry. I should have offered to help," he said. "Must be the fumes."

"Ha-ha." As she handed him a cup, she could see the redness in his eyes. He was exhausted just like she was. They'd had no sleep the night before, and it showed.

Alex sat down in a chair across from him, next to the fireplace. It had a matching ottoman. She stretched her legs out and leaned back into the overstuffed cushion. It was still a little damp, but that didn't bother her. She was confident the germs were gone. The chair was so comfortable she was pretty sure she could spend the night there if she felt like it.

"I'm concerned that we're too late to save this last victim," Logan said.

"But the ME said victim number five had been dead for less than forty-eight hours. We're getting faster."

"But wasn't that because Walker sent us those clues for Union Station in his letter?"

She frowned. "Maybe."

"I think he's accelerating his plan, Alex. He was impatient for us to find his fifth victim so he gave us clues. And I think he's going to speed up this next one too. He's in a hurry to bring this judgment on the world."

"But Stephen said they couldn't find any message with the guy at Union Station."

"That's because he already gave it to us."

"He did?"

"Yeah, in his last letter. He capitalized all the letters when he said, 'LONG LIVE THE MASTER!' That was the message."

Alex sighed, trying to release all the tension from her body. "You're right. I should have seen it, and you could be right about his escalation. I don't know how many churches are in the Kansas City area, but the KCPD can't cover them all. Some of the victims were purposely chosen away from his base of operations. He didn't want investigators to know where he lived."

"That makes sense." Logan took a sip of his hot chocolate. "Hey, not bad," he said with a smile.

Alex nodded. "Could be worse." She set her cup on the lamp table next to her chair. "You know, I think we need to consider whether Adam has changed his appearance. He must know we've discovered his identity. The stakes are high. He can't take a chance that someone will pick him up and stop his destiny. I really don't think he looks like the photo we have from his employee file and driver's license."

Logan was quiet for a moment. "You're right," he said finally. "He has short, dark hair and is clean shaven in those photos. So his choices would be to dye his hair lighter, grow his hair longer, and grow a beard, which would also cover that scar on his chin. Maybe he hasn't made all those changes, but at least he's probably grown a beard."

"I think longer hair and a beard are a given. But he might also dye his hair. The police are looking for a dark-haired man. They might want to look for someone with blond hair. Or gray. Could he be trying to look older?"

"That would take a lot of effort," Logan said slowly. "Adding wrinkles, dying his hair gray . . . I'm gonna bet on blond hair. Not red, of course. Too easy to spot."

"So we're betting now?"

Logan chuckled. "No. I have a feeling I wouldn't win against you."

"Maybe we should call Harrison," Alex said. "I'm afraid the police might walk right past Walker because he doesn't fit the photo they have."

Logan shrugged. "I have to believe Harrison has thought of that, but if you feel it's important . . ."

Alex picked up her phone and called. As she waited for Harrison to pick up, she wondered if he was home in bed. It was almost eleven at night. However, he picked up on the second ring and sounded awake. Alex shared their concerns.

"Yeah, we thought of that," Harrison said. "The chief has

an artist working on possibilities. What's your opinion? How will he have changed his looks?"

"We think he'll have blond hair. Not sure if he's had time to grow it out much, though, so he could be wearing a wig. We also think he'll have a beard. Maybe a mustache too."

"Glasses?"

"A real possibility."

"This helps. Thanks, Alex. I'll contact the chief."

"Great. See you in the morning."

"Okay. And thank you for all the great work you've done. It's appreciated."

"Just doing my job, sir. Good night."

She clicked off and had barely opened her mouth to tell Logan what Harrison said when she realized her partner was asleep. She rose from her chair and went over to him.

"Hey, Logan. Better get up and go to your own room," she said. "I guarantee your bed will be more comfortable than this couch."

His eyes fluttered open, and he chuckled softly. "Wow. Sorry. Big, strong FBI agent brought down by a nice fire and a cup of hot chocolate. I suddenly feel a little vulnerable."

Alex laughed. "I won't tell anyone."

"Thanks." He got to his feet, then grabbed his bag and walked to the door. "Good night, Alex," he said. "I'm just down the hall if you need me."

"Thanks. Same here."

He grinned at her and opened the door. She stepped into the hall to watch him go, curious to know where his room was. He was just about to unlock one of the doors when Alex noticed someone walking toward him. It was Mike.

"Hey," Logan said. "Did you get sent to this hotel too?"

Mike smiled. "Yeah, but I'm surprised. I assumed all the nonessential personnel would end up at Cowboy Bob's Motel and Gift Shop a few miles from the CP. I was prepared to battle mice and other little varmints."

Logan laughed. Alex forced a smile, but Mike's words stirred the fear inside her. The thing she couldn't face.

"Are you going back to the CP in the morning?" Logan asked.

"That's the plan."

"Why don't we all go to breakfast first?"

"That would be great." Mike shrugged. "I have to admit I feel a little out of place among all these experts. In particular, you guys really make me feel dumb. I'd love to hear more about what you're thinking."

"You're not dumb," Alex said. "We're just strong in different areas." She pretended to stifle a yawn. "Sorry, boys. Hitting the sack. What time do we get together in the morning?"

"Six a.m. in the lobby?" Logan said. "Let's eat at the Waffle Palace across the street. I think we'll get better food than what they offer here. The idea of dry bagels and soured cream cheese doesn't thrill me." He looked at his watch. "Wow. It is late, but I'll call Monty on his cell and let him know." He looked down the hall. "I assume his room is somewhere on this floor."

Alex nodded. "Sounds great. Good night."

She closed the door, then locked it, turned around, and leaned against it. She put her hands up to the sides of her head and slowly slid down until she sat on the floor. She couldn't stop trembling, and she sat there until she brought the monster under control once again.

Why was it getting harder to fight it?

27

After saying good night to Mike, Logan just wanted to fall into bed. But he needed to shower first. After he grabbed sweats and a T-shirt from his bag, he gazed around his room. Alex's comments about germs made him a little uncomfortable. Should he buy some disinfectant spray too? Maybe she was right. Maybe the hotel provided some for guests to use.

He went into the bathroom and looked under the sink. Sure enough, he found a can of disinfectant spray. He took off the cap and sprayed the faucet and the doorknob. Then he went out to the main room and sprayed anything he thought he might touch. As he lightly sprayed the bedclothes, he suddenly asked himself what in the world he was doing. This stuff didn't smell like flowers. It smelled like . . . disinfectant. It reminded him of a hospital. He carried the can to the kitchen and opened one of the windows in the small living area. As the cold November air drifted in, the odor began to dissipate.

Logan sat down on the chair as the stink lessened. In all the traveling he'd done for the BAU, he'd never worried about germs. Most people who feared germs were actually afraid of something else entirely, like losing control. Was that the case with Alex? After thinking about it for a minute, he realized lots of people probably worried about germs in hotel rooms. That didn't mean anything was wrong with them.

He laughed to himself. "You're getting suspicious in your old age, Logan," he said quietly as he stood. Yet a small voice inside told him he was missing something.

He ignored the warning and got ready for his shower.

Alex knew Mike hadn't meant to upset her with his comment about rodents and bugs, but she wished he'd kept it to himself. And she should have waited for Logan to leave before spraying down everything that worried her. But she couldn't. Things were starting to spiral. She had to keep her PTSD under control. If she couldn't, she might lose everything she'd worked for.

"God, Logan thinks you're real," she whispered. "I don't. I prayed once when I was younger, but you didn't answer, so I don't think you're really up there. But . . . I don't know what to do. If you are real, I could use some help. If you're everything Logan says you are, I'd like to know you better."

She wiped her face with the back of her hand and sighed. What was she doing? Why in the world was she talking to some invisible being that didn't exist? If God was real, He would have helped her years ago when she prayed.

Suddenly she heard *You survived, Alex. And you're where you wanted to be. Are you certain I didn't answer you?*

NANCY MEHL   **211**

She looked around the room. Was someone in here? Was she hearing voices? She stared at the TV, but it was off. Was she in trouble? What should she do?

Then the words she thought she'd heard whispered in her mind. And as she thought about it, she realized she *had* made it through. She *had* survived. And she was living the dream she'd prayed for. She'd forgotten that part of her prayer.

She got to her feet and walked to the chair where she'd sat earlier. Was she hallucinating? God didn't really talk to people. That was nuts. She wasn't going to turn into Willow. The Master didn't exist, and neither did God. She was alone. She had to trust in herself. No one else would rescue her. She'd been on assignments where she'd spotted a bug or had to talk to someone who wore red lipstick or red fingernail polish. She'd managed to fight the panic that tried to push her back into her nightmares. She'd made herself strong—without any help from a therapist.

So why was she unraveling now? It had to be returning to Wichita and seeing Willow. And now that awful house was hers? She'd hire someone to clean it out and sell it. She had no intention of stepping back inside its walls.

And Mike was here. Even though she was glad to see him, he reminded her of things she didn't want to remember.

After a quick shower, she dressed in sweatpants and a sweatshirt before checking to make sure the door to her room was locked. Then, leaving on the kitchen and bathroom lights, she approached the bed. Although she fought the urge, she couldn't stop herself from pulling the sheets and bedspread down just to make sure bugs weren't hiding under them. She hadn't done that in years. She'd taught herself not to. But tonight she couldn't help it. How far would her fear push her? Could she keep her condition from Logan? From Jeff? If they realized the truth and revealed it, the FBI would probably force her into counseling . . . or even dismiss her. She couldn't let that happen.

Alex had talked to a therapist once when she worked in Kansas City. "Alex, PTSD isn't anything to be ashamed of," he'd said. "You went through an extremely traumatic experience."

"That's true," Alex had shot back. "But a law enforcement officer who goes bonkers if she sees a bug won't be looked upon as reliable."

"To be fair, it isn't just a bug," the doctor had said. "You have a problem with roaches, germs, the dark—red lipstick and nail polish. These are all triggers. They take you back to when your mother died as well as to the first few days you lived with your aunt. You were still reeling from finding your mother. You spent several nights in a dark bedroom with roaches crawling everywhere. And your germ phobia comes from trying to clean your aunt's filthy house. You became obsessed with cleaning."

He had paused before adding, "But it wasn't really about the germs. You were trying to control your environment. Your father's abandonment, your mother's suicide, and those first days at your aunt's are where your emotions are bunched up. Tightly woven into your psyche. Basically, your mind is at war with itself."

"So what am I supposed to do, Doc?" she'd asked. She was tired of hearing what was wrong with her. How about prescribing the pill that would fix it?

"It will take some time, Alex. But if you hang in there, we'll face your hidden pain together."

"How much time are we talking?"

"Don't think about the time it will take. Just accept that there's no other way."

"But could it take . . . years?"

"Yes. Some patients take that long to find coping mechanisms for their trauma."

"I don't have years," she'd said, rising to her feet. "Thanks for your time. I know you're trying to help, but I think I can handle this myself."

She'd walked out and never returned. And as the therapist had suggested it would, it did take years to control her fears, to teach herself to ignore the triggers that took her back to those days. It was harder than anything she'd ever done, but she'd done it. And now this case had caused her PTSD to roar back into her life.

She got into bed and stared up at the ceiling. *Did I look all the way down to the bottom of the bed?* The thought kept running through her mind. "Stop it!" she said out loud. "I will not look under the sheets again. I will not!" But as she lay there, she felt her body tense. Finally, she gave up and pulled the sheets back again. Nothing. She felt ashamed of herself.

As she got into bed again, she glanced at the window. The night, the darkness, always made everything worse. Evil things loved to hide in the dark. She turned on the lamp next to the bed.

Somewhere in the night, a train whistle blew, and Alex covered her ears.

Alex was silent while Logan, Mike, and Monty ate breakfast and discussed the case. She'd ordered a waffle and coffee, and she was trying to choke down the waffle. But she couldn't drink the coffee. The waitress had touched the side of her cup with the carafe's spout. Didn't she realize this was how germs were spread from one person to another? Alex had used hand sanitizer after handling the menu, but what if the silverware wasn't really clean? All she could do was wipe her fork with her napkin. She kept her hands under the table so no one would see her do it.

"Don't like the coffee?" Logan asked her.

She shook her head. "I'm sure it's fine, but I had coffee in the room. Too much caffeine makes me nervous. Decided I didn't need it after I ordered."

Logan nodded, but she caught the odd way he looked at her. Did he know? She took another bite of her waffle.

Thankfully, the syrup came in small plastic packets. She wiped them off with hand sanitizer, then tore them open. And she forced herself to stop wondering if the plate was clean or if the person who made the waffle touched it with unwashed hands.

She was aware that she was getting worse. She'd been able to control her germ phobia for years, although the COVID-19 pandemic had made her really paranoid. But she'd fought her way through that. At least she thought she had. She'd finally convinced herself her fears weren't real and ignored them . . . for the most part. She still sanitized hotel rooms and used hand sanitizer in restaurants. But that was it. Lots of people did that, right?

Last night the nightmare she'd had over and over since she was a kid had made a reappearance. It had been a while since she'd had it. In the dream, she walked up to her mother's open casket. Even though they'd applied a lot of makeup, it didn't completely hide the rope burn around her neck or the blueness of her skin. In contrast, her dark red lips and matching nails seemed to stand out as if a small spotlight were aimed on them. Her mother had never worn red lipstick or nail polish when she was alive. Why did they put it on her now? It looked like blood against her pale skin.

Suddenly, from beneath her mother's still body, roaches wrestled their way up from inside the casket. They poured out, running over the coffin's sides like water. They came for Alex, so she turned to run although her legs felt heavy, and she could barely move. As they got closer she screamed. And then she woke up gasping for breath. The nightmare terrified her every time. She'd spend the rest of the night sleeping fitfully, forcing herself awake. She'd never told anyone about it. It was disgusting. What kind of person has a dream like that?

Finally, the men finished their meals and left, driving to the CP in their separate cars. Styrofoam cups sat next to the coffee maker in the back room. She could take one from the middle of the stack and then pour her own coffee, never touching the spout to her cup. She used a napkin to pick up the handle of the pot. She'd lied when she said she'd had coffee in her room, and she really needed a shot of caffeine now. She was still tired. Before she met the men in the hotel lobby, she'd found the ice and vending machines and purchased an energy drink, which she guzzled down. That had given her what she needed to get going, but she was beginning to crash. Coffee would have to get her through the rest of the day.

Harrison waved them over, motioning to the table. But first Alex went over to the coffee table and filled a cup with fresh brew. Logan looked at her strangely when she sat down. She smiled and shrugged, hoping he wouldn't read too much into it.

"I want to bring you up to date," Harrison said. "We're still contacting churches in the area, giving them the photo of Walker as he was and several ideas of what he might look like now." He frowned. "I'm not sure about this idea that his next sacrifice might be a Christian. Seems a little far-fetched, but it's as good as anything else we've got."

He took a breath. "Got a call from the ME in Wichita. As you know, doctors there thought Nettie Travers would recover from the blunt force trauma inflicted during the attack, but she didn't, and the ME felt something was off. She did a toxicology screen, but it showed nothing. So she went back over the IV equipment Travers was hooked up to and found a small hole in the tubing. She looked closer at the body and now believes someone injected air into the IV and caused an embolism. That's what actually killed her."

"So she was murdered," Alex said. "I thought so."

Harrison nodded. "You were right. But by whom? You don't think it was Walker."

"No," Alex said. "For the reasons we already stated. The question is whether the person who killed both women was working with him."

"Like you said, not too many serial killers have partners."

"That's true," Alex said. "But we have to remember he's been part of the Circle, and they all believe there will be a Destroyer. That makes it more likely he might have help from someone who, like him, believes they're a demon, not an angel. The chemist in Ethiopia, who we think was part of the Circle, helped him. Why not someone here in the States too?"

"Everyone in the ICU that night was questioned. An orderly remembered a doctor he didn't recognize going into Nettie's room before you and Logan got there. Said the man was in there for only a short time. He didn't raise any alarms because . . . well, he was a doctor."

"I probably saw him," Mike said. "I was sitting outside the ICU much of the time." He shook his head. "Several doctors went in while I was there."

"Would you recognize him if you saw him again?" Harrison asked.

"Maybe." Mike sighed. "I'm sorry. I wasn't worried about Mrs. Travers because she was supposed to be safe in the ICU. It seems I messed up."

"I don't think that's true, Mike," Logan said. "You did every-thing you could. Our killer was really bold walking into Net-tie's room like that."

"And remember, we don't know everyone in the Circle," Alex said. "What if one of the nurses did this? It's possible."

"You said Nettie spoke to you," Harrison said to Alex. "What was it she said again?"

"She said, 'he's here.' I think she was telling us someone was in the ICU who shouldn't have been. Probably the person who attacked her."

"It's really hard to make that jump," Harrison said.

"Well, someone injected air into her IV. My guess is Nettie saw her killer."

"It still could be Jimmy Gedrose," Logan said, making Alex wonder if he'd had second thoughts about letting the man go when he showed up at their hotel. "After all, Nettie recognized Alex's sketch. That one young nurse said he was there, and then he admitted it to Alex and me when he came to our hotel in Wichita."

"He'll be here within the hour," Harrison said. "We'll question him then." He turned his attention to Mike. "We're sending you back to Wichita. As you've said, you didn't see Jimmy at the hospital, but you may have seen who killed her if it wasn't him. Being back there could trigger a memory. Maybe the killer interacted with one of the staff. Seeing them might spark something. I'm not ruling out that Walker did this, though, and you might be the only one who can tell us what he looks like now."

Mike frowned. "You know, I believe Nettie was collateral damage. Willow was the main target." He sighed deeply. "I'll never forgive myself for allowing her death to happen." He looked at Harrison. "Of course, I'm more than willing to go to the hospital if you think it might help."

"We never asked. Who sent you to the hospital that night?" Logan said.

"The WPD needed someone to interview any of Nettie's relatives or friends who showed up. See if they had any idea who the attacker might be. I volunteered to do it because I knew her. Since the department is so mired down in the drug case they're working, they accepted my assistance." He took a deep breath. "I talked to Nettie's sister-in-law when she arrived. Nice woman. She had no idea who might have done it. She did mention that Willow had some strange ideas, but she never mentioned anyone else Nettie knew."

"Well, I'm glad you were there," Harrison said. "Right now you're our best shot to find out who killed Nettie in that hospital. Wait until after Gedrose shows up before you leave, though. Seeing him in person might help you remember something. Special Agent Thompson will take you to the hotel so you can get your things and then he'll drive you to the airport."

"And, Mike, you're sure you can't recall anything else that might help?" Alex asked. "Something we missed?"

"No. Like I said, I saw a few doctors go into the ICU. That nurse in charge, Ruth, let me go back to Nettie's room a couple of times, but I saw only two doctors enter it. Both times I was on my way back to the front desk and just turned around when I heard footsteps. One was the doc who told us Nettie had died. I only saw the side of the other one's face. To be honest, I don't remember seeing him leave. I think I was getting coffee." He put his head down and was quiet for a moment. "He was tall. Maybe six feet? Dark hair. I . . . I think he wore glasses." He closed his eyes for several seconds. "I'm sorry," he said when he opened his eyes. "That's all I can remember."

"Thanks, Mike," Alex said. "Just do your best and don't blame yourself for anything."

"I just wish I could do more."

Harrison sighed. "We need a break. We've got to find Walker quick." He looked around the table. "Before a lot of people end up dead."

He knew her name now. He'd followed her to the restaurant where she worked. She'd taken his breakfast order, so he'd seen her up close. Her name tag read *Laura*. No tattoos that he could see. Very little jewelry. Light makeup. Hair fashioned into a bun. She was perfect.

Of course, he had no idea how she'd lived her life before she was "washed in the blood." He didn't care. He was convinced she fulfilled the Master's needs. Revulsion slithered through him anytime he thought about those self-righteous hypocrites who believed in some master other than *the* Master. What fools they all were.

He had to take a deep breath to push down the rage that almost choked him. He would have to wait on the last sacrifice. He couldn't take her during the day. He only worked in the dark. He'd have to wait for nightfall.

Alex, Logan, Monty, and Mike all stayed at the table after Harrison left. Logan looked through the open doorway to the large room where even more people were working than yesterday. Harrison had told them an assistant U.S. attorney stood by, waiting for updates. A ViCAP analyst had come in to oversee other analysts working hard to find something— anything—that would help them find Adam Walker. Personnel from the FBI's Crisis Management Unit and the Crisis Negotiations Unit also stood by to help.

Logan noticed several people around Dr. Greene. CDC staff, no doubt. They were still worried. No one could be sure how virulent the sample Adam Walker had was. If Martin Kirabo really had engineered this thing to be more deadly than Ebola, the consequences were unimaginable.

He was also more certain than ever that Walker hadn't taken any chances. He was determined to carry out his assignment. He was an organized killer. That meant he'd probably planned this down to the smallest variable.

"So can we update our assessment?" Alex asked. She had a notebook in front of her, a pen poised to write.

"I don't see that it changes much based on what's happened," Monty said.

"Maybe not," Alex said. "If Adam Walker is responsible for Willow's and Nettie's deaths, he must have had help. Could one person have attacked Willow and Nettie and yet another killed Nettie in the hospital? Let's work on that and see what we can come up with."

"You're talking about more than one person helping him?" Mike asked.

"We've seen that before," Monty said. "Although not very often."

"I think there's at least one. I still don't think Walker committed either murder in Wichita himself," Alex said. "For one thing, he would have to have changed his MO, which rarely happens. Remember, these deaths are holy sacrifices to his god. They were carefully orchestrated even though his victims were random. He waited for the right opportunity. Knew exactly how he was going to kill them."

She frowned. "It still bothers me that Willow's killer used a weapon at hand rather than bringing one with him. *That* doesn't sound planned. Wouldn't someone from the Circle prepare better? I guess they could kill with the kind of anger we saw in Willow's house. It's possible they're angry with me for taking her copy of The Book and bringing law enforcement down on their heads. Yet helping Walker would only bring more attention to them. They're a very secretive society. It just doesn't make sense."

"So you're both still convinced Walker didn't kill Willow and Nettie," Monty said.

"Yes. We also have to remember that Walker is driven by a book he believes mentions him," Alex said. "It's his identity. He is the Destroyer. Therefore, it makes sense to him that he has minions. People who will do his bidding. They might not know everything he's planned. He may not have told them about the virus."

"I wouldn't give you a plug nickel for anyone who helps him once he's completed his mission," Logan said.

"What do you mean?" Mike asked.

"I believe Adam is incredibly narcissistic. The world is being shaped by him. He won't hesitate to get rid of anyone he thinks is a threat to him." Logan shrugged. "If he does have helpers, maybe he's convinced them to take their own lives after they carry out the assignment he's given them."

Mike frowned. "Why would they do that?"

"If they believe their involvement might put the Destroyer at risk, they could kill themselves to protect him. He probably promised them some kind of wonderful afterlife. It's been done before. Remember the Peoples Temple and Heaven's Gate?"

"Christians believe in heaven and hell," Alex said, "but The Book doesn't teach that. Like with Heaven's Gate, everyone goes to a planet where they spend eternity. Angels go to one planet, and the demons go to another one. I can't remember the names of those planets, but at some point, the Master will end their war and bring them all together to rule the earth."

Mike grunted. "That's nuts."

"No more nuts than what Christians believe. Look how many of them are out there." Her gaze moved to Logan. "You believe this, right?"

"I believe in heaven and hell, but not that we will all end up on another planet or that demons and angels will rule the earth together. If you think I'm crazy, then so be it." Logan felt a flash of irritation, but as soon as the feeling came, he pushed it back, remembering a Scripture that said the message of the cross is foolishness to people who don't know God. It wasn't their fault. Without God in their lives—changing them, teaching them truth—he realized he really did sound foolish to them.

"I'm sorry, Logan," Alex said. "I didn't mean it to come out quite like that."

He smiled at her. "It's okay. I've been challenged before. That's where the nickname Preacher came from."

"It's said with respect . . . and a little fear," Monty said. "Logan's pretty good with his gun. He got top scores in firearms training at the FBI Academy."

Logan laughed. "Yeah, but I've heard not as high as Alex. I wouldn't make her angry."

"Think I'll be extra nice to both of you," Mike said with a grin.

"Let's get back to Walker," Alex said. "With what we know, where is he?"

"I don't think he'd be too far from his family," Logan said. "According to the people he worked with, they were important to him." Logan was a little confused by this guy. It was like they were dealing with two different people. The psychopath intent on destroying millions of human beings. Men, women, and children. And a loving husband and father with a wife and two kids.

"I still don't get the family component," Alex said as if reading his mind. "Doesn't fit his profile. I know we've already mentioned this, but I can't shake it."

"Dennis Rader was married, right?" Mike asked.

"Yes," Monty said. "But that was unusual. He was adept at hiding his life from his family. They had no idea what he was doing. For the most part, serial killers are loners. That makes it easier to act out their proclivities."

"By all accounts, Rader had some kind of feeling for his family," Logan said, "although it wouldn't be the kind of love we understand since psychopaths are incapable of real love. His differences are what made him so interesting. He was able to live a divided life. Not easy. But it seems Walker is able to do that too."

"I think his helper—assuming he has one and only one— also believes in The Book," Alex said. "He's probably a member of the Circle."

"You said *he*. How do you know it's not a woman?" Mike's

cheeks reddened after his question. "I'm sorry. I need to shut up. You guys are the experts on human behavior. I don't know anything. I should stop interrupting."

Alex laughed lightly. "Don't stop. It actually helps us see Walker more clearly. We need to be able to defend our ideas. If we can't, it may be a sign we're on the wrong track."

"Are you sure?"

Alex nodded. "Let me try to answer your question. Could it be a woman? Sure. Profiling is often based on statistics. Not very exciting but true. Most killers are men, especially the perpetrators of the kind of attack Willow and Nettie endured. It was violent. The crime scene made it clear that the women fought for their lives but were overpowered. Their attacker was physically powerful. Even though the women were older, adrenaline would have made them stronger. Even so, they were both subdued."

"So it was probably a man," Mike said. "I get it."

Alex nodded. "Back to Walker, he probably intends to get his family to safety, out of the area where the virus is originally released." Alex took a quick sip of coffee before continuing. "He has a family because *he* wants them. In other words, God help them if they become an inconvenience or stop fulfilling his vision of what a family should be." She paused for a moment. "Like Logan said, a psychopath doesn't know what *real* love is. His family may be there only to feed his ego and give him what he believes he deserves."

"That's . . . chilling," Mike said.

"Yes, it really is," Logan agreed. "But psychopaths are a special breed. Everything and everyone around them is there for their pleasure. They kill because it brings them satisfaction."

"This guy is like Rader," Alex said. "But still different. Rader wasn't killing because of some great destiny."

Monty nodded. "In fact, he was a deacon in his church. Sitting in services week after week, listening to what's right, what's wrong . . . It still didn't stop him."

"He believed he killed because of something called Factor X," Alex said, "an evil force that unleashed a character inside of him he called the Minotaur."

"Like the Train Man?" Mike asked.

Logan pointed at him. "Yes. A character controlled by something else . . . whether it's Factor X or instructions in a book. The Minotaur carries out the desires of Factor X, and the Train Man obeys what he reads in The Book."

"One last question," Mike said. "It still seems like you guys are working a profile, even though you say a profile is used only when you don't know who your subject is. Why is that again?"

Alex smiled at him. "That's true, but if using profiling techniques helps us understand more about Walker, we might be able to figure out his next move. For example, we think he's looking for a Christian woman to be his final victim. That fits the description of the virgin to be sacrificed in The Book. It's not impossible that he's had someone picked out all along, but it's improbable. For one thing, he doesn't have close relationships. Second, how would he know for certain that a woman is a virgin? The final reason we're leaning toward that scenario is because he hates other religions. He believes his god is the only true god, so he wouldn't hesitate to kill a woman who believes otherwise."

She shrugged. "It's an educated guess, but it makes sense."

Logan had another explanation, but it wasn't one he'd

share with this group. The voice in Walker's head was the same as the Minotaur's—Satan's. That's why Walker hated Christians so much, and that's why Logan was almost sure they were right about the next victim being a Christian.

"KCPD is contacting churches in the Kansas City area," Alex continued. "Warning them. But just like all the trains that travel through Missouri can't be watched constantly, the PD can't protect everyone who attends church."

"Let's pray this doesn't go public," Monty said with a sigh.

Mike stared at him. "Because it would cause a panic and impede the investigation. I get it. I've seen this before. Right now finding that virus is the most important thing."

Harrison walked up to the table, a woman with him. "This is Special Agent Alvarez," he said. "She thinks she's found the origins of The Book."

Alex smiled at her. "You mean it wasn't brought to earth by divine aliens?"

Alvarez returned her smile. "Unfortunately, no. That would have made for a much more interesting story." She placed some papers on the table in front of them. "I made you copies of everything I found. I searched for some of the phrases from The Book and found every single one was ascribed to a Horace Austin Jennings."

"Does he admit to writing The Book?" Alex asked.

"Not to my knowledge, but according to people who knew him, he talked a lot about a divine calling. A man named Arthur Adair wrote about him in 1890. Adair was an evangelist, and he was rebuking Jennings. It seems Jennings believed that angels and demons had been sent to earth by beings in the skies. According to him, one day the demons and angels will be at war, and one third of the earth will be annihilated."

She took a breath. "Then I found records of a woman who claimed to be Jennings's niece. She said when he died he left behind a book she planned to copy so others could share in his divine vision. I believe someone got hold of this book and printed several copies. My guess is they were passed down in families. I couldn't find any newer information." She turned to look at Alex. "I understand your aunt said it was forbidden to talk about The Book to anyone outside of the Circle?"

"Yes, that's what she said."

Alvarez shrugged. "That might explain why I couldn't find any newer references." She placed her hands on the table and leaned in. "I wish I could have found more information. I know we're doing all we can, but it still feels like we're walking on eggshells, just waiting for the sixth victim to be killed. She might be alive right now, enjoying her life, unaware she's the target of a monster."

Alvarez turned and walked away, but her words echoed through Logan's mind. They needed a breakthrough soon. The woman Alvarez mentioned was living on borrowed time.

30

With Mike helping, Logan, Monty, and Alex worked all morning, going over and over all the information they had and trying to determine if they'd missed anything. It was close to eleven when the back door opened and Jimmy Gedrose walked in, flanked by two police officers.

When Jimmy saw them, he halted, then spoke to the officers as he pointed toward their group. The older man nodded, and Jimmy joined them at their table.

"Nice to see you again," he said, smiling at Alex and Logan. "Nice to see anyone." He cocked his head toward the men who had protected him. "Great guys. Made sure I kept breathing."

"Good to see you too," Alex said. She gestured toward Mike. "This is Agent Monroe." She watched as they shook hands. No flicker of recognition from Jimmy, so maybe he was at the hospital before Mike got there.

Jimmy turned his attention to Monty, who stuck out his hand. "Monty Wong," he said. "I work with these two."

"Nice to meet you," Jimmy said. "Any progress? Have you found this guy?"

"Jimmy, do you know a man named Adam Walker?" Alex asked.

"Not by name. And if you mean someone from the Circle, remember, we didn't use real names. Just pseudonyms."

Alex pulled a file closer to her, then opened it and took out a photo. "How about now?" she asked.

Jimmy's eyes widened. "Yes, I met him. He came to a couple of Circle meetings."

"In Wichita?" Alex could hardly believe they might be able to place Walker there. Maybe that's where his family was. But she still didn't think he attacked Willow and Nettie.

"Yes, in Wichita. But the last time he was there, he told us we weren't true believers. Frankly, he was rather strange, which I guess is why I remember him. He called himself . . . what was it? Oh. TM." He laughed. "At first I thought he said his name was Tim. He got so angry that I kept getting it wrong. He'd say, 'My name is TM,' and I'd say, 'Tim?' Boy, I thought he was going to hit me there for a while."

"You said he left the group after coming only a couple of times? When was that?" Monty asked.

"Oh, not long before I left, about ten years ago. We weren't sorry to see him go. He talked about this war that was supposed to break out between the angels and the demons. It was *all* he talked about. The Book mentions it, but there's a lot more to it. About self-worth. Walking in peace. Ignoring those who don't agree with you without losing your cool. That was a big one. Circle members are taught to hide their true selves from others unless they become convinced they've found an angel. Then you're allowed to tell them something about the group. However, if they don't seem interested or they think you need counseling"—he grinned when he said this—"then you have to back off. Make them think you're kidding or something. No matter what, you never reveal who you are to others who won't believe. It's expressly forbidden."

"Jimmy, do have any idea where this guy might be? Maybe somewhere in or near Wichita?" Alex asked.

Jimmy frowned. "Not right off the top of my head. It's possible he said something, but I'd have to think about it. For the most part, we just discussed The Book. Kind of like Christians do with the Bible."

"I thought people in the Circle hated the Bible," Monty said.

Jimmy nodded. "They do. But like I told Alex and Logan back in Wichita, after my wife died, I read the Bible and realized it made sense. The Book never did." He smiled widely. "I found God, and I finally felt some peace."

What is all this stuff about God? Alex wondered. Every time she turned around someone was talking about Him.

"He wants me to tell you that He saw your tears, and He's been watching over you all this time."

She suddenly remembered her prayer.

If you are real, I could use some help. If you're everything Logan says you are, I'd like to know you better.

Was God answering her? She shook that thought away. She needed to concentrate on the case, not God. But this time when she tried to clear her mind, it wasn't as easy as before.

Harrison joined them. "We need to ask Mr. Gedrose some

questions," he said. "I can send him back to you when we're done. Has he helped you any?"

"He recognizes Adam Walker," Logan said. "Walker was definitely part of the Circle, but not necessarily only in Kansas City or even Independence when he and his father lived there. He attended Jimmy and Willow's group in Wichita a couple of times."

"That's new," Harrison said. "Maybe he was traveling around looking for minions. Or maybe that's where Walker and his father lived in those missing years between Kansas City and Independence. Follow up on that, Alex."

"Yes, sir. We will."

Jimmy leaned forward. "It turns out some members of the Circle are anything but angels. If any of them were in this room, you would have just signed my death certificate. Like I said, no one is allowed to reveal the real name of any member. But if they do, the *demons* will make sure their ticket gets punched."

"I think you're safe," Mike said, smiling. "No Circle members here. Just law enforcement personnel who will do everything in their power to protect you."

Alex was trying to get the timeline straight in her head. "When did you say you quit going to Circle meetings?"

Jimmy scrunched up his face, making it clear he was thinking. "Let's see, I want to be sure I'm telling you right. Yeah, it was ten years ago. After my wife died."

So about the time Walker had probably finished college and his father died.

"When did you start going?" Alex asked.

"Twenty-five years ago."

Just before I arrived at Willow's, twenty-four years ago.

"So you went to meetings for at least fifteen years," Logan said, a look of surprise on his face. "That's a long time."

"It sounds like it, but we didn't have meetings very often." His forehead wrinkled. "I just remembered something else about this guy." He stabbed a finger at the photo of Walker. "He told us Circle meetings were every week when he was a kid. He couldn't understand why we met only once a month. I don't think we were committed enough for TM."

"I need you to come with me now," Harrison told Jimmy. "Hopefully, it won't take too long."

"He didn't seem to recognize me from the hospital," Mike said in a low voice as Harrison led Jimmy away.

Alex turned to stare at Logan. "Did you catch it?" she asked.

"Yeah."

"We all did," Monty said. "TM. Train Man."

31

I t had taken him several days to decide exactly when he was going to take her, but he was ready to move. Laura had gone to church this morning, and they had a Sunday evening service too. He would wait to see if she attended that one this evening and if she went alone. If so, he would grab her after the service. He couldn't take her at the church. He would wait outside her apartment, which he'd learned was over the garage at the house where he'd followed her before. It would be dark, and the treelined street would provide the perfect covering.

Excitement bubbled up inside him. It was almost time. He'd created the perfect way to disperse the virus. No one would suspect a man carrying a package. He planned to bump up against passengers waiting for planes and trains. They probably wouldn't feel the tip of the needle pierce their skin. If they did, he doubted they would pay attention to it. But they would carry the virus to other states, other countries. It was so virulent it wouldn't take long for many people to be infected.

Planes were hothouses for germs. His victims would be touching the overhead compartment, their seats, the armrests, everything in the bathrooms. So many others on the plane would touch the same surfaces. Then they would change planes and carry the virus onto the next flight.

Then back to Union Station. A few pricks here and there. His last visit would be to area hospitals. When patients began to pour in, they'd discover that nurses and doctors had already infected hundreds of people. It would be a pandemic beyond anything ever experienced.

He smiled to himself. But first the last sacrifice.

Tonight the world would change forever.

Alex spent Friday and Saturday working at the command post. She, Logan, and Monty continued assessing what Walker's next move might be, even though she felt they'd done just about everything they could with the information they had. Jimmy was still being questioned. Alex could tell he was tired, but everyone was doing all they could to find Walker's sixth target before it was too late.

They'd also come up short exploring Walker's connection to Wichita. Other than Jimmy's news that Walker had attended a couple of Circle meetings with his and Willow's group, they had nothing. Jimmy didn't even know how Walker knew about their group, let alone why he chose to check it out. Maybe Harrison had been right. Maybe Walker was looking for minions to help him fulfill the prophecy even then. Just like he'd somehow managed to connect with the chemist in Ethiopia.

Walker's fifth victim, the one found at Union Station, had been identified—Gerald Gregg. He was a maintenance worker at the station. The police and railroads had clamped down so tightly that Walker had clearly been forced out of his comfort zone.

The maintenance supervisor hadn't tried to contact Gregg when he didn't show up for work. He was a single man that no one might miss for days. That was sad.

Alex realized she had a lot in common with him. She had no family. Well, a father somewhere who wanted nothing to do with her. And no real friends. She didn't really care. She had her work, and she had Krypto. She missed him so much. She wondered if he was missing her too. He loved the Stewarts, the neighbors who cared for him when she had to leave town. The FBI would let her take him on assignment when possible, but this time she knew she would have to be in both Wichita and Kansas City. Bringing him along would have been too difficult. She'd been certain he would be much happier staying with the Stewarts.

It was important to her that Krypto felt safe. He'd been badly abused by his previous owner, and when he was dumped at the animal shelter, his chances of being adopted were small. He was timid and afraid, and he sat in the back of his pen, refusing to look at anyone. Being a pit bull made finding a home for him even less likely. But when Alex went to the pound to find a dog, she was drawn to him. She returned several days in a row, sitting in his pen with him, talking to him. Eventually, he moved out of the corner and put his head in her lap. The first time she looked into his sad eyes, that was it. He was hers. She took him home the next day and named him Krypto, determined to ensure he'd never be hurt again.

After some time of healing and learning to trust, he'd turned into one of the sweetest dogs Alex had ever known. He won over the Stewarts when one of their house cats got out. When they realized Maizie was gone, they looked all over the neighborhood. They finally found her in Alex's backyard, curled up with Krypto, both of them sound asleep. Maizie and Krypto were now great friends, and the Stewarts treated Krypto like their own.

Mike had answered every question he could before heading back to Wichita. He wasn't scheduled to come back to Kansas City unless he remembered something important and they needed him there. Frankly, she felt useless. Harrison had told her, Logan, and Monty to stay at the hotel Sunday and rest. They were all exhausted, so they were relieved to have some time to recharge. But they were also frustrated. They'd pulled the information they had apart and put it back together so many times it didn't make sense anymore.

They'd read through most of The Book too. That had been disappointing. Most of it was nonsense about how the world was formed by the Master, who planned to reign after the angels and demons fought in that final war. They found several mentions of the God worshiped on the earth that was considered false. The writer of The Book clearly hated other religions. They also scanned the pages Walker had referred to in his letters. Nothing new there either.

Alex recognized several sections Willow had quoted to her. Frankly, it bothered her to read them. It was as if she could hear Willow's voice speaking the words.

She woke up around ten Sunday morning. The nightmare had tried to come back again. She'd fought it, waking up several times with tears streaming down her face. Finally, about four in the morning, she'd fallen asleep, passing out from sheer exhaustion. She swung her legs over the side of the bed and sat there a moment, getting her bearings. Then she got up and went into the bathroom to shower.

She'd picked up some milk and cereal on the way back to the hotel last night. The three of them weren't meeting until lunch because they all wanted to sleep late. She'd stuck all the dishes on the kitchen shelves in the dishwasher and washed them as soon as she had a chance. They might have been clean, but who could tell? She dumped some cereal into one of the bowls, then grabbed the milk out of the fridge.

A few minutes later she was sitting on the couch in the living area, watching TV. She'd also made coffee, but she wouldn't drink much because she hoped to catch another nap. She'd put a note on the door asking the maid service to come by after eleven to change the sheets and towels. She wanted to be there when they did it. She suspected they sometimes just left the dirty sheets on the bed. Clean sheets made her feel safer.

She was flipping channels when she stumbled across a service from a large, nationally known church. She wasn't going to watch, but the minister started talking about how much God loves people. How they're the apple of His eye. Alex chuckled. She'd met some people she doubted God would love.

As if he'd read her thoughts, the minister said, "That means everyone. Even hardened criminals. Serial killers. Everyone. Every single person on the earth was born to be a child of God. For many reasons, you may find yourself far away from Him. Maybe you had an awful childhood. Maybe someone

you loved walked out. Maybe your friends have rejected you.
But if you give God a chance to be involved in your life, I
promise you, He'll never leave you. Never forsake you. You
will be loved completely. He will give you beauty for your
ashes. He will heal your broken life."

He looked into the camera, and Alex felt distinctly uncomfortable. It was as if he were talking right to her. "Will
you give yourself to Him today? Let Him change your life?
He's created a wonderful plan just for you. He wants to give
you hope and a future that's beyond anything you've ever
imagined." He pointed toward the floor in front of the stage.
"If that's you, come down front and let us pray for you."

A woman behind him began to sing a song about being
washed in the blood of the Lamb. Alex was riveted to the
screen. As if her eyes were opened and she could see into
the thoughts of the Train Man. What if Walker wasn't just
looking for a Christian but for a *brand-new convert*? A woman
who hadn't had time to lose her newfound virginity. It made
sense. Walker hated the Christian God, but he seemed to
have learned something about Christianity. He wanted to kill
one of God's virgins, and he had to be sure he'd found one.

She took a deep, quick breath and conjured up the memory of her one time in a church. The only way he'd find this
woman was to watch her make that commitment, standing in
front of the church and praying with someone for salvation.

She jumped up and grabbed her phone. Seconds later she
had Harrison on the line. "Look, I know this is a long shot,
but it might make our search a little easier." She quickly
told him what she was thinking. "What if the police contact churches in the area we believe Walker is working and
ask for the names of women who came forward for salva-

tion Wednesday night . . . or this morning. I think Walker watched for them at a church, and he's probably already targeted one."

"It's not such a long shot," Harrison said slowly. "Like you said, it makes some sense. Walker hates Christians, and the description of the virgin being 'washed in blood . . .'" He sighed. "We need to check it out. We don't have anything else. Thanks, Alex." He paused for a moment. "You stay there. Get some rest. If I need you, I'll call and let you know."

"I'd rather come in if it's all right with you," she said. "I want to be there to help in any way I can. I'm meeting Monty and Logan for lunch, and I'll head your way after that."

"All right. But tell Monty and Logan they don't need to come back today."

"Sure. Thanks."

Alex disconnected the call, then sat down on the couch again and turned up the TV's volume. The camera showed people gathered in front of the stage. All kinds of people. Young, old, different ethnic groups. All of them appeared to be truly touched. Tears streamed down the faces of most of them. How was this any different from what people in the Circle believed? Her own words came back to her. *From what I've heard about Christians, they believe people can change.* The Book said nothing about that. People's lives had been decided for them. They had no choice. Adam Walker believed he was fulfilling some destiny already designed for him.

Christianity gave you a choice, though. It was probably one of the reasons he hated it. But what about this "plan" the preacher talked about? Was it the same thing? Did God have your life all planned out? Alex had felt such a tug at her heart when the minister spoke, but she knew what she wanted out of life. What if God called her to . . . be a missionary in some other country? She shivered at the thought. Might be nice for some people, but not for her. She doubted she could ever be a Christian if she had to surrender her future to God. She didn't know Him. Didn't trust Him. Didn't trust anyone.

She'd just downed the last of her coffee when her phone rang. Logan. She didn't really want to go to lunch with him and Monty. She was still fighting her fear of germs, and it continued to be a struggle.

"Stop it, Alex," she said out loud. "You don't have to do this. You can stop. You've done it before." But when she answered her phone, her hand shook.

"Good morning," Logan said. He sounded sleepy.

"Good morning," she answered back, trying to sound chipper.

"Hey, I just got up. It will take me a while to get ready. Where do you want to have lunch?"

"Why don't you and Monty go without me? I'm going back to the CP." She shared her thoughts about Walker and new converts to Christianity. "I called Harrison and suggested that Walker might be trolling churches, looking for a woman who . . . who . . ."

"Accepts Christ?" Logan said.

"Uh, yeah. I guess so." It sounded odd to hear him say it like that. She'd never felt Logan was pushy about his religion. Still, something about the vernacular embarrassed her. It sounded so . . . hokey.

"What did he say?"

"He thought they should follow up on it. Once again, he's

having the police contact churches in the area where we think Walker is hunting, this time for information about recent converts. It seems like a stretch, I know, but we've run out of ideas. The strange thing is it matches Walker's psychology. He wants a woman he's certain is a virgin—who knows about a woman who converted years ago?—and it helps him to strike back at the God he hates and thinks is false."

"So he hates Christians, but he's willing to accept the belief that someone who converts to Christianity is cleansed? Wow. That really doesn't make sense."

"I think it might to him. Gives him a perfect way to offer a sacrifice to his god. In his delusion, Walker sees this as a truly divine sacrifice."

Logan was quiet for a moment. "Well, it's worth looking into, I guess. Hey, if you'll wait a bit, I'll go in with you."

"What about lunch?"

"We can pick up something on the way. I want to see if we can help identify Walker's sixth target before it's too late. I'd like to look more closely at your new-convert idea."

"Okay. How fast are you?"

"Faster than you think. I'll come over when I'm ready."

"You'll call Monty?"

"Sure. My guess is he'll want to come."

"Yeah, probably." Monty had worked tirelessly since he'd arrived in Kansas City. She was certain he'd want to be with them.

"You okay?" Logan asked.

Fear slithered up her spine. "I'm fine. Why are you asking?"

"Because of the other night. If you need to talk, I'm always here."

"I appreciate that, but I'm fine. Let's just concentrate on finding Walker, okay?"

"Okay. I'll be by in a bit."

When he hung up, Alex stared at the phone. She should have kept her life private. Why had she shared any of it with Logan? Had she made a terrible mistake? The answer to that question terrified her.

32

S ure enough, Monty wanted to come with them. They decided to go in one car so they could talk over how they'd approach the rest of the day. As the sixth sacrifice grew closer, all three of them had become more and more concerned. Behavioral analysis could only help to narrow a search so the actual investigators would have a better chance of finding their target. All they could do was try to give law enforcement clues to find the victim Logan was certain had already been selected.

They swung by a fast-food taco restaurant on the way to the CP. Logan watched as Alex ordered and then paid for her food. She seemed fine today. Maybe she'd just had a problem with the Waffle Palace. It really wasn't the cleanest place he'd ever seen, and he understood the side effects of the COVID-19 outbreak too. It took time to adjust to normal again.

He wished Alex would talk to him. He was fascinated by

her. She was smart, insightful . . . and injured. He really wanted to get to know her better. Be a sounding board for her. She didn't seem to have anyone in her life to really talk to. He'd like to be that person if she'd let him.

When Logan pulled into the CP, he was struck by how few cars were there. Had everyone left for lunch? They'd just stepped through the back door when Harrison waved them over.

"Did the team go out to eat?" Logan asked as they approached the ASAC.

"Hardly. The police needed help covering churches, trying to stop Walker from taking his next victim. They pulled in their own detectives, and some of our agents went with them." He grunted. "The mayor wants to warn the public about Walker—and the virus."

"This thing will go south if he does that," Logan said.

"Our only hope lies with the governor," Harrison replied. "He seems to be listening, but he hasn't made a final decision."

"But if just one person from the mayor's office decides to leak this, we'll lose control," Alex said. "Everyone and their neighbor will think they're living down the street from Walker. People will panic. We'll have a mass exit from the area. The highways will be blocked with all the traffic."

"And the Train Man will be able to do whatever he wants because he'll know the police are forced to deal with the fallout. They won't have time to look for him."

"So what can we do?" Logan asked.

Harrison sighed. "I honestly don't know. All the files, all our notes, are back there on the conference table. Can you just go over everything again? I know it seems like a waste of time. But maybe we missed something. A clue that will tell us where he's going. Where he's living."

"Of course," Alex said.

Logan could see the tension in Harrison's face. He had dark rings under his eyes. Logan wanted to ask him if he'd gotten any sleep, but that would probably make him angry. Logan wasn't his mother. Harrison would have to decide on his own if and when he needed rest.

"By the way," Harrison said, "I got a call from the police chief in Addis Ababa. Seems the ME there determined Martin Kirabo wasn't murdered after all. He committed suicide."

"Suicide?" Alex said, her eyes wide with surprise. "That's . . . I don't know what to think about that."

"Maybe he felt remorse about what he did?" Monty offered.

Alex shook her head. "No, that doesn't fit. You spend months designing a deadly strain of the Ebola virus, you send it overseas to a guy you know plans to kill thousands or millions of people, and then suddenly you feel bad about it and decide to take your own life?"

"Are they sure?" Logan asked. "Could someone have murdered this guy and tried to make it look like a suicide?"

Harrison shook his head as he sat down on the corner of an empty desk. "No, I'm not sure why they thought it might have been murder in the first place. But now they're certain it was suicide. His hand had gunpowder residue on it, and they found no signs of staging. They've also found a suicide note in Kirabo's handwriting."

"Maybe he was forced to do it," Logan said.

"Possible, but again, they found no sign of another person where he was discovered. It had recently rained, and only

Kirabo's footprints led to his body. No sign someone had tried to cover up their own footprints. Authorities are convinced it was suicide."

"You said there was a suicide note," Alex said. "Do we have a copy?"

Harrison pointed toward the back of the room. "Faxed over a few minutes ago. It's on that table." He stood. "Your food smells good. I'm going to run down the street and get some lunch. I won't be gone long. SSA Ortega is in charge while I'm gone."

Harrison left to inform his second-in-command he would be gone for a while.

"Speaking of food, let's sit down and eat this stuff while we have the chance," Monty said. "My stomach is growling." His dark eyes narrowed. "You took away my nice lunch. At least let me scarf down my fast food before I spend my day going through all this paperwork—again."

Logan smiled at him. "Sounds fair."

He carried the bag of food over to the table and deposited it in the middle. Logan kept glancing at Alex, but she still seemed fine. She grabbed a plate from the stack on the table that held plates, cups, and plastic utensils. Then she sat down and pulled out her order. Maybe he'd been too hard on her. He was tired and not at his best. He sighed to himself. He needed to concentrate on the case, not on whether Alex Donovan had a germ phobia.

But of course it wasn't just that. He was a trained behavioral analyst, and he felt strongly that something else was going on with her. Sometimes she looked . . . haunted. He could see it in her eyes.

He grabbed the suicide note and brought it to their table. "Do you want me to read this?" he asked.

Alex and Monty both nodded.

"'To my dear family, I have done something that will bring great shame to my name. I cannot allow you to pay for my actions. I love you all too much. Please remember me with love. Martin.'"

Logan heard only the sounds of chewing as no one said anything.

"Sounds like he's sorry for his part in spreading the virus," Monty finally said after taking another large bite of his burrito. Monty didn't usually talk with his mouth full, but when you're trying to stop a serial killer, manners go out the window.

"I noticed he didn't say he was sorry for what he did," Alex said. "He's just sorry it will bring shame to his name."

"Yeah, his concern is for his own family." Logan sighed. "I don't see anything in this note that gives us new information about Walker."

"Except it seems Walker might not have known Martin as well as he thought he did," Alex said. "Or did he know this guy would commit suicide?"

Logan stared at her for a moment. "Good question. Was that the plan? I mean, now another way of finding Walker is gone."

"The Circle seems concerned with tying up loose ends. Even if this was a suicide, it may have been . . . encouraged by the Circle, if not by Walker."

"So now what?" Monty asked. "Are we going to rework our assessment . . . again? I'm beginning to have nightmares about this thing. Last night, I dreamt Adam Walker was stalking me, and the only way I could stop him was to answer a series of ten questions about serial killers."

Although the comment wasn't meant to be funny, Logan burst out laughing. Alex joined in, and finally Monty grinned. "I'm glad you find my nightmares amusing."

Logan smiled. "I think we all have dreams like that. I had one once where I was in a classroom, taking a test to retain my spot in the BAU. As I worked hard to answer the questions, I looked down and realized I was dressed in pajamas my mom made for me when I was in kindergarten."

Another round of laughter caused the few people working in the larger room to look their way.

Alex got up and closed the door, then sat back down. "We don't want to disturb them. If either one of you shares another one of these bizarre dreams . . ."

"It's your turn, Alex," Monty said, smiling. "Do you have any strange dreams?"

Logan saw Alex's lips thin, then she looked away. "No," she said. "Nothing as amusing as yours."

"Okay, enough," Logan said, trying to get the attention back to the case. "So what do we do now?"

"We look for some piece of information we skipped over because it didn't seem important at the time," Alex said. "This guy has to have a base of operations. Geographic profiling tells us he lives somewhere in this area, despite his having once lived in Independence and attended a couple of Circle meetings in Wichita. Kansas City is where he was born and lived until he was seven, where he worked in that lab." She got up and pointed at a map stuck on the large corkboard behind them. A circle had been drawn representing Walker's comfort zone.

Monty sighed. "Again, the guy had an apartment near his work, but that's been completely cleared out. No forwarding address. The Evidence Response Team found only a few fingerprints, a couple on the window blinds and one on a lightbulb he changed. That's it."

"No other fingerprints?" Alex asked.

"Only the apartment manager's."

"And because he could tell us when Walker moved out, we also know he lived there while he killed his first four victims and then moved somewhere else before killing his fifth victim at Union Station. That was only a little out of his comfort zone, no doubt because we were watching the rail yards. But I still don't think that means he'll stray far for this next killing."

Alex said all this slowly, as if turning the information over in her mind. "My guess is he went home to his family, wherever they are. Now he's searching for the last victim—unless he's already found her."

She stopped eating and looked at Logan, her eyes narrowed. "All the other killings were done either on or near a train. But this last victim . . ."

Logan immediately understood what she was thinking. "This is special. He can't kill her where he grabs her. He has to prepare her. Display her somewhere that has meaning. Every single victim has been staged. He wanted them to point to the Train Man. But . . ."

"Maybe he'll find a place still worthy of the Train Man but even more worthy of the Master?" Monty said.

They finished their meals in silence. Logan was sure they were all trying to think of someplace Walker might take his next victim.

"It has to have *something* to do with trains," Alex said.

"Or The Book." Logan took a drink of his pop and grabbed

a large folder. He thumbed through the pages. "Okay, here's the part about the virgin.

> "'When the Virgin who shall be washed in blood, the final sacrifice, is offered to the Master, the demons will be unleashed, and the angels will make war with the evil ones. This sacrifice will be holy, and the one who offers it will be elevated in the Master's kingdom. He is the Destroyer. The one called to fulfill the will of the Master. Long live the Master!'"

"This sacrifice is *holy*," Alex said. "It's different from the others. They weren't called holy, were they?"

Logan searched through the pages copied from The Book. "Listen to this.

> "'When the time comes for the Master to send judgment on the earth, he will choose a servant, one who has been prepared. This demon will become the Destroyer. He will offer six perfect sacrifices before a plague is unleashed. Destruction will come upon the angels and the demons. Only those true to the Master will survive.'"

"I'm confused," Monty said. "Is this Master on the side of the angels or the demons?"

"I guess he reigns over all of them," Alex said.

Logan shook his head. "That doesn't make much sense."

"Right. Willow told me good cannot exist without evil. That demons were necessary. Some of them will be preserved through this war that's supposed to begin after the plague."

"Boy, the Bible is a lot easier to understand," Logan said in a low voice. "Demons bad. Angels good."

"But you said some angels fell."

Her remembering he'd told her that caught Logan by surprise. "Yes. There are fallen angels. Lucifer was one."

"So the Bible and The Book have some similarities."

"But God doesn't send demons out to hurt people," Logan said. "He loves us. This god of Walker's hates humanity."

Alex gave him a strange look. "The Book teaches people are either angels or demons, and they have no choice. Their fate has already been determined. So Walker would never be able to accept God's redemption as long as he believes his fate is locked in, right?" She looked away.

Monty stayed quiet, and Logan didn't respond. But something stirred in his heart. Did Alex think she was locked in somehow? She had obviously been thinking about the Bible and its message of redemption. Could she be seeking God?

33

Laura was tired. The restaurant had been busy all afternoon, but it was always packed on Sundays because so many people liked to eat out after church. That crowd gave the largest tips, though, and they were always the nicest people. It was rare to find a grumpy customer on Sundays. She enjoyed talking to everyone, but her feet were starting to hurt.

Amy, one of the other waitresses, nodded at her, letting her know she'd cover Laura's table while she took her break. Laura smiled at her and headed for the kitchen. She waved at Terry, who worked the grill, and told Meghan, another one of the servers, she'd be outside for a few minutes. She walked into the small hallway connected to the kitchen and took her purse out of her locker. After grabbing her cigarettes and lighter, she put on her coat and shut her locker door before stepping outside.

The closed-off alley was usually quiet. Only once in a while did someone from the dry cleaners or the insurance company in the same strip mall come out to throw trash away or grab a smoke. The only other smoker seemed to be a part-time guy who worked for the cleaners. He'd never talked to her, just looked at his phone while he smoked. That was okay with Laura. She wasn't looking for a boyfriend. The last one had hit her, and she'd promised herself she'd never put herself in a situation like that again. Besides, now that she was a Christian, she wanted something new. Someone new. Someone who would treat her with respect and love her even if she wasn't perfect.

She knew smoking was bad for her. She'd told the person who prayed with her at church this morning that she was worried she couldn't stop smoking right away. She could still see the kind smile on the woman's face. What was her name? Shirley? Yeah, that was it. "Give it to God, honey," she'd said. "He loves you just the way you are. He'll give you the strength to get free when the time is right. He's the deliverer, you know. You're not." She'd put her hand on top of Laura's head and prayed that God would deliver her from smoking. As she prayed, something had flowed through Laura. It was like . . . warm, liquid love.

Tears sprang to her eyes. She wanted to believe God wasn't disappointed in what He was getting. She'd gotten involved in drugs and drinking when she was younger. Even though she was clean now, her mistakes had caused a rift with her parents. After they divorced, Laura tried to reconcile with both of them. Her mother lived in another city, but they kept in touch by phone. Her father remarried, and Laura had to share him with a woman named Sheila. Although Sheila pretended to like her, Laura knew better. She tolerated

Laura because she had to. Sheila was busy trying to add her father to her own family. Laura didn't fit in anymore. She'd given up a couple of years ago. Her father had never tried to contact her after that.

She wiped a tear from her cheek. She'd gone to church only because Amy had invited her. She liked Amy and wanted a friend. It was fun getting dressed up and going out with someone—even if it was to church. First was what Amy called praise and worship. The music had touched her heart. She'd looked around at other people, and they seemed so happy. It was as if the music was alive. As if it seeped inside her somehow and touched all the hurt in her life.

Then came the sermon. She'd gone to church once. Before her mother and dad divorced. They went on a vacation and visited an uncle in New Mexico. They all went to church one Sunday, and the minister talked about all the rules people were supposed to follow. He'd talked for only a few minutes before Laura tuned him out. She was already having a hard time doing everything her mother told her to do. She knew she couldn't follow all the rules the minister talked about. But the pastor on Wednesday night talked about a God who already knew everyone's weaknesses. He wasn't asking her to be perfect. He was just asking her to allow Jesus to love her.

Before she knew what she was doing, she found herself at the front of the church with several others. Even though she couldn't explain it, when she walked out the front door of the church building, she knew she was different. That life was different.

Church had been a joy this morning, and she could hardly wait to go back this evening. Amy couldn't pick her up because she would be coming straight from work. Laura was grateful she would have time to go home, wash up, and change clothes before meeting her tonight. She felt grungy.

She took another long drag on her cigarette before dropping it on the ground and stamping it out. She usually smoked down to the filter, but today she just didn't want to. She walked back to the restaurant door and started to open it. She stopped at the last second and looked around her. She thought she'd seen something out of the corner of her eye, but no one was there.

Once inside, she entered the dining room and smiled at Amy. She could hardly wait until six o'clock. Life was changing, and she welcomed it with all her heart.

Adam hurried back to his car. She smoked. He wasn't thrilled about that. This was a holy sacrifice. How could a smoker be holy? He'd only carried cigarettes and a lighter with him on his hunts because a lot of drifters smoked. But this sacrifice had to be different.

As he drove away he argued with himself, but in the end, he decided to go forward with his plan. His father had smoked the last few years of his life, and even though it killed him in the end, Adam was proud to be his son. If he rejected this sacrifice because she smoked, did that mean he was saying something was wrong with his own father? The man who had helped make him who he was today? No. The sacrifice would happen, and it would be perfect.

The trio had finished eating their lunch hours ago, and Harrison still hadn't returned. Alex was poring over Walker's work performance records yet again when she suddenly closed her file and stood. "Where's that page from The Book that talks about the sixth sacrifice?"

Monty sorted through some pages in front of him, then pulled one out and handed it to her. "Something new strike you?" he asked.

"Not exactly." She searched through the page until she found what she was looking for. "I just want to go back to what The Book says about the sixth victim. 'This sacrifice will be holy, and the one who offers it will be elevated in the Master's kingdom.' We were talking before about how this sixth sacrifice will be holy." She stabbed at the page with her index finger. "So what's holy to Walker?"

"Trains?" Monty asked.

Alex leaned back in her chair and thought for a moment. "But he knows the trains are being watched closely as well as Union Station. And I know we said some form of a train can be found at zoos and amusement parks, but those wouldn't qualify as holy."

"He could use an out-of-state train, but I don't think he'll leave this area," Logan said. "For something this important, he'll stay within his comfort zone."

"I agree. But I think this decision will connect to The Book more than to a train. I could be wrong."

"So what does that mean?" Logan asked.

Alex was quiet for several seconds before looking up at Logan, her eyes locked on his. "I don't know," she said. "But we'd better hurry and figure it out. We're running out of time."

34

lex stared at the files on the table. Should they go through them again? Had they missed something? As she considered their options, SSA Ortiz came into the room.

"I've got a call for you, Agent Donovan," she said. "A Randall Burkhart? He says he has some information for you."

"That's the cousin," Logan said.

Alex nodded. "This would be a good time to pray, Preacher."

"I'm way ahead of you."

Alex followed Ortiz to her desk. She pointed to her phone. "Line three," she said.

Ortiz walked away, so Alex sat down in her chair. She picked up the phone and pressed the line Ortiz had indicated.

"This is Supervisory Special Agent Donovan," she said.

"I was told I needed to talk to you," a man's voice said. "I'm Randall Burkhart. My cousin is Adam Walker?"

"Yes, Mr. Burkhart. I know who you are. What can I do for you?"

"The police questioned me about Adam, but I couldn't help them. I only met him once when we were kids, and I had no idea where he might be."

"Yes, they told us they'd talked to you."

Burkhart paused. "I don't know why law enforcement is interested in Adam, but I assume it's important. So after talking to the police, I looked in the attic and found my mother's papers. I went through them, hoping to find some kind of information that might help. I'm not sure, but I . . . I may have found something."

Alex could feel her heart beating in her chest. "Tell me about it," she said.

"It seems there's a cabin. Our family owned it once, I believe. I found a note about it. It reminded me of a conversation my parents had when I was a kid. More of an argument, I guess. My dad was against giving away a cabin—one that my grandfather built—but my mom insisted. It didn't mean anything to me at the time. But now I wonder if they were arguing about giving the cabin to Adam's mother." He paused for a moment. "This may not pan out. I hope I'm not wasting your time. I just thought . . ."

"You're not wasting our time, Mr. Burkhart," Alex said. "This may be a big help. What did the note say?"

"It's like . . . well, like my mother was documenting a transaction. It basically declares that she'd transferred ownership of a cabin to my aunt Agnes. There's no deed. Nothing legal. Just a statement. I can't explain it except that my grandfather may have built the cabin on someone else's property. Not illegally or anything. Someone may have allowed him to rent the land so he could build a cabin. I understand that used to happen a lot."

Alex's hope began to fade. "You don't know the location of this cabin?"

"Not exactly, but my mother's note mentions the south side of Lake Lotawana. A lot of nice homes are in other areas around that lake. A friend of mine has a house there, and he told me some of the old cabins have been abandoned. The county is tearing them down to make room for new construction. That means this cabin might not even exist anymore. Sorry I can't be more encouraging, but I'm fairly sure Adam's family lived there at some point. Maybe that's where he is now."

Alex tried to control her excitement. After asking Burkhart if he could tell her anything else, she thanked him and hung up. Then she hurried back to the table where Logan and Monty waited and brought them up to speed.

"Shoot," Logan said. "I was hoping he could tell us something more solid. But if there really is a cabin, Walker could be there. Maybe his family too."

"Could be," Monty said. "But without a clue of some kind, it would be hard to find."

Alex stepped over to the map on the corkboard and drew a circle. "Burkhart said it was near Lake Lotawana. In the woods. Probably on the south side." But even that left a large search area. Alex stared at the map, looking for anything that would put them closer to finding Walker. Then she walked over to the door and gazed around the larger room in the CP. Except for Ortiz, some analysts, and them, the building was deserted. She'd never seen a CP with so few agents working. She realized even the people from the CDC were gone.

"I'd rather be out helping find Walker or his sixth target instead of sitting here, doing nothing," she said firmly. She turned around to stare at Logan and Monty. She could see the frustration in their expressions.

"Well, we're not doing much good here," Logan said. "I can't keep looking at this stuff. I think I've memorized most of it."

"Look, this is the only lead we have. A cabin on the south side of Lake Lotawana. We need to get someone out there." She selected a number from her directory and tapped it.

"Are you calling Harrison?" Monty asked. "Isn't he helping the police contact area churches? I'm not sure—"

Alex held up her hand to stop Monty from talking. She didn't need his permission to call Harrison. This was important.

They may have found the Train Man.

35

Logan didn't say anything as Alex called Harrison, but he tended to agree with Monty. Finding some old cabin that could have been torn down years ago wasn't as important as saving a woman's life and stopping Walker from releasing his superbug.

Alex put her phone on the table and pressed the speaker so they could all hear. When Harrison answered, he sounded rushed and aggravated. Alex quickly explained about the cabin.

"We don't have time to try to find a record of this cabin, especially on a Sunday," she told him. "So I think you need to send some people out to Lake Lotawana and see if you can locate it."

He was quiet for a moment before cursing loudly. "Listen to me, Agent Donovan. We're trying to warn churches in Walker's hunting ground. If we can stop him from this next killing, we've stopped him from using that virus . . . at least for a while. He has to have the last sacrifice before he begins to infect people. I don't have the time or the personnel to send on some wild goose chase." He took a deep breath. "Look, I appreciate the effort, but this isn't important right now."

"I disagree, sir," Alex said sharply. "Maybe that's where Walker and his parents lived after they left Kansas City and before he and his father lived alone in Independence. And if that's the last place his mother was with him . . . I think it could be his sacred place. The spot where he plans to offer his holy sacrifice."

"But you don't know that," Harrison said, anger obvious in his tone. "And you've said yourself it's far more likely he'd stay in his comfort zone."

"I don't *know*, but let us check it out," Alex said, pleading now. "The three of us. We're just sitting here. We could do it."

"You're not field agents. You're behavioral analysts. You don't belong out there."

"Is that your final word?" Alex asked.

"Yes."

Harrison hung up. Alex stared at her phone as if she'd never seen it before. Finally, she clicked it off. "He's wrong," she said. "We need to find that cabin."

"Absolutely not," Logan said just as sharply as she'd spoken to Harrison. "He told us to stay here, Alex. And he's right. I know you've spent a lot of time in the field, but now you're part of the BAU. What you're suggesting . . . We could lose our jobs." He hated telling her not to follow her gut. He couldn't be sure she was wrong. What if she wasn't? Still, he couldn't disobey Harrison's order. None of them could.

"I agree with Logan," Monty said. "The Bureau has assigned agents to different divisions. We each have to do what we're called to do. If we don't, we cause confusion. You gave him the information. We need to stay here and wait."

"He may think about what you said and change his mind," Logan added. "Let's just sit tight for a while, okay?"

The expression on Alex's face changed. Logan had seen this look before. Stoic. Unreadable. He didn't care as long as she listened. If she went against the ASAC she could be out of the FBI. They ran a tight ship. Going against orders wasn't looked upon kindly.

"Okay," she said. "I just hope he does change his mind." Her eyes locked with Logan's. "I'm right about this."

"Maybe you are. But we can't go rogue. Let the system work." He glared at her. "I mean it, Alex. Leave it alone."

She walked to the table with the coffee and poured a cup, then stayed there for a while, just sipping her drink. Finally, she turned around. "Let's at least talk about this cabin. I doubt he'd take his wife and kids to a ramshackle place like that, but it sounds like he may have spent time there as a child. How would that affect him?"

Monty started to answer her, but Alex shook her head. "Hey, can you hold that thought? I need to make a run to the little girl's room. I'll be right back."

"Sure."

After Alex left, Monty leaned closer to Logan. "Do you think she's right?"

"I don't know. The cabin could be important. Unfortunately, it's not my job to determine what's important and what isn't. We've got to follow orders. We have no choice."

"But it is our job to understand this guy—to understand him so the agents in the field can find him."

Logan shook his head, but his gut told him Alex was right. She had an amazing instinct for understanding criminals.

"What should we do?" Monty asked.

"I think I'll call Harrison myself and try to impress on him that this could be really important. Ask him again to find some people to send out to the lake." He shuffled through the papers on the table. "The KCPD looked up Walker's car registration, right?"

Monty nodded. "I think he has a silver Honda Accord, although none of the alerts have turned it up. My guess is he may be using a different car now. He has to know we're looking for it."

"Yeah, here it is. A 2016 model." Logan stared at the information for a moment, then looked at Monty. "I agree with you. Maybe he parked it at the cabin. If we spotted it, we'd have that clue we need."

"Look, Logan, I'm willing to stick my neck out if I have to. But this does seem like a wild goose chase. This cabin might not be standing anymore. We're going on just a hunch."

"I know, but it's Alex's hunch, and she's done some incredible work in the past." He took a deep breath and held it for a moment before saying, "Walker is looking for a *holy* place for the last sacrifice. What if Alex is right? What if . . ."

Logan felt like a diver getting ready to jump off a high board. Alex was in the water, and Logan was next in line to take a leap.

"Walker's mother had disappeared by the time he and his father moved to Independence, the place he lied about Agnes leaving them. What if the family lived in that cabin those missing five years? And what if Charles killed Agnes?"

He took in a deep breath. "And what if Adam saw that killing as somehow holy based on The Book's teachings? Maybe something like that could have set a twelve-year-old on the path Walker's on now. Propelled him toward this book his family believed in. And now, here he is, fulfilling his so-called destiny. So he takes this sixth victim to the place where everything changed for him. He offers her as a sacrifice where he became the Train Man. Everything has come full circle."

Monty leaned back in his chair and studied Logan. "I don't know," he said finally. "A lot of *what ifs* in your supposition. Not sure this has anything to do with behavioral analysis."

"Sure it does," Logan said more harshly than he meant to. "We create profiles so law enforcement can capture criminals. If we have an idea where one might be, based on our training and experience—"

Monty made a fist and hit the top of the table. "But that's the problem. This is a guess, nothing more. If we keep pushing this—"

Logan stood. "I'm calling Harrison. I'll make sure he knows you're not in agreement with us."

"Don't do that," Monty said with a sigh. "I'm in. I just hope this doesn't go badly." He pointed a finger at Logan. "My Chinese grandmother will get very upset if I get kicked out of the FBI. If that happens, *you* will explain it to her. And trust me, you've never faced anything as scary as my grandmother when she's angry."

Logan laughed. "Okay, I'll face her if I have to. So you're in?"

"God help me, yes."

"Okay, I'm going to ask him once more if we can try to locate the cabin. We're just spinning our wheels here. If he says no, I'll tell him we've done everything we can for now, and we want the rest of the day off. Then we'll look for the cabin on our own time. Maybe that will protect us in the end."

"Yeah, maybe. But I'll call Grandmother and set a date for your meeting."

"Let's wait a bit on that," Logan said with a grin.

He took his phone from his pocket and called Harrison. His call went straight to voice mail. Should he leave a message? As busy as Harrison was right now, it seemed all right to let him know they were taking off. When he heard the beep, though, he felt a sense of panic. Was he making a mistake?

"Sorry I missed you," Logan said. "Hey, I really think Alex is on to something about that cabin. I know you're super busy, but this actually could be important. Just thought you should know that Monty and I agree with Alex. Well, we're not accomplishing anything here, Boss, so we're taking off. I'll keep my phone with me, so call me if you need to. Anything more we can do, just let us know."

Logan quickly hung up. He didn't actually say they were going to look for the cabin, but Harrison was no fool. He'd figure it out. Was Logan about to throw away his career? This was all he ever wanted to be. But he felt something stirring inside him. Was God telling him to keep going? It sure felt like it. God had protected him many times by telling him to stay away from certain things or particular people. And a few times he'd experienced a tangible sense of peace when he prayed about something in his life he wanted to do. That peace was always right.

He walked back toward the coffee counter to pray silently. As he finished, that sense of peace enveloped him, and he knew he was supposed to look for the cabin.

"Okay, let's go," he said to Monty. "I guess we'll search the south side of Lake Lotawana, and maybe we'll find a silver Honda Accord parked next to a cabin." He frowned. "This is a great way to spend our time off, huh?"

Monty didn't respond to the sarcasm, and his expression was grim.

"Have you changed your mind?" Logan asked.

"No, but where is Alex? Unless she has some kind of physical problem, shouldn't she have been back from the bathroom already?"

Now it was Logan's turn to be concerned. He'd started for the restroom when he noticed the keys to their rental car weren't on the table where he'd left them.

"Did you pick up my car keys?" he asked Monty.

"Of course not."

"Where's Alex's purse?" It was more like a satchel. She carried personal items in it as well as case notes and research documents. He looked next to her chair and was relieved to find it. "It's here," he said. Why had both of them jumped to the conclusion that Alex had taken off on her own? He knew the answer before he even asked the question. When Alex made up her mind about something, it was almost impossible to get her to change it.

Monty stood and grabbed the bag from Logan's hand. Then he put it on the table and unzipped it.

"What are you doing?" Logan said. "That's Alex's personal property. I don't think—"

Monty pushed the bag toward Logan. "Where's her wallet? You've seen it when she pays for anything. It's purple. She has her credit cards and her driver's license in it. It's not here."

Even before Monty finished, Logan realized Alex was really gone. She'd taken the car and was headed to Lake Lotawana to find that cabin—and Adam Walker.

36

aura sat in church feeling so grateful she'd found the Lord. Several people came up to talk to her, and just before praise and worship started, Amy plopped down next to her on the pew. She'd asked Laura to save a place for her.

"Whew. Made it," she said with a sigh. She plopped her purse onto her lap and set her Bible down. "Hey," she said, still a little breathless. "I ran by my apartment before coming here." She removed something from her purse. "I want to give you this. It's a Bible. Brand-new. My mom gave it to me for my birthday, but I don't need it."

"Oh, Amy. Your Bible is falling apart," Laura said. "You should use this new one."

Amy leaned closer. "I have no intention of getting rid of my Bible. I've spent four years making notes and highlighting passages. Besides, it was a gift from my father before he died." She straightened up. "This beautiful new Bible needs someone who will mark it up and highlight Scriptures important to her." She handed Laura the lovely blue leather Bible. "Besides, I had your name engraved on it. That means no one else can use it."

Laura gasped when she saw her name printed in gold in the lower right corner of the cover. "How . . . I mean . . . where . . ."

Amy laughed. "I went to the shop where my mom bought the Bible. They were thrilled to engrave it. I told them you were a new believer. Oh, I almost forgot." She reached into her purse again and pulled out an envelope. She handed it to Laura, who opened it. Inside was a short note congratulating her for her decision to follow Christ. With the note was a twenty-five-dollar gift certificate toward anything in the store.

Laura couldn't stop the tears that filled her eyes. "Thank you, Amy," she said quietly, her voice choked. "I've never been treated like this before."

Amy gave her a hug. "No matter what life throws at you, you'll never be alone again, Laura. God loves you. He's a good Father."

When Laura was seventeen, she finally got out of the house, away from her stepmother, Sheila. A cousin let her stay at her place until Laura could get on her feet. Now she had her own small apartment over her landlord's garage. It might not be much to anyone else, but she loved it. She'd been there for only a couple of weeks when she came home one night and found a sick, scraggly kitten in front of the house. She took it to the vet's the next day. Thankfully, the kitten was only hungry and flea infested. They cleaned her up, treated her for fleas, and gave her the shots she needed. Then Laura took the little kitten home.

At first she had to feed the kitten through an eyedropper. She'd considered all kinds of names, but for some reason the name Sabrina seemed to fit the little black kitten the best. Laura had fallen in love with her. It was great to come home to someone who was excited to see her.

The landlord had a pet policy. When Laura called to tell him about the cat, he thanked her for saving a kitten that would probably have died without her help. He waived the pet deposit and offered to help her if she ever needed it. The landlord was a Christian, and so was her cousin. She'd begun to see a difference between Christians and other people even then. When she met Amy at work . . . Well, all these people had shown such compassion and kindness that Laura had decided she wanted what they had. And now she did.

Laura was filled with joy. God was a good Father, and who knew what He would do in her life from here on? She also felt something else she'd never felt before. Hope. Hope that God really did have a plan for her life. She put the Bible down next to her on the pew as the praise and worship musicians took the stage. She loved worshiping God, and tonight it would mean even more. She couldn't wait to see what the Lord had for her next.

He drove slowly by Laura's church. He'd noticed police cars stationed at several other churches, and he knew why they were there. He gave them credit for figuring out that the virgin would come from a church. But they were still a day late and a dollar short. He was sure they hadn't realized she'd be a brand-new convert.

He laughed to himself. Outfoxing the police was easy. They

wouldn't halt what must happen tonight. No one could halt what was already set in motion. The virgin would be sacrificed tonight, and then the world would be judged.

Alex wished she'd been able to come out here when it was still light out. Night fell early in November, and the narrow roads leading to Lake Lotawana were more than precarious. No streetlamps. No stoplights. Some stop signs if you saw them in time. Alex had to watch out for other cars coming around steep curves and deer that might suddenly step onto the road. She hated this. Why hadn't she stayed at the CP? What if she'd just thrown away her career for nothing? It was almost impossible for her to find this cabin—if it was even still standing.

But she couldn't just sit around if there was any chance she could stop this man from killing an innocent woman and spreading a deadly disease. Saving thousands of lives was more important than her job . . . or even her life.

She drove for quite some time, searching for a cabin that might be Walker's base of operations. Something ramshackle. She wasn't sure why she was so convinced Walker was here. He could be holed up anywhere. Was she on a wild goose chase like Harrison said this would be? But she kept going back to the passage from The Book that said the sacrifice of the virgin was holy.

Just before she'd slipped her wallet out of her bag and grabbed the car keys, it had occurred to her again that Adam's father could have been a killer too. Could he have murdered his wife at this cabin before he and Adam moved to Independence? And if he'd told Adam killing her was somehow holy . . . She shivered, then shook her head. "You might be losing it, Alex," she said softly. Hearing her own voice gave her some comfort. She felt alone in this darkness.

She'd passed a small convenience store—the kind that also sold gas—before she'd started her search. Wondering if she could get some help there, she'd turned around and driven back. Before getting out of the car, she slipped off her jacket to make sure nothing identified her as FBI. She could tell this was a small mom-and-pop operation, and she didn't want to cause a stir.

Once inside, she saw they had maps of the area, and she bought one. She'd also asked the elderly man working there if he knew anything about the properties on the south side of the lake—especially about any cabins.

"There's some smaller places stuck around there." He'd jabbed at the map she'd opened. "These are real fancy homes. No cabins, so you don't want to go there." He moved his finger to an area west of that area. "My guess is what you want is around here somewhere." He rubbed his stubbly chin. "I think there's a few cabins there. Some of them's pretty old, though. Empty too. No folks been there for a long time. Mighta been pulled down by now. I never go down there. But if you do, look for Waywind Road." He pointed to a spot on the map. "It's about here, as I recall."

Alex had thanked him and left. But now, here she was, pretty much lost despite the map, looking for a cabin with no real clue as to its location.

She slammed on her brakes when she saw a sign. Backing up a bit, she pointed her headlights at it. It was old and worn and sat crookedly on its splintered wood pole, but it said *Cabins* and had an arrow pointing to the right. She turned that way, hoping it was the right thing to do.

It was even darker now, so she switched on her bright lights, frightening a doe and her fawn who ran into some trees. Forming a forest, they lined both sides of the narrow road.

When the first few raindrops fell, Alex didn't pay much attention. But when they turned to tiny pellets of ice, she halted the car. This might be the dumbest thing she'd ever done. She picked up her phone to call Logan. She didn't feel safe going any farther by herself. But as she found his number, she realized he would just tell her to come back, and she wasn't willing to do that either. Or maybe he would come find her. If he was here, surely he'd understand how important it was to keep going.

Sweat broke out on her forehead, and she started to breathe faster—as if her body had a will of its own. She hated the dark, and right now she was enveloped by it. She clicked on Logan's phone number, but nothing happened. No signal. She was in the boonies, surrounded by a forest so dense that she couldn't see into it. She began to really panic.

"Stop it, Alex," she said out loud. "You're not going to give in to this fear. Nothing will happen to you. Just keep going."

The ice pellets, which seemed to taunt her, began falling even faster. She turned on the fan for her windshield and turned up the speed of her windshield wipers. Should she turn around and go back? Or should she keep going? She looked at the clock on her dashboard. Nine thirty. Shoot. Most churches would have let out by now. Hopefully, the police had put a kink in Walker's plan.

She put her car in gear and drove slowly down the road that supposedly led to some cabins. She'd come this far. She couldn't turn back now. She wished she'd been honest with Logan. Maybe if she'd tried harder he would have come with her. She had a strange urge to pray, but she ignored it. People tended to call on God when they were in trouble.

Suddenly, Nettie's words played in her mind. *"He wants me to tell you that He saw your tears, and He's been watching over you all this time."*

"Okay, God," she said out loud. "If you really exist, which I doubt, help me find Adam Walker and stop him before he kills an innocent girl. One of yours, by the way. And stop him from releasing this virus, which would probably kill more of your people." As silence filled the car, Alex sighed. "Show me you're real, God, and I'll follow you . . . or whatever. Logan believes in you, and he's pretty smart. Maybe—"

What was she doing? *You really are losing it.*

But what if?

37

Laura tried to open her eyes, but it was difficult. She struggled until she was finally able to raise her lids a little. Where was she? What happened? She tried to remember, but her memory was hazy.

She remembered walking out of church. Amy had asked her if she wanted to get something to eat, but she'd turned her down. She was tired. She wanted nothing more than to go home and cuddle up with Sabrina.

Laura tried to move but couldn't. She turned her head and looked around her. Was this a basement? Why couldn't she move? Then she realized she was tied down. Her arms were raised above her head, and her wrists were bound with rope attached to the legs of a large table. Her own legs were tied to the other end of the tabletop.

What was going on? Fear coursed through her. How did she get here?

She searched her mind again, although it was like fighting

through a thick fog. Laura remembered driving home. She got out of her car . . . What next? She tried hard to find her memories. There was a voice . . . and nothing after that. She thought about calling out for help, but what if whoever did this heard her? She fought against the terror she felt. She remembered what Amy had said—that she wasn't alone anymore.

As tears fell down her cheeks and dripped into her hair, she silently cried out to God to save her. As she prayed, fear turned to hope. Hope that God would get her out of this. She wanted to get married. Have children. Live the kind of life she once thought was impossible. She wasn't the useless, unwanted girl her parents had rejected. She had a new Father, and He loved her. He'd adopted her. Laura decided to believe He would rescue her.

As the words from a worship song they'd sung at church began to play in her mind, she sang along in a whisper. And as she thought about the words, the fear dissipated until she was certain God had heard her. That He had a plan for her life, and no one could stop it. No one.

───

Logan and Monty had borrowed an SUV from one of the computer analysts trying to track down Adam Walker. He'd checked in a couple of hours earlier and was prepared to work all night. Monty told him someone had borrowed their car and that they needed to follow up on a lead. It wasn't really a lie—although they didn't tell him they'd probably be driving in pretty tough terrain.

When they opened the back door of the CP building, they stepped into a cold rain, then ran to the car. Monty threw himself into the passenger seat.

"Turn on the heater," he said as Logan got in. "It will probably take a while to warm up." Logan started the car and pressed the button for the car's heating system. Cold air blew out of the vents. Logan turned on the car's GPS system and put in the address of Lake Lotawana, a small town with the same name as the lake. Finding it would lead them to the lake.

"It's going to take about thirty minutes to get there," he said, putting the car in gear and heading out of the parking lot.

"I wish we knew what was going on with the churches," Monty said. "We're going into this blind. Are we looking for a kidnap victim? Or are we just trying to find Walker?"

"Just assume we're looking for a kidnap victim and a man who may be planning to unleash a deadly pathogen." *And Alex.* "If we find this guy, we find the virus. And if we find the virus, we've saved many, many lives."

"And if we don't, we may be working at McDonald's."

Logan snorted as he looked over at Monty. "Hey, I like McDonald's. Don't be a hater."

Monty grunted, then looked out the windshield. "Uh . . . is that still rain? It's looking more like sleet."

"I guess we better hurry up and get there, then." Logan didn't like driving in ice, but what choice did he have?

"You didn't tell Harrison where we were going, right?"

"No, but I think he'll figure it out—if he checks his voice mail. If we find something, I'll call him immediately." He glanced at the clock on the dashboard. "It's a little after nine forty-five. Most church meetings will have dismissed by now."

"I would feel a lot better if you'd actually talked to Harrison," Monty said. "What if they've already caught Walker? We may be doing this for nothing."

"But Alex is out there. We need to find her. Try her again."

They'd called Alex's cell phone several times, but it went straight to voice mail. Monty nodded at Logan when he got the same thing again. "Hey, Alex," he said, "this is Monty. Logan and I need to talk to you. We've left you several messages, and we're getting worried. Assuming you've gone to the lake, we're headed your way. Please, please call us so we know where you are, okay?"

He disconnected and sighed. "She obviously doesn't want to talk to us. And I don't think she'll be pleased to know we followed her." He sighed again, this time more loudly. "Let me get this straight. We're all driving into the woods, it's dark and sleeting, and we're not even sure the guy we're looking for is where we're headed. Can this get any worse?"

"Actually, it could get much worse. I looked over some information about the lake while you were in the restroom. A lot of the roads around the lake are dirt, especially on the south side where we're going."

Monty turned to stare at him. "Super. Let's add that to the list. Woods, darkness, ice, no one will know where we are except a woman who won't return our phone calls and a man who might or might not figure out where we've gone. A man who could ruin our careers. Who told us not to do this. Good." He slumped down in his seat. "Now dirt. We better find this Walker guy, rescue Alex if she needs it, and save the world. Unless we can pull that off, those jobs at McDonald's are looking pretty good. Maybe I can be a fry guy."

Logan was certain they were doing the right thing, but he understood the point behind what Monty was saying. They needed a win here. But first they had to find Alex. Logan hadn't mentioned she was gone in the message he'd left Harrison. At least he could keep her out of it if the situation went south.

He tried to tell himself he would do the same thing if Monty had gone off on his own, and he believed he would. But something about Alex had wriggled itself into his mind. She was an exemplary agent, but she was also fragile. He hadn't worked closely with her before this assignment, but he'd been around her enough to know the way she was acting was new. It seemed to have started after she went to Wichita. Something was clearly wrong—something beyond what she'd told him about her past.

He suddenly realized she reminded him of someone. His great-uncle Jasper, who served in Vietnam. Alex had the same look in her eyes he'd had. His wife told Logan's mother Jasper had PTSD. Jasper saw a counselor several times, but two years ago, he'd taken a gun into the bathroom and killed himself.

A chill went through Logan that had nothing to do with temperature. The car was warm enough now. Was Alex going through PTSD from her experiences with her aunt? She certainly had been through more than most children should ever endure. A father who left and a depressed mother who killed herself, leaving Alex to find her body. And then she was thrust into the home of a strange aunt who allowed Alex to be the adult while she spent her time espousing crazy teachings. It would be almost impossible for anyone. And finding that aunt standing over your bed with a knife? The more Logan thought about that, the more bizarre it sounded. No teenager should feel she had to hide a gun under her pillow to protect herself.

Logan sighed to himself. He should have seen it sooner. Put the pieces together. He was trained in analyzing people's behaviors. Why hadn't he seen PTSD as a possibility? Was it because he had feelings for Alex? Although he had no intention of acting on them, he finally admitted to himself that he did. He was attracted to her. But to be honest, he wasn't sure if his attraction was romantic or merely a desire to rescue her from herself. Damsel-in-distress syndrome.

They were almost there when Logan pulled into the small parking lot of a convenience store, not far from the entrance to the lake according to his GPS. They were almost out of gas. The guy who owned the car hadn't mentioned he was low. Thankfully, Logan noticed it before they got too far into the woods surrounding the lake.

"I want to go inside to see if there's a map of the area," he told Monty. He took out his wallet and handed Monty his debit card. "Do you mind getting some gas? Just fill it up."

Monty waved away Logan's card. "Nah. Alex has put herself at risk to find a serial killer, and you've put your career on the line for the same reason. I should at least buy gas. That's my contribution to your heroic efforts. Besides, if this blows up on us, I plan to blame it all on you."

"Gee, thanks. Not sure they'll believe that, though."

Monty shrugged. "I intend to tell them you forced me into this car. I tried to get away, but you threatened to make me eat snails."

Logan laughed. "I happen to like escargot."

"You really are weird, man. You know that?"

"Yeah. I do. Thanks for the gas. I'll be right back."

As Logan carefully made his way across the slippery lot to the door of the small building, he couldn't help but worry about fallout for his team. He wasn't in charge; Alex was. But here he and Monty were, following her into a situation that could be dangerous. If they needed backup, would they be able to contact anyone? They might not have cell phone connection the deeper they went into the woods. Maybe Alex didn't now. Were they all putting their lives at risk?

He didn't know the answers to those questions, but he had no intention of leaving Alex out here alone. No matter what happened.

When he opened the store's door, he found an old man sitting behind a counter, his head down, snoring. Logan hated to wake him, but he didn't have much choice.

"Excuse me?" he said softly.

No response. The snoring just got louder.

"Excuse me?" he said with a little more volume.

This time the old man's head shot up, and he glared at Logan. "You don't have to yell at me, young man," he snapped. "I ain't so old I can't hear."

"I'm sorry. Do you have a map of the lake area?"

The man got up from his stool and pointed to a table near the window. Logan noticed a name stitched on his shirt. *Elmer.* "Maps is over there." He looked toward the large window at the front of the store. "Is it icin'? What in the world are you doin' out in this?" He stared at Logan's jacket. "FBI? What's the FBI want out here? Ain't nothin' illegal goin' on."

"Looking for someone. I don't suppose you've seen another FBI agent, have you? A woman with long black hair tied back in a ponytail?"

The old man stared at him for a moment. Logan could tell he wasn't sure what he should tell him, so he reached into his inside pocket and pulled out his creds, then waited while he looked them over.

"Okay," he said. "I guess you're the real deal." He coughed a few times and then spit into an old paint bucket behind the counter. "I didn't know she was FBI, but she was here about . . . an hour ago maybe? Lookin' for a cabin on the south side of the lake." He nodded toward the maps, then held out his hand for one. Logan picked up a copy and gave it to him.

Elmer opened it up on the counter and pointed at a spot. "She wanted old cabins, so I sent her here. There's also a couple of small houses there, but they were deserted years ago . . . I think. No one goes down there anymore. Now that I think about it, though, someone told me they seen a light comin' from one of them old properties. But I wouldn't drive down there, young man. The roads are terrible. And in this?" He pointed at the window, and Logan's eyes followed. The ice was coming down faster. "You could get stuck real easy."

"You say that area has old cabins *and* a couple of houses," Logan said. "There's a difference?"

"They all look like small houses, but only the houses have basements. Cabins might have a cellar, but that's it. 'Course, everyone calls them all cabins." His eyebrows knit together, causing even more wrinkles than the old man already had. "I'm pretty sure one of them houses was torn down a couple of years ago."

The mention of a basement got Logan's attention, although

he wasn't sure why. "Can you tell me where that house with the light might be?"

Elmer pointed to another spot on the map. "Probably on Waywind Road. That's the road I told that woman to watch for."

Logan pulled out his phone and scrolled through his photos until he came to the one he'd taken of Adam Walker's employee photo.

"What about this guy?" he asked, holding the phone up so Elmer could see it. "Do you recognize him?"

"Hmm. No, he don't look familiar."

"Thanks."

Logan was putting the phone back in his pocket when Elmer said, "Can I look at that one more time?"

"Sure." Logan retrieved his cell and reloaded the photo. He handed the phone to Elmer, who stared at the screen for several seconds.

"I ain't seen him as a man, but I think he used to live around here when he was a kid. I wouldn't have thought it was him except for this." He pointed to the scar on Walker's chin. "His family was in here once in a while to buy some of the staples I carry—milk and the like. But one time the father brought him in here and asked for antiseptic and bandages so he could treat a gash on the kid's face. Never said what happened. I told him he needed to take his kid to the hospital. Get him fixed up proper."

Elmer shook his head. "I still remember him lookin' back at his car. The woman I always assumed was the kid's mother was sittin' there starin' daggers at him. Then he said he couldn't do that." He sighed. "I gave him what I could, but I was concerned that gash weren't gonna heal right. And sure enough, it looks like it didn't if this is that kid all growed up."

"So you didn't really know the family?" Logan asked.

"Nah. I could count the number of times they stopped in here on one hand. They bought their gas somewhere else, though. I kinda worried about the kid after that gash thing. And then one day I realized they must have moved away because I hadn't seen them for a long time. Never seen them again."

"Are you pretty sure the boy you knew is this man?"

"Well, how sure can anyone be? Nah, I can't say I'd write it in blood. But if I had to bet my store on it, I'd say, yeah. It's him." He sighed. "Sorry I didn't figger it out when you first showed me the picture. It's been maybe . . . twenty years? Guess it slipped my mind."

"And you think the boy and his family lived on the lake?"

"I think so. I mean, they always came from that direction. But I don't know for sure. I ain't connected to the lake. Just run my business near it. Sorry."

"That's okay. I understand. You've been very helpful."

Logan jammed his phone back into his pocket, then paid for the map and turned to leave. But before he made it to the door Elmer called out, "Hey, FBI agent. I sure do hope the kid turned out all right. I don't think his childhood was anything to write home about."

Logan turned back and grappled with what to say. "He's certainly made an impact with his life. Went to college. Got a good job. Has a wife and two children."

Elmer nodded. "That's good. Thanks. You know, he had such sad eyes. That's somethin' I'll never forget."

Logan pushed the door open. It took effort since the wind pressed back with intensity. He hurried to the car, ice pellets stinging his face. He pulled his hood as far over his face as he could, trying to protect himself.

When he got into the car, Monty said, "You talked to that guy for quite a while. Did you learn anything helpful?"

"Yeah. Alex was here and got some directions from him. And he recognized Adam Walker from his photo. Knew him when he was a little boy, although not by name."

"Did he know where they lived?"

Logan shook his head. "No, but the few times he saw the family they came from the direction of the lake. And he mentioned a small house where someone thought they saw lights recently. We need to find it. My gut tells me that's where they lived and that's where Alex will end up."

"We need to call backup," Monty said.

"Not yet. We don't know for certain we're going to find Walker. If we're wrong and we pull people off what they're doing now . . ."

"It could be disastrous for all of us."

"Yeah. Let's find the house. See if Walker's there. If he's not, we'll find Alex and tell her we have to go back to the CP. Maybe I'm wrong about Harrison figuring out what we've done. Maybe we can just stay mum about this whole thing."

"But if Walker is there, Logan, we've got to call for backup before we go inside. If we handle this wrong, we're putting Alex and ourselves in danger. And if Walker has the virus, we could set off something more devastating than losing our careers."

Logan turned on the windshield wipers, but they just smeared the ice across the glass. He adjusted the fan to blast the windshield, and as it warmed up, a portion cleared enough for him to see the road.

"Okay," he said finally. "I'll call Harrison and tell him where we are. But if he tells us to turn around, what do we do?"

Monty turned his head and looked out his window. After a few seconds he said, "Okay. Keep going. But as soon as we either find Alex or decide there's something here that rates backup, we call it in. Agreed?"

"Agreed."

"Then let's go." Monty took a deep breath. "This is the craziest thing I've ever done. You know we could get stuck out here. Then what?"

Logan grinned at him. "We call a tow truck?"

"Not funny. Really not funny."

Logan pulled back out onto the road. He drove as slowly and carefully as he could. It wasn't long before they came to the lake. Although no streetlights were out here, they did see lights along the lake. Really nice homes sat on one side, and their lights made it possible to see the water even though it looked like a puddle of black ink in the darkness.

"There's a sign," Monty said.

Logan slowed down. He had to squint to see it through the ice now falling in sheets, but he was certain it said *Cabins*. Next to the word was an arrow pointing to the right. He consulted the map. Looked like this might lead to Waywind Road.

He held his breath as he turned the car toward whatever lay ahead.

39

Alex didn't so much drive down the dirt road that hopefully led to the cabin she was looking for as she slid her way down it. Thankfully, it was covered with small rocks that gave her just enough traction to control the car.

She passed four small cabins but saw no lights or cars. Either they were abandoned or the owners didn't think November was a good time to take a vacation. They all looked pretty rundown anyway. She finally saw a street sign. *Waywind Road*. The road that old man, Elmer, told her she should find.

After she turned, she noticed a mailbox on a pole and slowed down. It was hard to see clearly through the sleet, but there was no structure behind the mailbox. Just a concrete foundation. Obviously that place had been torn down.

She wanted to turn on the interior lights of the car in an attempt to overcome the blackness that covered her, but she fought the urge. It would make her visible to whoever might be out there—although the chances of anyone except her being out in weather like this were slim.

As she headed down an incline, her car suddenly turned sideways and slid into a ditch. Alex tried and tried to get the car out, but her tires just kept spinning. Wondering what to do, she peered down the road. She was certain she saw a light glowing from a small house. Someone was there. What should she do next?

A sense of panic started to set in. She was alone in the dark. Just like she'd been at Willow's. Visions of the first night in her aunt's house worked their way into her brain. She'd cried herself to sleep lying on the bedspread because the sheets looked dirty. Finally, she was so cold she decided to risk it and get under the covers. The bed smelled. Not like urine or anything. It just smelled dusty. Old. Like it had never been cleaned. She started to fall asleep again when something crawled up her neck and onto her cheek. She'd shrieked and brushed it away.

Then something crawled up her leg. She jumped up and ran over to the light switch. When she flipped it on, she was shocked to see roaches running across her bed. They scattered, hiding under the bed's frame. Alex stood shaking, next to the wall. Fear caused her to wet herself.

She'd pulled her suitcase out of the closet and took out clean underwear and another nightgown. After she changed, she put the soiled clothes in a zippered part of the suitcase and stuck it back in the closet. Then she spent the rest of the night shivering and crying, sitting on a chair with all the lights on, visions of her mother's body slipping into her thoughts even though she didn't want to remember. The mother she'd adored despite her shortcomings had deserted her, and now she was here. Alone and unprotected. She promised herself that when morning came, she'd take care of herself and never rely on another human being again.

"Stop it!" Alex shouted. When would she get past all that? When would she overcome these fears? A young woman's life might be at risk if she gave in to this terror that wrapped around her now like a shroud. The stakes were huge here. If Adam Walker was in that house, she might be able to thwart his plan. Her stupid fears couldn't be allowed to hinder her mission.

She checked her gun. Fully loaded. She wished she'd brought another clip, but slipping her wallet out of her satchel had been the best she could do without alerting Logan and Monty. She wasn't worried. Walker was just one man, and he wasn't trained like she was. She donned her FBI-issued jacket again, then took her knit cap out of one of its pockets and slipped it on her head. She was thankful she was wearing jeans and a thick, warm sweater. And that she'd chosen boots over pumps this morning.

She pulled up her hood, then took a deep breath and opened the car door. She struggled to get out of the ditch, slipping several times before she finally made it. Then she lowered her head and pushed against the ice that pelted her as if trying to keep her away from her destination. Her jacket was lined, but it didn't offer much protection against the bitter cold and ice crystals that felt like tiny knives flying toward her with ferocity.

It seemed to take forever to get near the house, but she finally stepped onto the property. She was right. Someone was here. The light she'd seen came from inside. Maybe a lamp. Did they have electricity for this place? She made her way to a side wall and leaned against it. Her legs felt like limp spaghetti, but she pushed herself off and inched her way toward the front of the house. She stepped lightly onto the porch and carefully looked through a window. The drapes were partly closed, but as she peered through the crack, she saw a lantern close to the back of the house. It was still too dark to make out anything, though.

She edged her way off the porch and walked around to the other side of the house, which provided more protection from the weather. She noticed a car and an SUV parked behind the house and crept near them. The car was a silver Honda Accord. The SUV had to be the vehicle he'd been using undetected—or at least one of them.

This was it. She'd found him.

After taking her phone out of her inside pocket, she discovered she still had no reception. Between the trees and the fact that she was at the bottom of a hill, there was no way a call was going out.

She put her phone back, then took out her gun. She'd started back around the house when she noticed light coming from a window near the ground. A basement window. Alex knelt to look inside, then gasped at what she saw—a large wooden table with a young woman tied to it, the only light coming from a few lanterns. A dark-haired man stood to the side, looking down at the girl. Alex couldn't see his face, but he had to be Walker.

Although the last thing she wanted to do was face the Train Man alone, she had no choice. He was going to kill that woman, and then he would begin his plan to murder even more people. She had to stop him. No one else could.

She stood and crept back to the front porch. As the ice

hammered down around her, drowning out any other noise, she quietly tried the door and was surprised to find it unlocked. She was about to push it open when something hard touched the back of her head.

"I wouldn't do that if I were you," a male voice said. "Put down your gun and kick it away, or I'll pull this trigger."

"Okay," she said. "Whatever you say."

Alex hesitated, trying to find a way out of this. If she could get him off his feet and grab his gun, she had a chance to subdue him. But if she tried that and failed, helping the woman in the basement and finding the virus would be impossible. At least Logan and Monty would know what she'd done by now. And Harrison knew about Lake Lotawana. Were they on their way? Would they get here in time?

She needed to stall. Her best move was not to provoke this guy. Make sure the woman downstairs stayed alive and hope the cavalry showed up soon. She put down her gun and kicked it away.

"Good. Now go inside. We'll join our friends in the basement."

Walker was his friend? What did that mean?

"He's had help, I see," Alex said. "We've been wondering about that."

He pushed her through the door, then stopped and put his hand on her shoulder, turning her around. This was Walker. As they'd guessed he would, he'd dyed his hair blond and grown a beard. She'd forgotten he'd probably be in disguise. To untrained eyes, he wouldn't look anything like himself, especially not with those big thick glasses.

So who was the other man? His "friend" in the basement?

"I'd appreciate it if you'd show some manners in front of my

wife and children," Walker said. He kept his gun trained on
her with one hand while with his other hand he made a wide
sweeping motion toward a couch. "This is my beautiful wife,
Sally. And these are my adorable twins, Gabby and Trey."

Alex looked around. Even in the dim light, she could see
the room was in shambles. In fact, the entire place looked
ready to collapse. Dust covered everything, including the old,
tattered couch he'd indicated. But no one was sitting there.
She looked at Walker to see if he was joking, but she found
only madness in his eyes. He was delusional. This wasn't a
man who could be bargained with, and that made him ten
times more dangerous than she'd expected. They'd profiled a
psychopath, but they hadn't anticipated his psychotic break.

Walker jabbed her with his gun. "Say hello."

"H . . . hello," she said to no one, keeping her eyes trained
on the couch. "It's very nice to meet you."

Only silence returned to her, and Walker jabbed her again.
"Answer my wife's question," he growled.

"I'm sorry. The sound of the ice is so loud, it makes it hard
to hear."

Walker sighed with exasperation. "She asked if you came
here to hurt us."

"No, Mrs. Walker. I only came to help the girl downstairs.
I have no intention of hurting your husband. Or you and the
children. I would never do that."

Walker grabbed her arm and twisted her around until he
could peer into her eyes. "That girl is the last sacrifice. You
can't have her. I have a destiny, and no one will keep me
from it. Do you understand?"

"Yes. Yes, I understand." She cleared her throat. The dust
floating up from the floor was beginning to choke her. "But

isn't she innocent? I mean, what if she were your daughter? Wouldn't you want her protected? She has parents. People who love her."

Walker drew back his hand and hit Alex in the face so hard she fell to the floor. "Sally, take the children to the playroom," he said. "I think they've seen enough."

Alex put her hand up to her face, then brought it away. Blood. She felt her jaw. Two of her bottom teeth were loose.

Walker paused for a moment as if listening to someone. "I love you too, darling. And thank you. I'm just doing what the Master asked of me."

Alex looked up to see Walker smile. His break was complete, and she was in real trouble. She tried to get to her feet when something ran across her hand. A roach.

She fought back a scream. Her nightmare was becoming reality.

40

alker reached down and yanked her to her feet. "Great. Now you've got blood on my nice carpet. Sally will have to clean up after you." He dragged her into the kitchen. Alex gagged at the sight of it. Old food on the counters. Crusted dishes in the sink. Roaches ran everywhere. She could see them by the light of the lantern sitting on an old table.

"Please," she said, hating the pleading in her voice. "Please. I can't . . . I can't . . ."

"Shut up," Walker snapped. He reached toward an empty paper towel dispenser. "Wipe off your face with this."

As he spoke, a roach ran up his other arm and sat on his shoulder. Alex's body convulsed with terror, but she reached for his empty hand, then pretended to wipe her mouth.

"Th . . . thank you," she choked out.

He smiled, his empty eyes burning with lunacy. "That's better." He transferred the gun to his other hand and scratched his shoulder, which sent the roach scrambling. It disappeared behind him. "My wife keeps an immaculate house, but there's something here I must be allergic to." He shook his head. "Makes me itch." He put the gun back in his left hand. Walker was indeed left-handed, just like the Train Man. Not that the confirmation would help her now.

Walker pointed to an open door in the kitchen. "Let's go downstairs. I want you to witness the final sacrifice. It's an honor to force an angel to watch the war begin."

"I'm . . . I'm not an angel," Alex said. "You've made a mistake."

"Don't lie to me!" he screamed. He held the gun over her head and moved closer to her.

Alex tried to think. Tried to come up with a plan to deal with him, but her mind was fuzzy. Fear had her in its grip. She forced herself to look away from the roaches scampering over the dirty dishes and filthy counters. She got a quick glimpse into a bedroom. An old bed, also layered in dust, was the only piece of furniture.

"I'm sorry," she forced herself to say. "I am an angel. You know that some of us will survive the war. I . . . I think I'm one of those."

His eyes narrowed. "We'll see, won't we?" He gestured toward the door with the gun. "Go."

Alex walked slowly. She didn't want to go down there. She'd be trapped, and it would be much harder to get away. But she had no choice. Besides, the girl was there. If she had a chance to save her, she had to take it.

As she reached the stairs, another roach ran across her boot. She grabbed the side of the doorframe to steady herself, chiding herself for her unreasonable fear. She was an

FBI agent. Trained. Valuable. Smart. She couldn't allow her training to evaporate because of a stupid bug. It was beyond ridiculous.

Even as she tried to convince herself she could handle this, a voice in her mind told her she was in way over her head. The horror of her childhood couldn't be reasoned away so easily. She could feel the beginnings of a panic attack, and she began to gasp as she fought to breathe. Dizziness tried to overtake her, and she knew she was going to faint. But if she fell down the stairs, she could be seriously injured . . . or killed.

It took every bit of inner strength she had to put her foot on the first step leading to the basement and to try to calm down. As she took the next step, she prayed to a God she wanted to believe in. She would give Him her life if He could help her now. But that would take a miracle.

Slowly the dizziness began to recede, and she was able to catch her breath. She paused on the stairs as the fog in her brain started to evaporate. Then she clearly heard a voice say, *Just trust me. Everything will be all right.* Alex looked back at Walker, who glared at her. Who had spoken to her? Was she having a psychotic break too? This was the second time she'd heard a voice. Was it possible—

"Hurry up," Walker said. "No one can help you. You can go down the stairs on your own, or I can push you the rest of the way. Like my father pushed my mother before he killed her, just like I killed my first five sacrifices. With a knife. Just like I'll kill this one."

So this was where Walker's mother died. When Alex reached the bottom of the stairs, she focused on the woman tied to the table. She turned to look at Alex, her eyes wide with terror. A piece of duct tape covered her mouth.

Then her own eyes shifted to the man she'd seen through the basement window. He was still standing near the table, his back to her and Walker. When he didn't turn around, Walker said, "That woman whose picture you showed me? She's the one we heard prowling around outside. I've got her."

"I see," the man said. "I'm sorry you decided to join us, Alex."

She recognized the voice even before he turned around. Mike.

"This is nuts," Monty said. "We're gonna get stuck. Our phones probably won't work. We're going to freeze to death out here in the middle of nowhere."

Logan glanced at him. "Remind me never to come to you when I need encouragement, okay?"

Monty didn't answer, just kept his eyes on the road in front of them. A mile or so back, they'd switched places because Logan wanted to keep an eye on the map himself.

"You can get out here if you'd like, Monty. I can drive again."

"You're really funny. Ha, ha, ha."

Although he wouldn't admit it, Logan had to agree with his negative friend. This was looking worse and worse. Monty slowed down as a mailbox was reflected in the car's head-lights, which were now set on bright. It didn't take long to see there was no house here. Was this a fool's errand? Logan was just thinking maybe they should go back and call for help when he saw an old street sign that said *Waywind Road.*

"Look," he said to Monty. "There's the road the old man told me to take." Monty slowed the car, although it continued a few yards after he touched the brake. "Let's go down this road a little way. If we don't see anything, we'll turn around and drive until we have cell service or we make it back to that convenience store."

"If it's still open. It's getting pretty late."

"I'm thinking Elmer lives there. I noticed an area behind the store with lights on. If he's closed up, we'll knock on his windows until he lets us in. Then we'll use his phone to call Harrison and ask for help."

"Okay. But we can't drive too far down this road. We could get so stuck we might not be able to get out."

"We won't go too far. I promise that if we don't see a house with lights on, we'll go back."

Monty shrugged. Logan knew he was worried. He was concerned too, but he couldn't just leave Alex out here.

Monty put the car in gear and turned down Waywind Road.

Harrison tried again to reach Alex, but the number went immediately to voice mail. Frustrated, he called Logan and then Monty. The same thing. He'd received Logan's voice mail message and was worried.

He'd come back to the CP after the operation with the KCPD. They had no idea if they'd prevented Walker from kidnapping a woman for his last sacrifice. They'd shown up at most of the town's churches with Sunday evening meetings, making sure they were seen in an attempt to scare him off. Then after the meetings, they showed Walker's photo to the people leaving, but no one remembered him. One woman at a large church said he looked slightly familiar, but she couldn't be sure. She didn't have enough information to help them.

Every law enforcement officer in the area had a photo of Walker and a sketch of what he might look like now, but no one had seen him. Harrison hoped they'd at least been successful in deterring the monster, but there was no way to know.

Logan had said they were taking the rest of the day off, but he would have left his phone on. They all would. What if they'd taken Alex's suggestion seriously? Ice from the storm was coating the area, and road conditions were dangerous. If they'd defied him and gone to Lake Lotawana trying to find that cabin, they could be in serious trouble.

He stared at the dry-erase board. What if Walker really was in a cabin out there? These agents were trained behavioral analysts. Maybe they were right. He picked up the phone and called the police chief. If he was going down dirt roads in the dark while an ice storm raged, he wanted SWAT with him.

Alex couldn't believe her eyes. "I don't understand," she said slowly, horrified to feel tears filling her eyes. Mike was her friend. How could he be involved with something like this? And why hadn't she seen it?

"You're probably wondering if I'm part of the Circle. I am. And you're why I joined," Mike said. His expression changed from one she recognized to one filled with rage. "You left," he said, clearly angry. "You just left. Not a word before you took off. If we'd really been friends, you would have told me you were leaving and where you were going. But apparently I wasn't worth the time."

She had to think quickly. What was the best way to handle this? "I'm sorry, Mike. I didn't want Willow to know where I was. I . . . I just wanted a new life away from her. I realize I should have told you. I didn't mean to hurt you. I was just so . . . confused."

"You thought I'd tell her where you were? I did everything I could to help you. I even got you a gun."

"I know. You're right. I wasn't thinking."

"Willow was really upset when you left. You always had her wrong, you know. She might have been a little different, but she wasn't a bad person."

"She stood over my bed with a knife. You know that. What kind of human being does that to her niece?"

"The rest of the time she was kind to you."

Alex realized this argument was going nowhere. Willow hadn't been *kind* to her. But Alex couldn't show her anger now. She didn't want to set Mike off.

"Look, I should have talked to you before I left. I really am sorry. You were a good friend. In fact, you were my only friend. I was wrong."

"I'm glad you two are having such a nice reunion," Walker said loudly, "but we have something important to do here. Let's get on with it."

"Mike, are you really going to let him kill this innocent woman? The Mike I knew would never have allowed something like that."

"The Mike you knew is gone, Alex. I visited Willow often over the years, at first to comfort her, then just because I cared about her. Around ten years ago she finally told me about the Circle. I joined, and it's brought fulfillment to my life."

"So you and Jimmy Gedrose really never met?"

"He'd just left the Circle when I joined, which might be one of the reasons Willow finally decided to recruit me. He visited her a lot after he quit, but I made sure our paths never crossed. He was helping your aunt, but he was no longer part of our group."

He cocked his head toward Walker. "Adam had been to Willow's Circle meeting not long before Jimmy left, which was how Jimmy recognized his photo. But I didn't meet Adam until a few years ago, through a wider Circle connection. He intrigued me. Later, he convinced me he was called to fulfill the prophecy. I wanted to be part of that. Something important."

She frowned at him. "But you're an FBI agent. That's something important."

He shook his head, and his eyes narrowed. "I'm stuck in a resident agency in Wichita. I tried and tried to get transferred somewhere else, get a promotion, but I was told I'd gone as far as I was ever going to go. Then Adam gave me an opportunity to be involved in something . . . magnificent. I could finally be someone."

"But you have great parents. You were brought up in a good home. Why—"

Mike laughed, but there was no joy in it. "If you'd stayed in touch with me, you'd know my father didn't die in an automobile accent. The truth is he got a girlfriend and walked out. I have no idea where he is, and I don't care. Mom died a few years ago, way too young and way too lonely."

Alex knew what it was like to be abandoned by a father. This time her regret was real. "Oh, Mike. I'm so, so sorry. I should have been there for you."

"I don't need your pity. I don't need anything from you." He glared at her.

She had to try one more time to reason with him. "Why are you working with this man? You say you cared about Willow. But he killed her. And Nettie. Or at least had someone else do it. Now he wants to kill thousands or millions of people. Please help me stop him."

Walker stepped up next to her.

"I'm the Train Man, little lady. The Destroyer. I was called to offer six sacrifices, not kill anyone else. That would derail the prophecy." He laughed, no doubt at the use of the word *derail*. "So you're right. Someone else killed those women."

"Who?" Alex asked. Then she was struck with a terrible truth, and it made her feel numb.

Mike just smiled.

41

Harrison cursed and clicked off his phone. Dealing with bureaucrats was his least favorite part of the job. Calls to the mayor and city administrator were a waste of time. All they'd done was give him the number of the Lake Lotawana Association president. Maybe neither of them had ever been to the lake. Either that, or they were afraid they might have to leave their warm homes and venture out into the storm.

He called the number, preparing himself for another dead end. But when the president of the association answered, he was encouraged. Marge Meadows was not only an expert on the area around the lake but it was clear she also wanted to help.

"The place you're looking for might be the old house on Waywind Road we plan to tear down in the spring. It's become an eyesore after being deserted years ago. It's the only one I think anyone could be squatting in."

After getting directions from her, Harrison phoned the SWAT commander, who was waiting for instructions. "We'll meet you at the entrance to the south side of the lake," Harrison told him.

"Okay. But why don't you ride with us? Our rescue vehicle can handle the ice. You'll be safer."

Harrison didn't need to be convinced. He was grateful and accepted the commander's invitation. "We'll also need a containment device in case we find the missing virus sample," he said. "Better suit up your guys appropriately."

There was a silence from the other end of the phone. Then the commander said, "That will take us longer to prepare."

"I don't know how much time we have. Can you hustle?"

Another brief silence. Then the commander said, "I understand."

Harrison sighed as he disconnected the call. He wasn't sure whether he needed to discipline the BAU team or thank them. If he'd listened to them, he and the SWAT team would have headed out to the lake hours ago. It's possible he'd made a huge mistake. If he had, how many people would have to pay the price for his blunder?

As he headed for the door, his phone rang again. After hearing what the person on the other end had to say, he called the SWAT commander back.

"Look," Logan said as they inched their way down Waywind Road. "It's a car in the ditch." As they got closer, Logan grew excited. "It's Alex's."

Monty pulled up next to the car and Logan got out. Had Alex been injured? A quick look told him the car was empty.

As he headed back to the SUV, he stopped and stared down the road. Even though it was hard to see through the falling ice, he could make out a light. It looked like a house.

"There's a house up the road," he said to Monty as he got back into the car. "Let's check it out. If she's not there, we'll go back to the CP. Okay?"

"We're in it this far, we might as well go all the way," Monty said in a low voice. "But if we get stuck out here and freeze to death, I'm coming back to haunt you."

"I don't think your plan will work. I'd be dead too—"

"Oh, shut up." Monty shook his head. "I never want to be paired with you again, you know."

"You don't mean that." Logan smiled. "You can't help but like me. I'm a lovable human being."

In spite of himself, Monty laughed. "Okay, lovable human being. Once more into the fray . . ."

"You know the rest of that poem from *The Grey*, right? From that film?"

Monty nodded. "'Into the last good fight I'll ever know. Live and die on this day. Live and die on this day.'"

"Let's live, okay?"

"Okay. Sounds good."

Monty put the SUV in gear and started for the house.

Mike forced Alex into a chair. He pulled a gun out of his waistband and trained it on her. "Sit there and don't move. If you do, I will shoot you. I won't hesitate for even a second. Do you understand me?"

Alex nodded, then looked the room over, trying to find a way out. She wasn't going to just sit there and watch this girl die. The poor thing hadn't taken her eyes off Alex ever since she'd walked into the room.

"Secure her," Walker said to Mike. "I don't trust her."

"My handcuffs are upstairs," Mike said. "I don't think I should leave you alone with her."

"I'm the Train Man," Walker shouted. "I can keep her here."

"But if you kill her, she'll have to be the sacrifice," Mike said evenly.

Alex could tell he was trying to placate Walker. Keep him calm.

"You can't let that happen," Walker said, his eyes wild. "We're so close to the end."

"Then let's get on with it."

"Wait a minute," Alex said. She'd been trying to discern whom she should manipulate, and now she decided Walker was the better choice. He was psychotic and delusional, but if she appealed to his ego, he might be more willing to listen to her. His own sense of importance was driving him now. On the other hand, Mike was fueled by zeal and anger. A dangerous combination. He was more likely to respond with violence.

"What?" Walker said, his tone almost that of a petulant child. "No more delays. The world is waiting for me to fulfill the prophecy."

"I can't figure out how you intend to spread the virus to a third of the world," Alex said quickly. "It's impossible, you know. It will be contained before it gets out of hand. You'll never be able to pull this off."

Walker's expression turned to one of superiority. He looked at Alex as if she were just too simple to understand his exceptional mental acuity.

"Don't listen to her," Mike said. "She's trying to stall you."

"Don't be ridiculous," Walker said. "She obviously came alone. If the police knew about this place, they'd be here already. Good thing they didn't follow you after you took the virgin."

Alex stared at Mike. "*You* kidnapped this girl? The police were looking for Walker. Not you. Not an FBI agent."

"You're right," Walker said, cackling. "I located her, but Mike brought her here. We've fooled you all along the way."

"But you killed the five victims, right?" she said to Walker.

"Yes," he said. "I had to do it for the prophecy to come to pass."

"And you have to kill this girl so you can release the virus. And the Circle supports this?" Alex asked. "They believe you're the Destroyer?"

Walker's face transformed to an image of uncontrolled rage. "They're weak. They don't want anything to do with the prophecy. They're false!" He pointed at Mike. "That's why we're working together. We know the truth."

Alex needed to calm him down again. She needed information in case backup came. Knowing Walker could be killed, she wanted to know where the virus was and what he had done already. "So explain it to me. How are you going to do this? There's no way one sample can infect so many people. You would have to design an incredible plan to make this work."

Walker smiled as he walked toward her. "You just don't get it, do you? I'm the Train Man. The Destroyer. I've been chosen. The Master guides me with his strength and wisdom. I know what I'm doing. My friend in Ethiopia created a strain of the Zaire Ebola virus so powerful that it takes very little to infect one person. And it's so contagious that one can spread it to a hundred."

"Not everyone has a hundred friends," Alex said. She tried to keep her tone level. She didn't want to make Walker think she was making fun of him. That would really set him off.

"They don't have to." When Walker laughed, his high-pitched tone was almost feminine. "You see, this strain is airborne. All anyone has to do once they have it is . . . breathe."

"Ebola isn't an airborne virus."

"But this one is. After this last sacrifice, I intend to infect people in airports, train stations, even hospitals. My friend Mike has already proved that anyone can easily infiltrate a hospital. Once we infect patients, the nurses, doctors, everyone there will be contaminated too. And each time they treat a patient—"

Although she wanted to keep Walker talking, at the mention of hospitals, rage toward Mike flared inside her. "Why did you kill Nettie?" she spit out at him, unable to keep the anger out of her voice. But then she sat back almost in defeat. "My aunt too. You said she was your friend."

"But she didn't protect The Book. She showed it to Nettie. And then Nettie gave it to you." He shrugged. "They both had to be punished."

Although Alex accepted that Mike believed what he was saying, she realized his rage wasn't for Willow and Nettie. It was for her. And not just because she'd left Wichita without telling him she was going. It was because he wanted to "be someone," like he said. Alex had been promoted to the BAU. It was an honor to work for one of the FBI's most elite divisions. But Mike had been belittled by someone at the

FBI. Told he would never be promoted. Instead of blaming himself, he'd turned his fury toward Alex.

It was her fault. That explained his frenzy, his anger, when he killed Willow and tried to kill Nettie. It also explained why he'd written her name on the wall. Even though she was certain he didn't know why he'd done it, she did. He'd written the name of the person he blamed for the murders he'd just committed. In Mike's twisted mind, Alex was to blame for everything he did. The reason he was acting out.

Alex forced herself to turn her attention back to Walker. He was the one she feared the most. "You said something about doctors and nurses becoming infected. But when they become sick, won't they stay away from patients?"

Walker stared at her as if she were pitifully stupid. "The virus has an incubation period. It can take two days before symptoms appear. Just think how many people can be af-fected in that time. And airline passengers take the virus to all different places and countries." He shook his head. "I'm sure you can see the brilliance of my plan."

Alex kept listening for any sound from upstairs that told her help had arrived. Nothing. Was she hoping for something that wasn't going to happen? "How are you going to infect people?" she asked. "You can't just walk up to someone and say, 'Excuse me, may I inject you with a virus that may kill you?'"

"This is taking too long," Mike snapped. "Come on. I'd like to get out of here someday."

"I don't think you're going anywhere for a while," Alex told him. "There's ice everywhere. My car went off the road. Yours will too."

"My SUV is equipped with snow tires. I'll get out of here without any trouble."

"Be quiet," Walker said to Mike. He was basking in the attention he was receiving from Alex. He wanted to share his brilliance, a characteristic of serial killers. They needed to feel special, and they wanted everyone to know how smart they were.

He walked over to a wooden shelf attached to one of the basement walls and picked up a box. It looked like a package waiting to be mailed. He set it down on the edge of the table where the girl remained tied down and muzzled.

"Let me show you something that will answer all your questions." He lifted the wrapped lid off the rest of the box. Then he tilted it so Alex could see inside. Some kind of cylinder was held in place by padded supports.

"There's a button hidden here. When I press it"—he turned the package and pushed a spot on the side, making the tip of a needle pop out—"the virus will be loaded into this syringe. All I have to do is bump into someone. They probably won't even feel it. If they do, they'll think they were bitten by a bug. I'll be walking away, looking completely innocent. And that's all it takes."

Alex swallowed hard. His plan was ingenious. And the worst part was that it would work. She didn't know what to say.

"I can tell you're impressed," Walker said. "You know what? I'm going to let you be part of the prophecy. You say you're one of the angels that will rule with me someday? Let's find out."

He giggled like a girl and then walked over to something that looked like an ice cream freezer. He took some gloves from a box on another shelf next to it. "This is a medical freezer for storing vaccines." He lifted the lid and reached in. "I've already prepared one of the syringes I'll be using for my holy mission." He pulled up a syringe with something inside it. "Only a little bit of the virus is added to this liquid, but it's enough to kill thousands of people. And I can make hundreds of these vials."

He walked toward Alex. "Lift her sleeve, Mike."

"No!" Alex tried to stand, but Mike pushed her down on the chair hard. She began to fight with everything in her. They'd have to kill her before she'd allow Walker to inject her.

"Stop it!" he yelled.

She started to rise again, but then she thought she heard a noise upstairs. "Help!" she yelled. Before she had a chance to call out again, Walker was shoving the needle into her arm, and then he pushed the plunger.

42

ogan had opened the front door as quietly as he could, but when he heard Alex yell, he moved quickly through the house, his gun drawn. Monty followed behind him.

Then he heard a scream coming from somewhere in the kitchen and found an open door. He hurried down the stairs and was surprised to be greeted by Mike Monroe, who pointed a gun at his chest. Logan started to lower his weapon, but then Alex yelled, "Shoot him!"

Logan pulled the trigger twice, and Mike fell. Logan shifted his gaze to a disguised Walker, who smiled at him. He walked around a large table and stood over a woman tied to it.

"Thank you for being here," he said. "I'm so happy you'll get to see the beginning of a war that will kill millions. But don't worry, angels. I'll ask the Master to allow you to live. You can reign with us."

He picked up a dagger and slowly raised it over the terrified woman. "Washed in the blood of the Lamb—and now her own," he said.

"Put it down!" Logan said.

Walker looked at him as if he couldn't understand what he was saying. Then he raised his eyes toward the ceiling. "Behold the last sacrifice, Master."

Before he could bring down the dagger, Logan shot him in the head. Walker looked surprised. As if he couldn't accept what had happened. Then he fell backward to the floor.

Alex shouted as he turned to look at her. "Logan, he's got the virus in a syringe. It can't break. The pathogen is airborne!"

He stepped to the other side of the table and looked around. Then he moved to the area of the basement where the syringe must have rolled. He stood and looked at Alex. "Too late," he said. He looked around and found a metal bucket, then covered the broken syringe with it.

"You're all probably safe for the moment." He pointed at Monty, who was standing near the stairs. "Get them out quick," he said. "Drive back toward that convenience store. As soon as you have cell service, call Harrison. Tell him I've been exposed."

"But—"

"Just do it, Monty. Okay?"

"Okay." Monty took a knife out of his pocket and cut the girl free. She pulled the tape off her mouth. "Thank you, thank you," she said, crying. "I prayed God would send someone to help me and you came."

Monty took off his jacket and put it over her shoulders as she sat up. "Let's get going. Come on," he said to Alex. But she didn't move.

"Did you hear me?" he shouted. "We've got to get out of here while we still have a chance."

"Monty, go," Alex said. "It's too late for me. Please. You may be our only hope for survival. Go."

"All right, all right," he said. "Just don't die."

"We'll do our best," Logan said.

Once Monty and the girl were gone, Logan turned to look at Alex. "What do you mean, it's too late for you?"

"Walker injected me right before you came downstairs."

"But you said it's airborne."

Alex smiled. "I think sticking it directly into my body works too." She shook her head. "I'm not sure they got out in time, you know."

"I know. Monty knows that too. He'll be careful and tell Harrison when he talks to him."

Logan sat down on the floor next to Alex's chair. She hadn't moved from it. He leaned his back against the wall.

"By the way, I'm pretty sure you'll find Agnes Walker under the floor somewhere," she said.

"Did he tell you that?"

"No, but I think his mother *was* living here when she died, probably at the hands of his father. Adam had to perform the sixth sacrifice in a holy place. If this is the room where his mother died, it probably qualifies in some twisted way."

"That sounds right."

"Small comfort," Alex said.

Logan shrugged. "Gotta take what we can get." He smiled at her.

He watched her face change as a roach ran out from beneath the cold, dead furnace in the corner of the room. Logan could see she was horrified. "It's just a bug, Alex. It can't hurt you."

"It's just . . . when I moved in with Willow, her house was infested with roaches. I . . . I hate them."

Logan had the distinct feeling there was more to the story, but he wasn't going to ask her about it now. "Just try to ignore them. We'll be out of here soon and in a nice, sterile hospital room."

She was silent for a moment. For the first time, he noticed the only light came from a couple of lanterns, and the flames were getting low. He watched as Alex scanned the floor, no doubt looking for bugs.

"What happened before we got here?" he asked, trying to get her focus off the roaches—especially since more and more would come out as it got darker.

"Walker thought he lived here with his family, but I don't think Sally and the kids ever existed. He experienced a complete psychotic break."

Logan was surprised. "So this whole family thing was only in his imagination?"

Alex nodded. "He found an identity through the Train Man and a calling as the Destroyer, but he still yearned for a family. The kind of family he never had. He was too damaged to obtain a real one, so he created his vision of the perfect wife and children. He had to break with reality to find happiness." She sighed. "I wish we could have kept him alive. Gotten him help. Maybe he could have found some kind of fulfillment in the real world."

Logan couldn't help but look at Adam's body only a few yards away. He wanted to move him so they didn't have to see him, but he couldn't. It would be tampering with evidence.

And he couldn't cover the body. Anything not completely clean could leave fibers and false evidence. Although the cause of Walker's death was obvious, he still couldn't go against his training and contaminate the scene.

"Sorry about Mike," he said, looking at Alex.

"Yeah, me too." Her voice broke, and she turned her face away from him.

He didn't know what to say, so he stayed silent.

"He blamed me for what he did. He killed Willow and Nettie." When she looked down at him, he saw tears in her eyes. "He was angry when I left without telling him. Then for some reason he tried to become the person I wanted to be by joining the FBI. But when he was never promoted, he became enraged about my success. Enraged with me. And then he joined the Circle and met Walker. . . ."

She shuddered. "It's my fault. He was a friend, and I shouldn't have left Willow's without telling him I was leaving and where I'd be. But I just wanted to get away from there. Away from her. I guess Mike thought we were closer than I did. If I could go back in time . . ."

"But you can't. And it's not your fault." He looked up at her. "Look, Alex. You, Adam, and Mike all experienced bad things. Especially Adam and you. But you all had choices to make. To give in to the hurt and pain and let it twist you or to fight back. To become something good. Someone who would add positive energy to the world. Adam had a terrible childhood, but he could have made a different choice. Mike was hurt that you left. He must have idolized you and wanted to become like you. He couldn't. But I suspect other things in his life went wrong too."

Alex told him what Mike said about his parents.

"I'm sorry to hear that." Logan sighed. "But it was still his choice to follow a dark path." He gazed up into her eyes. "Why did Adam and Mike go one way while you went another way?"

"Because some of us are angels and some of us are demons?" Alex's sardonic grin told him she was trying to be humorous. It worked. He laughed.

"Funny. But I'm being serious. No one *has* to choose a destructive path. God gave us free will. We choose. God addresses this in the Bible. Forgive me for paraphrasing, but it goes something like 'I've set before you life and death, blessing and cursing. Choose life that both you and your descendants may live.' That passage goes on to talk about how we can choose to love God or we can reject Him. He was talking to the children of Israel, but He still gives everyone that choice. What Mike did is not your fault, Alex. Blaming yourself is destructive. Stop doing that."

Alex leaned her head back on the chair and looked up.

The lantern began to sputter.

"I can't walk over there and add fuel to the lantern," he said quietly. "Can't tamper with—"

"The crime scene. I know." She stared down at him, her eyes locked on his. "Logan, I heard a voice."

"A voice?"

"Yes. It said, 'Just trust me. Everything will be all right.'"

Logan smiled at her. "Who do you think that was?"

"I know you want me to say it was God, but everything isn't going to be all right, is it? We're going to die." She started to cry. "I keep thinking about Krypto. What will happen to him? Will he think I abandoned him?"

Logan reached up and put his hand on her cheek. "I don't

believe we're going to die. We have no idea what this virus will do. Alex, if God told you we'll be all right, then I believe Him. He would know."

She finally looked away from him. "Okay" was all she said.

The lantern finally went out. Although he knew it was a risk, Logan reached for her hand. She didn't pull away. Instead, she held on so tightly it almost hurt.

"I . . . I hate the dark."

"Nothing can hurt you. I'm here. You'll be fine."

Logan leaned his head back against the wall again. How long would it take Monty to get help?

"Did you hear that?" Alex said.

"No, I—"

Then he heard steps overhead. Two men came down the stairs in hazmat suits. They held flashlights and swung them around until they found Alex and Logan. Alex quickly pulled her hand from his.

"Where is it?" one of them asked, his voice muffled by the mask.

Logan stood. "On the other side of the table," he said. "Under a bucket. We've both been exposed. And you need to check the other agent and the kidnap victim."

The men walked to the other side of the table. One of them took something out of a pack he wore around his waist. His partner had his flashlight directed toward him as he opened a small box and knelt down on the floor. Logan wanted out of that room, but he knew they would have to be escorted carefully so as not to expose anyone else. At least there would be no pandemic. Hopefully, this vicious virus would stop with him and Alex. He prayed silently for Monty and the girl who'd been abducted.

Logan wanted to look at Alex, to take her hand again. But he couldn't do it. She was trying to be strong. He needed to be strong too. To help her. Right now, he kept thinking about what he would say to his family. How could he tell them he'd been infected with a deadly virus? They'd all made it through COVID-19. Now this. At least they all had a strong faith. His mother was an intercessor. She spent more time on her knees than anyone he'd ever known.

Comfort and peace settled over him.

After what seemed like an eternity, the man looking at the broken vial stood, then nodded at his partner, who moved to the bottom of the stairs. He took off his hood, mask, and breathing apparatus, then called up to someone. "Come on down."

"You shouldn't do that," Logan said to the man, shocked. "You can't be sure you're safe in here."

"I'm fine."

Then the other guy removed his gear too. He lifted fuel and matches from a nearby shelf. Dumbfounded, Logan watched as he filled one of the lanterns and then lit it. He was just about to ask what was happening when someone came down the stairs.

Harrison.

"Sir, what's going on?" Logan asked.

"This virus could be dangerous," Alex added. "You all need to—"

"It's inactive," Harrison said. "There's no danger."

"What do you mean?" Logan asked. "I don't understand."

"I'll explain it to you later. Just know you're not in danger." He looked at Alex. "You're going to the hospital, though. You too, Logan. Just to be safe."

Logan didn't know what to say. He looked at Alex, who had a strange smile on her face.

43

One week later

Alex shoved her packed bag into the rental car's trunk, thinking about how eager she was to sleep in her own bed. She also couldn't wait to see Krypto again. This was the longest she'd been away from him.

She returned to her hotel room to check it one more time. She was worried she might forget something. After going through all the drawers and cabinets and looking under the furniture, she was finally satisfied.

She touched her cracked jaw. It still hurt, but it was mending. Those loose teeth had to be removed, and two brand-new implants took their place. Amazing how quickly the specialist could do that, but they looked great.

Trying to cover the bruising on her face with makeup, she was only partially successful. That was okay too. This ordeal could have turned out much, much worse. Besides, the discoloration was fading.

She turned off the light, closed the door, and took the elevator down to the lobby. Logan and Monty were waiting for her. They'd hung around for the week, but now they were all ready to go home.

When the three of them reached the CP, she noticed only a few cars were in the parking lot. Inside, they found most of the equipment gone too. About a dozen people were busy taking down the rest. Harrison was sitting at his desk. That would be the last thing to go.

He waved them over. "Find some chairs and have a seat," he said.

Logan grabbed two folding chairs pushed against the wall, and Monty found a chair behind an abandoned desk. He scooted it over and offered it to Alex.

"I'm fine," she said with a smile. "I don't think sitting on something padded will help my jaw."

"Just trying to be a gentleman," he said with a wink. He sat down and found himself several inches higher than Alex and Logan. He reached under the seat and hit the adjustment pedal. In seconds, he was level with them.

Harrison sat back in his own chair and studied them. "Everyone okay?" he asked.

"We're fine," Logan said. "Finding out you're going to live after you think you've been exposed to a deadly pathogen tends to put things in perspective."

Harrison smiled. "I understand. I wish we'd known the virus Walker had was inert sooner. It would have saved us all some worry."

"So Martin Kirabo didn't send a deadly virus to Walker after all," Alex said. "Why? Conscience?"

"No. Somehow the Circle found out about the plan and

ordered Kirabo to send an inactive sample to Walker but still convince him it was a virulent superbug. I can only guess that they wanted him to fail as a way of punishing him for operating without their oversight."

"But why did Kirabo kill himself?" Monty asked.

"Because he believed Walker was the Destroyer and he'd failed him and ruined the prophecy?" Alex said, directing her question to Harrison.

"Bingo. As we were assembling the SWAT team for our run out to the lake, I got a call. A second letter from Kirabo had turned up, and it went into more detail. He spelled out everything and asked his wife to contact the FBI for help. He was afraid his family might be in danger. Afraid the Circle would decide to exact revenge on a member who'd been willing to carry out such an act without their blessing."

Harrison sighed. "We actually have the Circle to thank for possibly saving thousands or millions of people around the world in case Walker had been successful. That just feels . . . wrong."

"So his wife found the second letter?" Logan asked.

"Yes. Kirabo put it in his filing cabinet at home with a folder that held his insurance policy. He knew she would look for it after his death. Sure enough, she found it and contacted us. She had no idea he was involved in the Circle. She didn't even know what it was."

"What happens to her and to their children?" Alex asked.

"We're bringing them here. They'll go into witness protection. New identities. New lives."

"Good. What worries me is that the Circle still has a prophecy to see fulfilled," Monty said. "What will they do in the future to make it come to pass?"

Harrison leaned back in his chair. "We're learning more and more about this cult. The Circle believes they're destined to take over the world. Though most call themselves angels, not demons, we believe that in its deepest recesses, the Circle is still dangerous. After all, it doesn't seem like they did anything to stop Walker or Monroe from killing people. For one thing, that tells us they weren't happy with Willow LeGrand and Nettie Travers either. The Bureau is setting up a task force to track down members, but they're so secretive it will take a long time to really put a chink in their armor. Your friend Jimmy Gedrose has been very helpful. He may be able to assist us in ending the Circle for good. We've hurt them, but we haven't destroyed them."

Alex wasn't sure what information Jimmy was giving the FBI, but she was pleased he'd turned out to be an important resource.

Harrison smiled. "You should know we've asked the WPD to take another look at that drug money charge against Jimmy. It doesn't pass the smell test. It was a long time ago, but if we can clear his name . . ."

He leaned forward. "Changing the subject, sorry about sending those guys downstairs in hazmat suits, but we had to be sure. Couldn't take a chance that Kirabo was lying about that sample."

"Not a problem," Logan said. "Facing imminent death from time to time keeps us on our toes."

Harrison chuckled. "I'm glad we could help. Oh, we did find Agnes Walker's body in that basement."

"I thought that might happen," Alex said. "Adam's father taught him well."

Harrison nodded. "Sad but true. What about your aunt's

house?" he asked her. "Are you going back to Wichita to clean it out?"

"No. I already hired a realtor there. She knows a company that sets up auctions. She'll oversee selling Willow's few possessions as well as her house. Most of the furnishings were Nettie's, though, and her relatives will come for those."

"All right. And when we're through with The Book your aunt owned?"

"Destroy it."

Harrison grunted. "You know we can't do that. It's yours. If you want it destroyed, you'll have to do it yourself."

Logan leaned toward her and said, "I'll help set up the bonfire."

"Me too," Monty said with a smile. "We'll roast hot dogs over it."

Alex smiled. "Sounds good."

"By the way," Harrison said, "we found Walker's copy in the basement. Hidden inside that old furnace. The utilities had been off in that house for years, making it a safe place to stash it. So now we have our own copy of The Book. We want to keep this one. Might help us if we come up against the Circle again."

He stood. "Keith is waiting at the airport. Let's get you out of here."

"I figured we'd be flying commercial," Logan said.

"I think you all need to get home as soon as possible. You've been through a lot. We'll ignore protocol this time." Harrison shook hands with each of them.

An hour later they were in the air, heading back to Quantico. Alex sat across from Logan. Monty had taken a seat in the back, and Logan noticed he'd fallen asleep minutes after takeoff.

"So it seems your voice was right," Logan said.

Alex nodded. "I can't stop thinking about that."

"Have you come to any decisions?"

"I still have a lot of questions."

"You can ask me anything, but I'm not sure I'll have all the answers." He sighed. "We're used to facts. Evidence. But God wants us to come to Him in faith."

"In other words, I'm supposed to believe in someone I can't see. What proof is there that He's really out there? That He cares about us? And what about the evil in the world? How do you explain that?"

Logan laughed and held up his hand like a cop stopping traffic. "Look, I'm not a Bible scholar. These are great questions. Give them to God. Read the Bible for yourself. You'll find your answers, and they'll come from Him. That way you'll know you can trust the responses you get."

Alex turned and stared out the window.

"If this helps you," Logan said gently, "God has never let me down. Not once. I trust Him with my life. Even more important, I trust Him with my eternity."

A voice in her mind warned her that trusting anyone was dangerous. She'd been burned too many times. What if it happened again? But she knew the voice that said *Just trust me* and *Everything will be all right* was real. No one would ever convince her it wasn't now. Her mind fought her, but her heart said something different.

"Okay," she said, turning to look at Logan. "I'm game. How do I get this God of yours involved in my life?"

Logan smiled. "I thought you'd never ask."

Acknowledgments

Thanks to retired Supervisory Special Agent Drucilla L. Wells, Federal Bureau of Investigation, Behavioral Analysis Unit. She makes Alex Donovan possible. I loved sneaking into Quantico, learning more about the BAU and the FBI Academy. Maybe someday you can show me the real thing. You're the best!

To Dr. Richard Mabry for the medical information. When you're trying to unleash a deadly virus on the world, you need someone with his expertise. (Not sure that sounds right . . . ha-ha!) I hope my readers will check out his medical thrillers if you haven't already. They're fantastic!

My heartfelt thanks to my friend Donita Corman for allowing me to borrow her wonderful husband. I hope I did him justice, Donita. I wish I could have met him. When we get to heaven, please introduce me. Lots of love.

Thank you to Raela Schoenherr for allowing me to write this new series. And once again, a big thank-you to Jean Bloom for her editing help.

Nancy Mehl is the author of more than forty books and a Christy Award and Carol Award finalist, as well as the winner of an ACFW Book of the Year Award. Her short story, *Chasing Shadows*, was in the *USA Today* bestselling *Summer of Suspense* anthology. Nancy writes from her home in Missouri, where she lives with her husband, Norman, and their puggle, Watson. To learn more, visit www.nancymehl.com.

Sign Up for Nancy's Newsletter

Keep up to date with Nancy's news on book releases and events by signing up for her email list at nancymehl.com.

More from Nancy Mehl

When multiple corpses are found, their remains point to a serial killer with a familiar MO but who's been in prison for over twenty years—Special Agent Kaely Quinn's father. In order to prevent more deaths, she must come face-to-face with the man she's hated for years. In a race against time, will this case cost Kaely her identity and perhaps even her life?

Dead End • KAELY QUINN PROFILER #3

You May Also Like . . .

When U.S. Marshal Mercy Brennan is assigned to a joint task force with the St. Louis PD, she's forced back into contact with her father and into the sights of a notorious gang. Mercy's boss assigns her colleague—and ex-boyfriend—Mark to get her safely out of town. But when an ice storm hits and the enemy closes in, can backup reach them in time?

Fatal Frost by Nancy Mehl
DEFENDERS OF JUSTICE #1
nancymehl.com

Attacked and left in a coma, FBI Special Agent Addison Leigh has no memory of the incident or her estranged husband when she wakes. Full of regret over letting his military trauma ruin their marriage, Deputy U.S. Marshal Mack Jordan promises to hunt down the man who attacked her, and soon it becomes clear that the killer won't rest until Addison is dead.

Hours to Kill by Susan Sleeman
HOMELAND HEROES #3
susansleeman.com

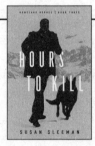

After one of her team members is murdered and the CIA opens an internal investigation on her, Layla Karam reluctantly turns to her ex-boyfriend and private investigator Hunter McCoy to help clear her name and uncover the real killer. With threats on all sides, Layla must put her trust in the man who broke her heart and hope they both come out alive.

Backlash by Rachel Dylan
CAPITAL INTRIGUE #2
racheldylan.com

BETHANYHOUSE

More from Bethany House

In 1928, Bonaventure Circus outcast Pippa Ripley must decide if uncovering her roots is worth putting herself directly in the path of a killer preying on the troupe. Decades later, while determining if an old circus train depot will be torn down or preserved, Chandler Faulk is pulled into a story far darker and more haunting than she imagined.

The Haunting at Bonaventure Circus by Jaime Jo Wright
jaimewrightbooks.com

When an accident claims the life of an oil-rig worker off the North Carolina coast, Coast Guard investigators Rissi Dawson and Mason Rogers are sent to take the case. But mounting evidence shows the death may not have been an accident at all, and they find themselves racing to discover the killer's identity before he eliminates the threat they pose.

The Crushing Depths by Dani Pettrey
COASTAL GUARDIANS #2
danipettrey.com

On a mission to recover the Book of the Wars, Leif and his team are diverted by a foretelling of formidable guardians who will decimate the enemies of the ArC, while Iskra uses her connections to hunt down the book. As they try to stop the guardians, failure becomes familiar, and the threats creep closer to home, with implications that could tear them apart.

Kings Falling by Ronie Kendig
THE BOOK OF THE WARS #2
roniekendig.com

◊ BETHANYHOUSE